I0768688

Mimic

For Rayna, who fills my life with lilac, warmth, and love.

Prologue

January 6, 1893 – Medford

William's eyes jerked open. He was in his bed, but something was wrong. The pit in his stomach urged him to action. He was unsure of the time, but it was still dark. He heard a creaking floorboard. Someone was here. Slowly, carefully, he looked for the gun that he kept on the nightstand. Where it should be was only a blank tabletop. He had to find it, but his arms felt sluggish. William didn't know if this was an after effect from a hard night of drinking or the result of his body not being ready to be awake. It had been a bad day for William, and he had hoped the whisky would prevent it from becoming a bad night. He was old, he thought. Too old.

"You won't find it in time" a voice rasped in his direction. The voice trailed off with a quiet chuckle.

William looked at the foot of the bed and saw the outline of a person. William urged his brain to focus. Capture the details, his training told him. Solve the problem. The intruder was medium height with a slender build. They must have been wearing a long coat with the hood pulled over their head. It was stifling in William's apartment, and William wasn't sure how the stranger wore the coat without collapsing due to the heat. That wasn't important right now. William focused, trying to find distinguishing physical features – some sort of tell or limp – anything that William could use against this intruder. The darkness of the night and the shadows of the hood made it impossible to see anything about this person's face and the coat masked the body. William couldn't even figure out if it was a man or a woman.

It was like the intruder could read his mind. "You can try and figure out who I am, but if you haven't by now, I don't think that you will. Don't worry, I'll show you my face just before we're done."

The intruder hauntingly chuckled again. William saw the intruder move, and they were next to him before William realized what was happening. Whomever it was moved quickly. Someone athletic, then. A distant corner of William's brain urged him to pay attention to the voice. The voice sounded vaguely familiar and had a masculine quality. Medium height, slender build, athletic, male. A worker in the brick factory perhaps?

Something hard and metallic was forced into William's hand, and he realized it was the gun he had been looking for. The stranger tilted the gun slowly upwards, and William tried to resist. Why were his muscles so sluggish? Yes, he was old, yes, he was still probably drunk, but this was more than that.

"I'll bet you're starting to figure out that you aren't able to resist me. Barbituric acid has quite a wonderful effect. It'll paralyze you, but its half-life is short. Anyone who checks your blood by the time they find you won't be able to detect it. I wanted to wait until July 2nd. That date means a lot to you, so it would make this even more believable. But you changed the timetable. You moved up your appointment."

This man knew the personal history William didn't speak of. It was someone he knew well. Or someone who had done their research. Someone intent on making this personal. William's eyes searched in the dark hood for an answer to a simple question – why?

"This way, between the empty whisky bottle by the side of your bed and the placement of this pistol, everyone will consider this to be a tragic suicide of a man who has lost everything. No one will give it a second thought. Our little game we've had will be the last thing you've lost."

Once again, the intruder was one step ahead.

"I'm doing this because I need to. I've had fun with you, William. You were a worthy opponent. I knew that since I met you. You outlasted all my other playmates, you know. But I can't have you getting too close to stopping me."

William mustered his strength and was able to get one word out between his parched lips.

"Why?"

The sound came more from his throat than his mouth, but his intruder understood.

"I have to have her. You were so close to figuring it out. The pieces fell into place for you, and there may even be the answer in that notebook of yours. I just burned your precious notebook so it's a little warmer in here. I've dealt with the need to burn evidence before. Back in London, a place you drove me. A place that would have swallowed me up, if it weren't for my brains and for my persistence. I'm not ready to leave Medford. Not yet. She will be mine before that. You would have taken me away. It was always meant to be Medford, and everything you've earned will be mine. If I didn't tie up this loose end, you wouldn't let me have her."

The mystery man spat these last five words at William, filled with vitriol and hate.

"You will no longer stand in my way. Oh, don't worry. I'm going to marry her after they find you. I'll murder half the town if I have to."

The hooded man brought the gun barrel under William's

chin and placed his finger on the trigger. William still couldn't resist, which he knew was now from the drugs the killer had put in his whisky. The stranger drew their hood back to reveal their face. The stranger held his gaze until the pieces fell into place for William.

"It's time, Chief Smith."

The killer watched William realize all the mistakes he had made. Every victim did this. William's confusion. This was the killer's favorite part. He cracked a small smile and let out a low chuckle in enjoyment. Time to clean up this loose end.

William had one last thought before the killer dropped the hammer and sent a bullet into William's brain.

Abigail.

Chapter 1

1825 – Medford

Medford in the early 1800s was economically anchored by a brick factory and supported by a wide net of farms around the towns of Medford, Somerville, and Wellington. The city grew with the help of new, smoother roads from Boston and a wider canal on the Mystic River. Progress was reaching the Boston suburbs, and the expanded infrastructure brought with it an influx of residents, hoping to capitalize on the town's potential.

Born in 1825, William Smith was the first-born son to first-generation General Store owners. His parents had left Boston shortly before William was born and bought a store front on Medford's High Street with their entire life's savings. They filled the store with general goods, eventually specializing in seeds for the local farmers and sundries for the townsfolk. They were gambling on the future, knowing that ruin would mean moving back to Boston and working long hours for little pay in the many Bostonian factories. The wider canal on the Mystic River had enabled Medford to build a rail yard and in 1830, construction began on the Boston and Lowell Railway. By the time it was completed in 1835, Medford was markedly different. William's parents had found the right time to capitalize, and the store was a success. Medford became an extension of Boston, but with less crime and lower cost of living. It was noisy, busy and filled with the latest advances. To a growing boy like William, it was heaven.

William's parents tried for years to add to their family, but for whatever reason God saw fit, no children other than William made it past 3. Four siblings were born after William: Todd,

Charlotte, John and Lydia. Each of William's siblings were born sickly and frail, and typically the first fever of the winter would be their undoing. William's parents still loved William dearly, but something between them died at the same time as Lydia, and William could tell that his parents didn't want to tempt heartbreak anymore. By the time William was 10, the Smith household was cold, even on the hottest summer days. There was just too much loss under one roof and William started to believe the house was cursed.

William grew older. He was a tall teenager but rail thin. No matter how much he ate, he would not gain any weight, but he never looked sickly like his siblings had. He had light brown hair and kind, striking green eyes. He had a calm disposition and was very slow to anger. William did well in school, especially in subjects such as science and math. He had a natural knack for details and seeing how things fit together. His parents and his teachers thought he might make a great engineer, working on the railroads as they expanded across America. William hated the idea but sunk himself into schooling all the same. He figured that the future would figure itself out. William's life settled into a routine of waking up, having a small breakfast in their home above the shop, heading to school, coming home to help in the shop for the afternoon rush, and then dinner and sleep. On Sundays the family would walk down the High Street to the Universalist Church and listen to the minister preach with the rest of the growing village.

It was at the Universalist Church where he first met Abigail Harper. She was the daughter of a dairy farmer who lived near Somerville, so the only time he could see her was when the Harper family trundled into church on Sunday. Abigail was not the tallest woman, but the way she carried herself made her seem at least 4 inches taller than she was. Classically beautiful, she had long flaxen hair and fair skin that William would get lost in. William watched with earnest as Abigail started forming in the right places, and it stirred new feelings within him. What enraptured him the most were her hands. Her hands were strong and callused from a lifetime on a dairy farm, yet he knew that if he was ever graced with their touch, it would be gentle and caring. Those were the types of hands you could form a life around. He was obsessed with her – her mind, her body, her hands, and her soul. He dreamed of her most nights and knew he needed a life with her.

Each week, William convinced his parents to sit next to the Harpers so he could be near her. They would pretend to protest, but exchange knowing glances before finally agreeing. They weren't as cold and unfeeling as William thought them to be. William sat each Sunday in church, listening to stories of the prodigal son, the loaves and fishes, the temptations of Christ, but missed the underlying message because being that near to Abigail took away his attention. Abigail, however, spent Sundays rapt to the minister's every word. William didn't think she even knew he existed once the minister started talking. That didn't matter to William, as it allowed him to steal glances at her without her noticing. It made his Sundays the best days of his week.

Over the next few years, the infatuation started to blossom into something a little more. Abigail had noticed him staring and had even started to return his advances. Their romance was fed by the times they could spend alone before and after the church service while their families and other church members talked about things that were mundane to two teenagers, like the weather and the crops. The Harpers and the Smiths were becoming friends with each other, and they would often joke with themselves about the foolishness of youth. William paid them no mind, though, as he knew that Abigail was the one he needed to make his life complete.

They married when William was 18 and Abigail was 17. On his wedding night, William was worried that the curse of a small family and sickly children would affect him and Abigail like it had his parents. William and Abigail both wanted a larger family than the one William had grown up with.

As the dowry, the Harper and Smith family built a new cottage on two acres of land in the woods. It was a quiet location near the land that Charles Tufts had just donated to the Universalists, but on the Medford side. William's father's store had connections that provided the brick from the factory at a discounted rate, and William and Abigail set about making the new house a home. William continued to work in the store, taking a larger workload from his father. Abigail would still help on the farm during harvest and planting season, but the newlyweds started a wonderful life together in their new home. William felt a long-dormant feeling: joy.

In 1844, Benjamin was born. He was a tall baby like his father but had the grace and inner strength of Abigail. He was not a sickly child, and he grew and put on weight faster than William could understand. With Benjamin's progress as a positive sign, they continued and had Charles in '46. Charles was a little sicklier, but a very tidy baby who rarely fussed. William and Abigail would have to check on him at night, as they were worried that he was sleeping too much or too long and might be dead. Charles stayed alive, though, and so finally William and Abigail welcomed Emma Elizabeth to the world in '47. Emma was the spitting image of Abigail as a baby, and William knew she would be gorgeous as she grew up. She took to food like Benjamin did, and soon the family had three bouncing children. The children grew, and the young family spent the days working or going to school and the evenings reading around the fire. All three children showed a zeal for learning and books, and they valued any education they could get. When their noses weren't crammed in a book, they played in the snow, walked in the woods, and above all they would laugh – all five of them. Over the years, Benjamin became Ben, Charles became Charlie, and William called Emma either Lizzie or Elizabeth. It was their nickname, only for the two of them.

When Emma was four, Charlie had tried calling her Lizzie, and soon after came running into the living room with portions of his hair missing. Tears were cascading down his face, and Abigail rushed to him to comfort him.

"Emma tore out my hair!" he declared through the sobs.

"What did you do, Charlie, to cause her to tear out your hair?" Abigail asked.

"Called her Lizzie," was all he could reply.

William and Abigail looked at each other and tried to stifle a laugh. Abigail's eyes clearly said "that tracks" to William, and William just nodded behind a sly smile. Emma came toddling into the room with a hand full of hair. She looked at Charlie, then up at her parents. She knew she was in trouble but believed her getting in trouble to be a grave injustice. She scrunched up her face and squinted her eyes in the direction of Charlie.

"Only da call me Lizzie."

From then on no one, not even Abigail, dared to call her Lizzie. These are the small conflicts that make the memories of childhood, and William knew the home was bursting with more love than he had ever felt as a child. He was happy.

Their family blossomed and grew. The only thing that faded at all in William was his belief in the weekly scripture. He would still go to church every Sunday to be with Abigail and the kids. He still believed that living a good life was a pathway to rewards, but he had a hard time sitting in the pews and being told he should feel regret for his happiness. If Jesus' life was truly about suffering, did his happiness make him a bad person? Given the choice between his family and his God, he would choose his family every time.

Chapter 2

May 1861 – Medford

As 1861 began, William was optimistic about the new decade. His parents had both died a few years before, after which he and Abigail sold their small cottage to Charles Tufts for a hefty profit. Charles Tufts had been using his profits from the brick factory to keep acquiring land. He was obsessed with expanding the newly chartered college in Medford that bore his name. Charles Tufts wanted the land more than the house, so the home that William and Abigail had built fell into disrepair.

William had looked into attending college to better understand the financial portions of the store but ultimately decided against it. William's parents had racked up debt by getting modern inventions into the General Store to attract a new type of client, and the sewing machines, gridirons, eggbeaters, dishwashers and new electric appliances had made the store look modern and new. It turned out the population of Medford wasn't ready for such modern times, though, so the new acquisitions sat in the store window accumulating dust and debt. The once profitable store had seen some leaner years as the progress in the store outpaced the clientele. William and Abigail had used the income from the sale of their cottage to pay off all of the debt and started fresh, owning the store outright. They made an excellent partnership and possessed parts of each other's brains. They always seemed to be able to ebb and flow to the work in an unspoken dance.

William and Abigail found that the demand for the goods in the store was even higher than the two of them could accommodate. They employed help from Ben, Charlie and Emma when the kids weren't in school and had restored the income levels to a steady state. The family was stable, unknown of the challenges to come from the civil war that was just drawing its first breaths. They read about revolts in Harper's Ferry and slave uprisings in South Carolina in the local paper, the Medford Mercury. For a while, they believed that the war may just miss their doorstep and stay in the south. As April rolled around and cannon fire was lobbed across the bay to Fort Sumter in Charlston, William knew the North would have to respond.

Lincoln's call went out for volunteers to serve the Union Army that same April. William read about it in the Mercury and felt a pull to serve and a calling to right the injustice.

"Maybe," he thought, "this is just the suffering that I need to restore my faith and bring me back to Jesus." An inner voice countered with another perspective. "Maybe this is just the hubris of the invincibility of youth." A third voice added another perspective. "Maybe you're just bored."

One evening in late May, William climbed the stairs to their home above the shop and found Abigail cross stitching scripture about the planting season in their armchair near the Franklin stove. This May had been colder than some, and there was still a nip in the air most evenings. She looked up from her chair expectantly as he walked into the room. William had thought all day about the conversation he was about to have and knew that it may jeopardize the joy he felt.

"Abi, I'm going to go to Boston next month to volunteer for the Yankee Army."

She stared at him, chewing her words. She didn't speak for a long while, figuring out the most effective way to respond.

William wasn't sure what she was thinking, but also knew after 19 years of marriage that it was coming. William stood in the living room, maintaining eye contact and waiting to hear what she said.

"You're too old."

"Abi, I'm only 36. I still have plenty of life left. If I volunteer, though, it may protect Ben and Charlie from having to get drafted. Lincoln wants 75,000 volunteers, otherwise he's going to start conscription. The boys are young – too young for war," William responded.

Abigail tried reasoning with him. "What do you think just one man would be able to do? You will be just another blue coat at the end of a rebel's rifle sight. Neither a bullet nor a cannonball cares for your morals."

William opened his mouth to interject, but Abi wasn't done yet.

"Here, with your family," she paused after this word, letting it sink in, "you are more than just a target. You provide. You are our literal and spiritual head and our authority. We cannot lose you."

"Besides," Abigail finished, "I love you too much, ya git."

William looked down into Abigail's lap at the cross-stitch and tried shifting tactics.

"If I do not do this, how can I defend my inaction to God? How could I stand at the gates and convince Him that I truly helped my fellow man? Abi, there is even talk from Governor Andrew of forming a Negro regiment. If they muster, what excuse would I have not to join?"

Abigail raised her eyes at William. They didn't talk about slavery in the house, but William knew both he and Abigail saw the injustice.

"Do you consider yourself to be more important than the Negro in this?" she responded.

"Now Abigail, that's not what I said. I said that I have a moral duty to fight for this cause. Isn't that what Minister DeLong talks about each week at Church? About how we must recognize the suffering of our fellow man and work to remove that suffering?"

"But why must it be you? Can't you wait for others to fight this war?" Abigail responded at a slightly louder volume.

William knew he was outclassed with the spiritual approach, but he had already thrown his lot down this road. He wished he had paid a little more attention in church. He scrambled for an answer.

"That's like saying the Good Samaritan should have kept walking and left that man beaten in the road. Are you asking me to turn a blind eye to the suffering of the slaves? I'm sure the South will realize their mistake once Lincoln gets his volunteers. This can't last through the Summer. The Mercury doesn't think that the South has the troops or the equipment," William responded.

Abigail knew William's faith had fallen off in the last few years and William knew she would see right through this line of logic. She may even accuse him of bearing the Lord's name in vain. William knew that he was at least bearing false witness. She tutted at him, and he knew that she saw through him.

"Proverbs chapter 20, verse 3 to 6 tells us it is to one's honor to avoid strife, but every fool is quick to quarrel," Abigail concluded.

William knew the conversation was over. Abigail had

quoted scripture and called him a fool. It made him angry, but he knew his wife enough to understand that no more discussion would be tolerated. She returned to her cross stitch, although William was sure that the needle and thread were not meant to be stabbed through the cloth that violently.

"I love you, Abi, but you'll see that I'm right. I'm going downstairs to sweep the floors," William said as he left the room. He didn't wait for a response.

Chapter 3

May 1861 – Medford

William went downstairs, flustered. He had already swept the floors that night and had no intention of repeating the chore. He just had to be alone for a while to cool his head. He didn't know how someone he loved so completely could drive him so insane.

"She doesn't understand me," he thought. He knew this was an overreaction, and he also knew she was scared of losing him. This was not a time for logic or reason, though. This was a time for anger. He kicked the counter in frustration, but this did not lessen the rage William felt burning within. All it did was leave him with a painful big toe.

He reached back to a shelf behind the register where they kept the alcohol and grabbed a bottle of whisky. William hadn't ever cared for the taste of alcohol, but his frustration got the better of his self-control. He needed something to numb the anger. He would hide the bottle when he was finished tonight, but he wanted something to take the sting out of the conversation he had just had with Abigail.

He took a large, deep swig directly from the bottle and nearly vomited as the liquid burned his nose and throat. The fumes wafted back up his esophagus and into his sinuses. All he could taste was burning. He coughed and felt as if he was breathing fire. He realized he was making a ton of noise, and he hoped that no one upstairs would come down to check out the source. He waited a tentative minute and went back to the bottle for another pull. This time he took a smaller sip, and the warmth of the whisky soothed his throat, and he felt instantly calmer. He took four more pulls and started to feel warm all over. He could understand why people became addicted to this stuff. The calm was, he thought, well, intoxicating. He cracked a smile and took another swig.

He ended up drinking about a quarter of the bottle, and at the end of the night, he sealed the top and hid the bottle in the back of a disused cabinet, hopeful that no one would discover his secret. He hadn't ever had specific conversations about alcohol with Abi, but it wasn't something he wanted to press. Perhaps it was better that it was his secret. Besides, if he only consumed whisky when she made him mad, he wouldn't have to hold the secret very often.

He walked back upstairs a little slower than normal to find that all the other members of his family had already gone to sleep. The fire in the Franklin stove was down to embers, and Abi had set out his dressing gown in the armchair next to the stove. Even when she was furious at him, she still showed him love. He was a lucky man. William undressed and put on his dressing gown in the residual warmth next to the stove. He grabbed the pile of clothes he had removed, and tip toed into his room and fell into bed next to Abigail. He listened to her gentle breathing, kissed her on her forehead, and drifted into a dreamless sleep helped by the alcohol.

For the next few weeks, communication between him and Abigail was terse. They stuck to what they needed to say to run a household and little else. William found himself retreating to the store about twice a week to pull from the hidden whisky bottle. William knew this tension had to break again, and he was hoping it would break to the positive.

The tension held for a month. Both William and Abigail were painfully stubborn, and both refused to cede the point. While time allowed them to slowly warm to each other, there was still a palpable tension under the surface. William's breath rose in his throat whenever they were alone, and the topic drifted anywhere close to the war. He held his breath when the headline of the Mercury was regarding the war. William was tired of being on the periphery of the love he had come to rely on in his life, so he proposed a bargain. He believed the war would be over by the end of summer, and summer was the busiest time in the shop. Therefore, William asked Abi to defer the conversation about joining the volunteer army to the fall, if the war was still on. In return, William would actively discourage both Ben and Charlie from even thinking about volunteering. Abigail accepted these terms, and the tension between them dissolved.

The summer came and went, and news of increasingly violent battles reached Medford. Business at the store started to slow as people started stashing money, fearing a long recession related to a prolonged war. It became clear that this war was not going to be over by the end of summer. William and Abigail had enough money to keep the store going because they had paid off the store debt when they sold their cottage. Luck had favored them, because without that relief, they would have faced harder times. Nonetheless, their expenses started to outpace their income, and the prospect of going back into debt was becoming a weekly conversation. William would steal away to the shop on occasion and have more whisky, drinking this time to ease the worry about the shop instead of the worry about Abi. It soon became a near-nightly habit to numb the pain and deaden the stress.

Through it all, William held up his end of the bargain and was sure to highlight the number of deaths to his sons and have an open discussion about the futility of armed conflict. However,

William felt disingenuous, as in his heart he still wanted to fight for his country and, if necessary, die for his morals. As summer gave way to fall, William steeled himself for what he knew was going to be another difficult conversation. His resolve had not wavered, and he was hoping hers had in some small way.

Luck favored William's convictions, as Abigail had come around and started to see the righteous and just cause of the North. She also wanted this war to be over so there was decreasing pressure on the financials of the store. As a final stroke of fortune, William's cause was aided by an unlikely source. There had been a marked shift in the sermon each Sunday as the minister had started to highlight the plight of the slave in his sermons. As a result, Abigail saw the anti-slavery cause as God's will.

Before Thanksgiving of 1861, William walked up the stairs again and found Abigail much as he had so many months before – sitting in their armchair and cross-stitching scripture.

"It's time, Abi," William started. "Time for me to serve my country."

"A time to love, and a time to hate; a time of war, and a time of peace," she responded, quoting scripture to start. William wasn't sure what this meant. Last time the scripture had called him a fool. He waited with bated breath until she continued, solving his confusion.

"It is now your time for war."

Just like that, the conversation was over. She had seen his morality, and he had fulfilled his end of the bargain. Come what may, they were united. That night they held each other for a long time, basking in the shared warmth and companionship that only two lovers can share. He never wanted that night to end. So it was for the rest of November, and they were some of the happiest moments of William's life. He felt complete, even though he knew there was a dark cloud brewing on the horizon that would require him to leave his heart and his home, potentially never to return.

In early December of 1861, William put on a coat, bought a one-way train ticket to Boston, and kissed his family goodbye. As he left, he once again made his boys promise not to follow him.

"If you break this promise, I will find you and it won't be the South you have to worry about," he said to each of them. He wanted to make sure they knew he wasn't kidding. He stared in their eyes, unflinchingly, until they both solemnly agreed.

Deep down, William still reasoned that the war would be over by spring, as he had heard the stories of winters in Valley Forge during the revolution and the way a winter can kill even the heartiest blood lust. He was hoping he'd be back to the store in time to support the spring planting season. He knew that Abigail, Ben, Charlie and Elizabeth could keep the store running until then without issue. They had enough money, they had experience, and if either of those gave out, they had the iron will of Abigail.

Abigail kissed him deeply before he left, passing off a pocket-sized bible to him. In the front cover was a folio she had made for him, showing her and the three children.

"Come back to me, William Smith" were the words she spoke as the train pulled from the station.

He arrived in Boston, found the volunteer regiment, and started his training with the Massachusetts 28th regiment. Training was unremarkable but by the time the regiment marched to battle, William felt like he had gained a second family.

Chapter 4

July 1, 1863 - Gettysburg

William ended up spending almost 3 years in service of the Union Army's 28th Infantry. The regiment saw a never-ending line of increasingly bloody conflicts. He was at the Second Battle of Bull Run, Antietam, Fredericksburg, and Chancellorsville. He lost so many friends, but somehow, he was never a blue coated target on the other end of a rebel's sights. As the time went on, he also formed a tight bond with these men. He escaped each conflict muddy and dirty but intact. Each progressive battle hardened him to the gory reality of war with the atrocities he saw. He had started to feel more and more invincible, and those feelings were quickly accompanied by an increase in faith. William saw that the fortune that shined upon him was God's plan, and he was merely someone to be the arm of His justice. The dormant faith within him for so long was awakened by the smell of gun powder.

He wrote to Abigail and the family as much as he was able, despite difficulties in finding dry paper, good pencils or a willing messenger. The letters from Abigail were a little less frequent. Nevertheless, William's heart would jump when a letter would come for him, and he would sometimes sit just staring at her wonderful scrawling lettering on the cover of the mail. It always smelled of Abigail's lilac perfume, and he would place the letters in his coat pocket to get a whiff of lilac throughout the day. She would send him updates on the children, the town, and the store. Everything was ok but not great. Wartime shortages were preventing people from spending money, and the store's profits were meager. They were helped by government spending that provided grain to local stores to keep farmers afloat. The kids were growing, and William enjoyed hearing stories about how Ben was taking a larger role in the store and Charlie was good at balancing the books and how Emma had kept them both in check. The letters served as a reminder to William why he was fighting – to make a better life and a better country for his children.

William's restored faith had him reading from the small bible Abigail gave him regularly. He could see the hope in faith but still struggled with the duality of the scripture: a vengeful God who wanted you to turn the other cheek.

In late June of 1863, William and his regiment were stationed in a small village called Taneytown with the rest of the 2nd Corps of the Army of the Potomac. They received orders to move from Taneytown to the nearby town of Gettysburg as the forward group for the 2nd Corps' artillery units. It was early in the morning on June 30th when the 28th regiment broke camp and started the march towards Gettysburg. The regiment sent three forward scouting parties, with the rest in loose formation behind. A river named Rock Creek bisected the area between Taneytown and Gettysburg. William was on the lead scout team, looking for a place to cross Rock Creek. It had rained on and off for the month of May, and the river was swollen. Command wanted the squad to find a dry crossing somewhere along the swollen river. After all, the Army strongly believed that there was no sense in risking wet feet. Rock Creek split the countryside and was surrounded on both sides with lush forest. The creek itself was 7 – 10 feet below the ridgeline in most places, so any location that a mass of troops and artillery could cross would have to consist of a traverse down the slope, across the river, and then back up the opposite slope.

Although the rest of the regiment was reliant upon them to

find the right way, the lead scouting party was not focused on their mission. They had been given strict orders to keep all but necessary noise discipline but there was no known sign of the enemy in this area. They walked through the woods with a false sense of bravado, believing that the enemy had run from their mighty regiment. The 12 men in the scouting party was made up of 8 soldiers who had volunteered around the same time as William and 4 replacement soldiers who had joined after the battle of Chancellorsville. The replacements still saw this war as a quest for glory, but the veterans had no such delusions. They had been through so many horrific scrapes to know that the only way you'd get to go home is if you got lucky. They were all dead men, just waiting for their appointment with the reaper. Superstition, fate, and even William's restored faith had nothing to do with it.

William's scouting party crested a small ridge and took a short break on an overlook near an oxbow of the river. The river was about 15 feet wide here, and from the current it looked to be about 4 feet deep. They were in the crook of the oxbow, and at the bottom of the overlook there was a gully with a beach of rocks littering the shallows. The steepness of the side of the gully, the depth of the water, and the rocks in the shallows made it so no wagons would have been able to pass through this location. William realized the rocks didn't look inviting for foot traffic either. There was a chance of turned ankles and twisted knees as people slipped off rocks into deeper water. Wet feet, twisted knees, and cranky infantry was not a way to win a battle. They would have to keep moving.

The scouting party finished their break and stood on the edge of the ridge for a few minutes, discussing their options in a low whisper. The squad knew they needed to head back into the forest to get back into cover so they could follow the river upstream to keep looking for a potential crossing but didn't really feel any urgency. Finally deciding to move on, they stepped back towards the forest, but the saturated ground peeled away from the overlook and gave way in a small landslide.

William and five other men awkwardly slid down the bank, bringing half of the ridge with them. The landslide formed a new beach near the river as the sandy, silty soil filled the shallows between the rocks. The 6 men at the bottom of the ridge looked at each other frantically. They realized this is something that could bring a rebel patrol down upon them. The good news, though, was that no one appeared to be hurt.

William looked back up the 7 feet that separated him from the rest of the squad. He knew they would need to climb back to the top of the ridge quickly to avoid delays or even a potential ambush. Their location made them in a natural shooting box, and they could easily be picked off from either side of the river. William attempted to scramble up the loose soil, but slid back down, bringing another portion of the ridge with him. Others in the squad tried as well, always with the same result. The squad members at the top of the ridge kept a watchful eye on the opposite bank, knowing the precarious position of the men on the beach. They were worried, and it showed on their faces. After another attempt to scale the bank, the frustration finally overwhelmed William.

"Arrrrgggghhhhh," William exclaimed loudly. Despite the hiss of 'quiet' from the other members of the squad, he continued, venting his frustration more than keeping his head.

"I'm tired of these little errands. Command probably already knows where they want us to cross, and the sooner we get across, the sooner we can get a hot meal. But our comfort doesn't matter, does it? We're just expendable pieces in the war machine. We march when they tell us to march, cut our leave short, won't let us send home more than one letter a week, feed us cold horse jerky instead of stew, and give us equipment that is worn out. We're led by morons and trained by incompetents. I've had enough and I don't care if my feet get wet. Let's just cross here and we can walk down BOTH sides of this God forsaken river."

The other members of his squad all looked at him in alarm at his sudden outburst. William was not known for irrational behavior. He was a quiet, calculated, and steady man. He kept his wits about him in battle. He was someone that all the younger soldiers tried to emulate. All other 11 members of the squad froze in their tracks while the sound of his exclamation died off. William knew he had made a big mistake.

His eyes started scanning the woods on the opposite bank of the river, realizing he had put his squad mates in danger. The rest of the squad on the beach started doing the same. It was unnervingly quiet. There were no noises from any birds or insects. The only sound in the entire forest was the rushing of the stream. Not even the wind dared make a sound, and it was like the entire forest was holding its breath in anticipation. Fear crept into William's subconscious. The members on the top of the ridge had dropped into low positions but soon arose and started to try and find a way to help the 6 men who were stranded below. William's hyperfocus noticed every creak, every crack, and every breath within the pregnant air. The humidity was suddenly strangling, and the air lacked any noticeable movement. William desperately wanted cover.

Spending so much time in the little cottage in the woods

with Abigail, William was never afraid of the forest. He recognized its power, and the noises of the forest were a comfort to him. They soothed his mind when it became overwhelmed with the pressure of life even better than the whisky had. All woods are alive, but at this moment the monster of the unknown threatened to unravel the psyche of all 12 men in the scouting party.

As William finally heard the scuttle of a squirrel, he felt himself let out a sigh of relief. It seemed they had come away from this, no worse for wear, and William said a silent prayer of thanks.

William felt the shots before he heard them.

The first was a punch in his chest, and the second was a blinding stab to his knee. His knee had shattered, and William collapsed to the dirt in a torrent of pain. As William fell to the ground, the woods across the river erupted in gunfire, decimating his squad around him. He awkwardly landed and struck his other knee on the top of a rock that wasn't yet buried by the dirt from the walls of the gully. He groaned in pain, but quickly suppressed the groan before the reverberation of the gunshots died away. He needed to be quiet and motionless. At this moment, a pretend death may save his life. As he lay there, he heard bodies from the soldiers on the high side of the overlook flop down the ridge onto the beach. William was sure that the enemy believed all 12 members of the first scout team to be dead. They may be right about 11 of them. The hubris of William's outburst had cursed them all. He looked around and saw shock and surprise on the dead bodies in the mud around him and waves of guilt overwhelmed him. This ambush and their deaths were his fault.

The reverberation of the shots fell away, and the air was still again, permeated with the smells of gun smoke and death. William didn't dare move. He was still exposed, and any movement would likely invite someone on the other bank to finish the job they had started.

The second scout team came up from behind and quickly dove into whatever cover they could find. William heard the command to open fire, and they sent a volley of return fire towards the source of the rifle smoke. William lay in the mud, bleeding from his knee and unable to move. He didn't know why he wasn't dead from the shot he had obviously taken in the chest. He would sort that out later, and lay motionless, trying not to make any sound. If the rebels assumed he was dead, he just might escape when there was a break in the battle. He wasn't ready to die, especially if his last words caused so many deaths. He needed to find a way to atone for these sins.

Chapter 5

July 1, 1863 - Gettysburg

The beach where William lay had turned into hell. His squad's blood trickled into the river, tainting the color of the Rock Creek to a deep crimson. The smell of sulfur from the gunpowder lingered in the summer Pennsylvania humidity, trapped as a fog over the river. A salvo of bullets rained on the second scout's team position from across the river and William heard the screams of men as the bullets found their targets. The screams were washed out by a volley of return fire. The back-and-forth between the second scout team and the embedded rebels continued for what seemed like hours. Bullets periodically struck the beach near William, but none were close enough to make him jump. He focused on his breathing and calming his muscles from the adrenaline. Sudden movements would surely be his end.

The second scout team had gotten a runner back to the regiment at large, and William could hear the noise of reinforcements bowling through the woods. Union troops started to mount a counterattack, but the Confederate soldiers were well positioned and well hidden. William knew that the body count was rising, and with it his guilt. His thoughts drifted to his family and to Abigail. He had to get out of here and back to them. Maybe the damage to his knee was enough to get a discharge, and he would be able to spend the rest of his days tending his shop in Medford with his wife and his children, never again having to think about an unexpected bullet from a soldier wearing a grey coat. He would see his grandchildren and watch Abigail grow old next to him.

He focused on every detail he could of Abigail. Her hair.

Her hands. Her smile. Her smell. They way her body curved above her hips and into her waist. The way she held him tightly in their bed. The way she nuzzled up to him when he held her. The small intimate hours. The way she gave way under his gentle touch and the way he gave way under hers.

This gulley would not be his end. He would see her again.

The rat-a-tat from the other side of the river gradually decreased, and an unsteady cease fire hung over the battle as both sides replenished their ammunition, reloaded their muskets, and dug into a little more cover. William drifted in and out of sleep, unsure of how much time passed. A combination of sleep, a loss of consciousness induced by the pain, and boredom blurred the hours.

He finally made the decision that it was time to hobble out of this ravine. He'd try and wade back up stream toward an area where the embankment wasn't so high or so steep, and then make his way back to the regiment. He brought feet together as the first step of standing up, but as he did, he heard a cry of "Fire the artillery!" in the distance. William froze, unsure if the call came from his side of the river or the enemy's.

The silence from the unsteady ceasefire was suddenly punctuated by a high-pitched scream. A blur of something flew over William's head and the trees in the woods behind him exploded into sharp, fragmented shards of wood. The artillery had come, and it was not a Union volley. They aimed high, but each time a volley came, William saw his chances of escaping dwindle. He lay there in the mud, still bleeding, still in pain, and the hopelessness of the situation caused him to break down into tears.

He finally realized after two and a half long years what a mistake it had been to go to war. No cause was worth this hell. He had to make it home to Abigail. He wept.

Volley after volley of cannon fire tore the trees to kindling until the ringing in William's ears drowned out all other noises. He covered his head to try and block out the ringing just as a large tree on the ridge burst into two. Time slowed down, and all William could do was think that it was probably a burr oak instead of a red oak. Burr oaks would be more dense than Red Oaks, so they would be more likely to crush him with their weight. The clarity of consciousness was a surprise to his beleaguered mind, and he laughed to himself. He wondered how long it would be until this majestic forest had regrown after the war. He wondered if Gettysburg and Taneytown would go back to being sleepy towns in Pennsylvania instead of the hell on earth they had become today. Time snapped back into focus, just as the upper half of the tree fell between William and the Rock River. It landed and rolled to a stop on top of William's damaged leg. The tree pinned him in the mud, and he was trapped. Bloody, alone, and trapped. He began crying again at the hopelessness of it all. He drifted back to thoughts of Abigail until he was out of tears to shed.

As night fell, William was done feeling sorry for himself and knew he had to take his escape into his own hands. Earlier in the day, William had used the cover of a gunfire volley to remove his belt and create a tourniquet above his knee to slow the bleeding from his wound. He had spent the last few hours using the cover of other fighting to dig his leg out from under the tree. It had been a slow process. He used the scream of a cannonball to create a channel with his good leg in the sand next to his trapped leg. The result was an increasingly wide swath in the dirt that enabled him to wiggle his leg free, inch by inch.

He didn't know if he would be able to put any weight on it,

but the darkness meant it was time to move. He pulled his leg back towards the ridge and away from the enemy's side of the river, hoping he would figure out a way to climb the eroded ridge and head back to the regiment through the woods. He stifled a scream of pain from his cramped muscles as blood rushed back into them. He had to get help if he was going to see his family again.

He leaned against the fallen tree trunk to catch his breath and to listen for any sound of the enemy. He gritted his teeth and pulled his belt tourniquet another notch tighter. He was without his musket, but he had freed his bayonet when he removed his belt. He would use it if he had to. No one would stop him from escaping this gulley. William waited and gauged the silence. He didn't hear any noise and moved to the second part of his plan. Laying pinned in one place for several hours gave him plenty of time to figure this part out.

He rolled onto the top of the tree trunk and shimmied up towards the top of the ridge, inch by inch. The dark blue of his coat and his pants allowed him to blend into the dark tree trunk in the low light. Every few minutes he would stop and listen. These breaks also allowed William to give his aching muscles and his tired mind a chance to rest. He traversed the tree trunk to the base of the embankment. He was on top of the tree trunk and still had about 5 feet to climb to the top of the ridge. He needed a foothold in the wall of the ridge and, if the foothold didn't give way, he would be able to climb to the top of the ridge.

He dug the foothold slowly with his hands and his bayonet, always listening to the forest to see if he heard any movement. Where the forest had seemed evil before, the nighttime had allowed it to return to the regular ebb and flow of life within the woods. It felt more like home than it had this morning. He dug the foothold about two feet above the tree trunk, which would then allow the top of the ridge to be at waist level. He was worried about being exposed for that long, but also worried about the ridge eroding again, sending him tumbling back down to the beach. He waited another few minutes, listening for any hint of any human in the forest, but the only sounds were the nighttime insects and a light wind through the trees.

"It's now or never," William thought.

He pushed himself to standing, balancing all his weight on his good leg on top of the tree trunk. He reached up and stabbed his bayonet into the top of the ridge to use as a handhold. He tested it against his weight and, satisfied with the result, pulled on the bayonet while switching legs on top of the tree trunk. The pain was nearly unbearable, and William saw stars flash at the edge of his vision as the pain in his leg threatened to cause him to crumple and fall. Mustering all the strength he could, he put his good leg into the foot hold and pressed up, letting his weight transfer from his bad leg. Miraculously, the bayonet held in the top of the ridge. He folded his torso over the edge. He half rolled, half dragged his lower body over the edge of the ridge and kept rolling for 5 or 6 feet. William was free of the gulley of death. He thought of the other souls he had started his day with and hoped they had found peace in the afterlife of their choosing. He would spend the rest of his life trying to make it up to them.

"I'm going to make it home to you, Abi," William said quietly to himself. He swore that the wind picked up through the trees at that moment, masking his promise from any other prying ears.

Chapter 6

July 2, 1863 - Gettysburg

William's ordeal was far from over, as he still had to creep through the woods without alarming any roving sentries and make it back to a medical tent. His knee was likely ruined, but he was hoping he could avoid amputation. He knew that if he wanted a chance at saving his leg, he had to craft a sling. He had stopped rolling away from the ridge right near two dead Union soldiers. He recognized them as Patrick and Edward. They had been with William since the start. Their eyes were still open, but they were long dead. William hoped their deaths were quick and mouthed an apology in the darkness while he reached his hands up and closed their eyes.

He quietly crawled and rummaged around in the underbrush for a musket and after about 10 minutes of careful searching, he finally felt the familiar butt stock of a Springfield rifled musket. He grabbed it, then crept on his belly back to the two dead Union soldiers. He removed their belts and stripped the brass buckles off the belts. He used the rifle and the two belts to craft a makeshift splint. He placed the rifle on the outside of his leg and tied it in place with one belt above his tourniquet and one belt near the ankle. He hoped it would hold. He had left his bayonet embedded in the top of the ridge, so he picked up Edwards' bayonet, knowing he may need to use it in the darkness. He crawled over to a large tree and put the tree between him and the river. He stood up tentatively, assessing his leg to see if it could carry weight.

He thought he would be able to carry on like this for a while, as long as he didn't put his entire weight on the leg.

"Move, Smith," he told himself through gritted teeth, and started back in the direction he had come so many hours previously. He used the sound of the river to try and stay a consistent distance from the edge and any potential danger. William had no idea if the rebel encampment was still there but knew it was prudent not to test his luck any further.

The going was slow, as the uneven terrain proved challenging. This was not a frustration, though, as William was happy to be alive and knew that each step brought him closer to relative safety. William estimated that he was traveling about 1 mile per hour but knew that he likely had about 3 miles to go to reach where he had departed this morning. Every step away from that river helped William feel a little safer.

Something cracked underfoot a short distance away. It had only been an hour since he started hobbling through the wood. It was too soon to be coming from any camp. It had to be a nighttime sentry.

But for which side?

He threw caution to the wind, knowing that if he got this wrong, it was almost certain death. He couldn't even crouch down due to the splinted leg.

"Please help me" he called gently into the dark abyss. "I'm a wounded Union soldier, and I need help".

The silence that followed was deafening. William held his breath, trying to think of ways he could get out of this if he needed to. He couldn't run and wouldn't be able to hide very well in the time it would take for the person on the other end of the noise to reach his location. He drew his bayonet and tried to replicate a ready position that he had been taught in training. He wouldn't go down without a fight.

Maybe he was mistaken. Maybe he hadn't heard that snapping twig. William lowered his bayonet and started to resume his journey when a response finally came.

"Don't move. If you move, I'll shoot."

William couldn't tell if the voice was friend or foe but decided to press his luck.

"Please. You don't understand. My entire scouting party is dead. I was trapped under a tree during the cannon fire. I have been shot in the knee and maybe the chest. I'm bleeding, hungry, and tired. Help me."

Again silence, but this time the response came back quicker.

"What unit are you in?" came the voice.

"Union Volunteer Army, 28th regiment, 2nd corps," William responded quickly.

His confidence grew every moment that he didn't hear the retort of a rifle or feel another punch in the chest. Surely an enemy wouldn't be stalling for this long. He was about to call out again when he felt the unmistakable presence of a gun barrel in the small of his back. A second person had crept up behind him. He was trapped. He felt the person behind him push against the gun barrel. The push from behind caught William by surprise and in his weakened state he fell forward. He hit the ground and rolled onto his back. Two faces loomed over him and as he studied the scene from his back, he was relieved to see familiar blue coats. He was with Union soldiers.

"Hey, guy. Mighty big risk you took there, calling out to us. How did you know we weren't rebels?" the second man asked.

William explained, "I'll be honest, I wasn't sure it mattered to me. I've been through hell, so I put my faith in God's hands and figured that whatever happened was meant to be. I couldn't go much further. I mentioned I was wounded so that if it was rebels, there was a chance I'd be captured and not killed."

"Well then let's get you some help," the first man said. "I'm Jacob and this is Jeb."

"Nice to meet you. William Smith."

"All right, William Smith from the 28th, let's head back to camp," the one called Jeb replied.

Jacob and Jeb each shouldered their rifles and took one of William's arms to help him back to his feet. Placing William between the two of them, they started hobbling in a different direction. William let them lead and just focused on maintaining the rhythm they developed. Good leg forward, drag the back leg while leaning on Jacob. Switch weight to the bad leg, lean on Jeb, put the good leg forward again. Repeat. After what seemed like an eternity, William saw the unmistakable lights of a camp flickering in the distance.

"What unit are you two in?" William asked Jacob.

It was silent for a bit, but eventually Jeb responded. "This is Major General Hancock's camp. Commander of the 2nd Corps. You are lucky that we came along, as this camp is at the end of the entire 2 corps. In the morning we're headed into Gettysburg to take over the command, and no one else would be here unless it was a scavenger or a wild animal."

Nothing more was said between the three men as they approached the tents, focused on each step.

"Identify yourself" yelled an unknown voice from near the

camps.

"Ahhh piss off, Ben," replied Jacob. "You're always so jumpy. You need to spend more time in the woods, city boy. It's just Jacob and Jeb. We found a survivor, though he's a little worse for wear. Come to think of it, he kind of found us. Come on over here and give us a hand. We need to get him to the Doc."

The one named Ben stepped out of the shadows with his rifle still trained on William. As they came into the light, a look of shock hit Ben. He dropped his rifle and ran at full tilt towards William. It took William a while to register what was happening.

How was it possible that a slice of home was here to greet him after his hardest day of war? Ben crashed into William, hugging him and knocking him down to the ground. Jacob and Jeb looked on, confused. William said just two words.

"Hi, son."

Chapter 7

July 2, 1863 – Gettysburg

After their reunion, William was helped back up by Jeb and Jacob and carried to the medical tent. Despite the lateness of the hour, the camp sprung into motion. By the time the surgeon burst into the tent, William was already on his back and on the operating table. The assistants had removed the makeshift splint and were cutting away his pant leg so the doctor could assess the damage to William's knee. It was efficient and orderly, and William could tell he was in good hands.

"Not bad thinking there with the splint, Smith," the surgeon said. "It probably saved your knee from permanent damage."

"I had to get away from that river" was all William could say in response.

Ben hadn't left his father's side and was working to assess any other parts of him for damage. "Check my chest, son. I felt something punch me in the chest – the left breast."

Ben's fingers searched until they found a hole in William's overcoat right near his heart. In what seemed like slow motion, Ben slid his finger through the wool material and wiggled it. William had to stop himself from laughing at the ludicrous visual. Ben quickly unbuttoned the rest of the coat buttons and looked for signs of blood from William's chest.

"No blood," he said aloud, though William couldn't tell if it was for the benefit of him or the surgeon.

Ben reached into the jacket pocket, trying to find the

explanation. His eyes went wide as he pulled something out of the inner jacket pocket. It was a small bible.

Realization came over William's face. "That's the bible your mother gave me when I left. How did it…"

William trailed off as Ben had opened the cover of the bible to find a musket ball embedded three quarters of the way through the book. Ben pulled out a stack of letters from Abigail from within the book and a picture fell to the floor. It was the picture of the family that Abi had made for him. Ben showed it to his dad, with all faces smiling back at him but one. The musket ball had gone right through Emma's face.

"Lizzy is going to be pretty upset about that one," William joked. "She's going to think I did it on purpose."

Ben chuckled in return. William was glad for Ben's presence, as it had lightened his mood. He was so tired from his ordeal, but the dose of home had given him another wave of adrenaline. Just then the surgeon appeared at William's head.

"It's mixed news, Smith," the surgeon explained. "Good news is it doesn't look like we'll need to amputate. The bullet shattered your kneecap, though, and we need to extract the pieces from the kneecap before they move into your blood stream. Then we'll need to do some repairs to the surrounding tissue and clean it out to try and prevent infection. You were hit with a Minié ball, which fragments on impact and usually brings bits of your pants with it. As a result, pieces of the lead ball are still in your knee somewhere, as well as bits of fabric. From the state of the rest of your clothes, I'd wager there's also mud in there. If we don't get it out, you may die from infection. We have to do this quickly, and it will hurt quite a lot. We're going to do what we can to knock you out, but I'm going to soak some rags in Bromine and put them on your knee to try and kill disease before it starts. It's experimental, but I've had good luck with patients not getting any infection."

"Do what you must," William responded.

Another person had entered the tent. William couldn't hear or see who it was, but their voice carried authority. "Before that happens, Doc, I need this soldier to tell me what he knows of the enemy position."

Through the pain, William recounted the basic details of the events. He talked about the ridge giving way, the kill box that formed, and the hiding position of the enemy. He discussed the accuracy of the artillery fire and his estimates of casualties. He left out his role in starting the fight.

As he wrapped up giving his story, the surgeon brought in two sets of soaked rags and a shot of whisky. The first rag had a very strong, unpleasant scent that the doctor laid on William's chest. The surgeon then gave William the whisky.

"Whisky with Barbituric acid. Barbituric acid is another experiment, but it's a paralytic and should help keep your legs steady when you're asleep. They've been using it on mental patients on the East Coast, without realizing the potential it has in medicine."

William downed the shot and felt the familiar whisky burn in his throat. It was like saying hi to an old friend. He hadn't had very much whisky since he joined in Boston, and it was one of the things he missed about his life back in Medford.

"Alright, Major General, I need you to leave this tent," the doctor said to the voice. He turned to William.

"This is Chloroform. Just breathe," he said, moving the unpleasant smelling rag closer to William's mouth. "When I see you go to sleep, I'll use the other rag soaked in Bromine and start extracting pieces of the bullet. The Bromine rags are going to burn fiercely, so if the chloroform and barbituric acid don't work, we'll know. Hopefully you'll be in a deep enough sleep that you won't feel it."

"Stay with me, Ben," William said as he drifted off into a drug induced slumber. Everything went numb and the darkness took him.

When William awoke it was light outside. He lay in bed but was not in the medical tent. The first thing he noticed was that his knee was wrapped tightly in clean, white cloths around a more durable splint. Ben was sitting on the other bed in the tent, looking like he hadn't slept all night. For the first time, William could clearly see Ben. The last two and a half years had been good to him, and Ben had filled out and grown more muscular. He was tall like William and fair like Abigail. He was a handsome man, and William could see intelligence and kindness in his eyes.

"Good. You're awake," Ben said. "I was worried we'd have to call the Doc to rouse you. We're striking camp in an hour. They've already torn down the medical tent. I should be helping get ready, but Jacob and Jeb said they'd cover for me so I could see you before we left. We are heading to town today to join the battle."

For the first time, William looked at Ben's uniform. He saw the unmistakable chevron of Sergeant, and knew his son outranked him and could even give him orders.

Ben continued. "The surgeon says everything went well and he thinks he got all the pieces. You are to watch for signs of fever and ensure that no one changes those dressings until you get back to the field hospital at Spangler's farm. Instruct the surgeon on duty to rewrap your knee in one layer of Bromine-soaked rags and then two layers of clean bandages. Do you understand?"

"Yes sir," William said, with too much formality and a twinkle in his eye. His lips cracked into an upturned smile.

Ben smiled back and they shared a moment of levity in the shadow of a cruel war. After a moment of comfortable silence, Ben snapped back into the present and gestured at a cane next to the bed. "You may need that cane for the rest of your life."

The noise of distant cannon fire crept into the tent, and with each salvo Ben looked out. He clearly wanted to go join the rest of his troops.

"Hold on, son. I realize I'm in no position to ask this question, but why are you in the army? We agreed that it wasn't safe for you and Charlie to follow me. What happened?"

"It was the letter we got from you after Chancellorsville," Ben explained. "It inspired us, and knowing the level of death and destruction made us certain the war was nearly over. No country should accommodate the death of their citizens like what you saw in the Second Bull Run, Antietam and Chancellorsville. One night when mom was asleep, I left a note for her, Charlie, and Emma and walked to the train station. I hid in the station that night and snuck aboard a train to Boston. I signed the volunteer papers and the 3-year commitment right after that."

"Did Charlie do the same thing?" William prodded.

"No. Charlie is helping ma run the store. He has a mind for figures and not for war. Emma is supposed to be helping as well, but mom says it's impossible to get her to pay attention when any man comes into the store. That girl is boy crazy," Ben continued.

"Why didn't Abigail tell me you had left?" William felt a

little betrayed by Abi. He thought that they told each other everything, and this was a pretty big lie by omission.

"I wrote her when I got to the training camp to let her know I was safe. I asked her not to tell you, as I was afraid of how you would react. She agreed not to tell you, but I don't think she's very happy about it. I convinced her that you'd be so upset that you'd leave your post and come fine me. You'd be shot as a deserter, da, and ma needs you after the war. She seemed to hear that."

William watched as Ben paused, clearly choosing his next words carefully. "The three of us children are going to move on from Medford after the war. You have to have predicted that."

"I hadn't thought about life after war," William responded. "I believe that all of us are dead men, whose actions during battle just delay our appointment with the reaper. I know, though, that ultimately the reaper will win. He always does."

Ben laughed slightly, taken by the naivete of his father. "You raised us to be independent and make our own ways. Did you think we'd just be comfortable taking over the shop?"

William must have had a confused look on his face, as Ben sighed and pinched the bridge of his nose with his fingers. "All three of us have talked about our plans. Everyone knows our plans but you. Charlie wants to move into Boston to make his fortune and Emma wants to try living in London."

William mulled these revelations over in his head. He should have considered that his children wouldn't always be with him at home, but in the rush to war and the focus on staying alive these last 2 and a half years, he hadn't really considered the future.

"What are you planning to do in the battle today?" William

asked, changing the subject.

Ben replied. "When I joined, they found out I was educated. I suppose I have you and ma to thank for that. I showed a natural gift for seeing the larger problem and I was promoted pretty quickly to Sergeant in training camp. Word got up the chain, and Major General Hancock selected me for his personal company. The hundred or so of us that are in this company are all from similar educational backgrounds and most are ranked Sergeant or above. Hancock is trying to put together something new. Something modern. He says the key to winning on the battlefield is faster communication. As a result, all us soldiers can read and write, and he's taught us some encryption. Our job is to get encoded information to generals faster than anyone else, while keeping it safe. We are all trained in basic bushcraft and have a level of understanding of strategy. As a result, we can creep through blockade lines and also change orders we have based on what we learn in the trip."

William paused to consider all of this, and Ben continued. "How do you think Jeb snuck up behind you without you noticing? Do you think Jacob stepped on that stick by mistake? They heard you coming a mile away."

"I hadn't considered it. I was just happy to hear another living soul," William responded, chuckling slightly at his luck.

Ben resumed, finally answering the original question. "Today I'll be running between one side of the infantry and the cannons. The infantry units are leading a counter charge after the cannons decimate the main Confederate force. The Major General is trying to time the cannon fire with the infantry charge, hoping to reduce casualties, even if the charge is towards cavalry. At least that's the plan. Between the cannon fire and using seasoned front lines, we're hoping to strike real change at this battle. There's a rumor among the company that President Lincoln may come to talk to the troops after the battle. He supposedly wants to deliver a message to inspire the troops after a great victory. We just have to win first."

William realized the man in front of him was unlike who he had left two and a half years ago. Ben had inherited the best qualities of both him and of Abigail. He was intelligent, confident and sure of his own skin. He exuded leadership and had a bright future. There was nothing more Ben needed from him on the journey to becoming a leader in his own right.

"Well," William concluded. "I guess I shouldn't keep you, then."

Ben nodded in agreement and stood to leave. As he rose, he laid the small bible on William's chest. The musket ball was still embedded within the cover.

"Keep this on you, da. It's done a pretty good job of keeping you safe so far."

William protested. "Carry it for me, then, Ben. Let it keep you safe. I'm sure that I won't be seeing battle again."

Ben shook his head and muttered something about extra weight slowing him down.

"Keep your head about you, then," William responded. "Don't forget it's better to be selfish than dead sometimes. Watch your back."

"I love you, da," was all that Ben replied.

"Love you too," William responded as Ben ducked under the tent flap and disappeared into the daylight. William wasn't sure if Ben had heard him or not.

Chapter 8

1863 – Medford

William got up and hobbled out of the tent shortly after he said goodbye to Ben. The cane took some getting used to, but it was a welcome relief from the dull ache in his knee and leg. William knew this pain would haunt him until his last day, but he was happy to be alive. The reunion with Ben and the escape from what seemed like certain death made him almost happy. As he reflected on his newfound happiness, though, guilt came crashing down on William as he remembered his role in the death of the rest of his squad.

He followed Ben's directions and went to Spangler's farm, which had been set up as a field hospital. Walking was easier than it had been through the forest, but it was still not the pace he had hoped. The slower pace allowed him to look around and see the Pennsylvania countryside. He continued to see signs of battle and he joined a stream of wounded pouring into the field hospital. The scene was backed by distant, never-ending salvos of cannon fire, with the closer rounds making William flinch. He waited in line with the rest of the walking wounded and eventually it was his turn to be examined by the doctors at Spangler's farm.

William told the doctors what the surgeon had said, and even though they looked at him with contempt, they changed his bandages per the instructions and sent him on his way. They needed the beds, and he wasn't in immediate danger of dying. On the way out, William stopped at the clerk's post and had discharge papers signed. The clerk granted William "honorable discharge due to injuries sustained in the line of duty," which enabled him to receive a pension for the rest of his life. The clerk directed him towards the closest troop transport and William sighed as he realized his time in the army had come to an unceremonious end.

William wound through Pennsylvania by train into Philadelphia. From there he made a short detour to the war office to file his final pension paperwork and onto another train to Boston. He spent the night in Boston at the barracks and caught the morning train into Medford. He got off the train and walked the familiar pathways that took him onto High Street and dragged himself into the General Store.

William was tired, dirty, smelling of Bromine, covered in dust, but excited to see his family. He opened the door and a bell over the door rang, announcing his presence.

A familiar voice called out "I'll be with you in a second."

William stepped into the store as Abigail looked up from the counter. She looked tired. She had lost some weight since William had last seen her and some of her flaxen hair had turned grey. William didn't care. Her eyes were still alive, and William immediately felt better just by being in her presence. She was the most beautiful thing in the world and his heart soared. A sudden terror gripped him.

What if she didn't love him anymore? What if she had taken another lover? What if she didn't want him in her life anymore? What if?

As he watched the blank stare of salesmanship turn into recognition and then finally joy, he heard her scream out for Charlie and Emma. Abigail leaped over the counter with a youthful exuberance and closed the distance between them quickly. He was laughing a deeper laugh than he had in a long time. She noticed the cane and corrected her course to avoid bowling him over in her embrace. It didn't matter. William braced for the impact and absorbed her as she crashed into his arms. They stayed like that for a long time. He was home. He greeted her with a deep and passionate kiss until it was interrupted by two others joining the hug. He drank them in. Their looks, their smells, their faces. He stared at Abigail the most and the longest.

"Da, you came home!" both children exclaimed.

Emma paused. "What IS that smell?"

"Hey Charlie, Hey Lizzie" he responded. "That's Bromine from my leg, but that doesn't matter. How'd you get so big?"

William nearly felt whole again, more whole than he had in two and a half years. He drank them in again and again. Charlie smelled of paper and ink. Lizzie smelled of grass and wildflowers. Abigail smelled of lilac and home. All the smells he hadn't been able to remember in the past two and a half years jogged his memory and the emotion flooded over him. He held Abigail in a tight embrace and buried his face into her shoulder, breathing in her essence. He didn't need to kiss her. Holding her tightly was refilling his soul.

Eventually, they broke apart and Abigail asked him for details since his last letter. William spent the evening filling them in on the stories from the last two and a half years. They dined over stew and cornbread, and it was the most delicious meal that William had ever had. He continued to recount his stories and ended with the story of Gettysburg – being trapped, being assaulted by cannon fire, his escape and his encounter with Ben. They asked after Ben, as he couldn't write home as much as William had. He recounted his time with Ben with immense pride.

He didn't reveal that everything in that gulley was his fault. He would never speak those parts out loud; in case the devil was distracted and had forgotten William's role in the day's events.

For the next few weeks, they waited for a letter from Ben to tell the story about how the rest of the battle went. They were anxious to fill the hole in their lives by proxy. Despite not knowing about Ben's fate, these were the happiest weeks of William's life. Each night was filled with stories and joy and good food and love. Abigail and he reconnected. Even William's newfound faith ended up deepening the bond between them.

Three weeks after William came back to Medford, they received a letter from Major General Hancock himself, addressed to the parents of Sergeant Smith.

The morning that William spent with Ben in the tent ended up being the last morning of Ben's life. He had left the tent and joined up with the rest of the forces mounting the attack on Gettysburg. He had made 3 trips between the cannon and the infantry and stopped to have some water from his canteen when the Confederate snipers caught up with him. He was found face up in the dirt after the battle, with a bullet in his knee and another through his heart. He never got to hear the Gettysburg Address and never got to see the end of the war.

The Major General detailed Ben's final hours and thanked them on behalf of a grateful nation. Sergeant Smith had died a hero, the letter said, and his actions of the day had saved countless Union lives. Hancock thanked them for raising such a wonderful person and expressed regret for his loss.

Ben was 20 years old and was buried in a mass grave in the fields of Pennsylvania.

Chapter 9
1865 – Medford

Something broke inside Abigail when the letter from Major General Hancock arrived. Ben had always been her favorite, and everyone knew it, even though it was never spoken. Just days after the letter arrived, Abigail sank into a deep depression and became a shadow of her former self.

She slept in Ben's room each night, and she and William drifted back apart. She grew more and more distant, and barely acknowledged that there was a family around her that still needed her. Gone were the warm embraces she used to give William and gone was the light in her eyes. She was a ghost of herself. She barely ate, barely slept, and refused to help in the store. She didn't brush her hair or apply her lilac perfume anymore. She was a person-shaped entity, drifting through her life.

The Smith family fell into a new daily pattern, held together by necessity instead of love. William learned how to cook and tried to help Charlie where he could around the shop. He didn't know how long Abigail's withdrawal from the world would last, but he would do what he could to get her through it and back to a life the resembled the normal he was used to before the war. William figured there wasn't a reason for him to survive the war if he didn't get a happy ending.

William's knee continued to bother him, and he needed the cane for anything more than 3 steps. Ben's prediction from the tent on that morning had come true. His knee just wouldn't support his weight. As a result, William only went upstairs at the end of the day, as the stairs were too much effort. The pain was constant, and William found himself slipping into the whisky bottle he kept behind the downstairs counter. Before the war he'd only fed this habit when he and Abigail fought. Now it was a near daily occurrence, and he'd take a few pulls before walking up the stairs to try and figure out how to make Abigail better. Abigail would typically stay upstairs all day, which didn't help close any of the distance between William and her. Grief had driven a wedge between them, and the coldness that William remembered from his parents' marriage was starting to replicate in his own.

1863 gave way to 1864. The war was still a strong economic driver to Massachusetts, and the railyard in Medford served as a hub for the outlying areas. Women went to work in the brick factory and the shop's profits started to recover. The Union Army was an ever-hungry mistress, buying up all the surplus food and supplies that Medford had to offer. The extra money trickled down to all the citizens, who in turn trickled it into the shop. A fragile peace fell over the Smith household as Abigail's routine didn't change. The days quickly melded into a routine. William would wake up and make breakfast for Charlie, Lizzie, Abigail, and himself. Then he would head down to mind the store with Charlie. William enjoyed his time in the store, though, as the constant stream of people through the store gave him some social interaction and let him hear about all the events that hadn't made it into the Mercury. Lizzie usually was gone most of the day but would return before supper. William had no idea where she went and didn't ask, either. William would head upstairs to the residence above the General Store while Charlie finished the daily books and cleaning so William could cook the evening meal. Sometimes Abigail would join them and sometimes she wouldn't. After dinner

Abigail would sit in her favorite chair and stare at the wall, giving one-word answers if she was asked a question. Then at 9 pm it was off to bed with William in his room and Abigail retreating to Ben's room.

The only real time she left the house was to attend church on Sundays, but she refused to sit next to William. William racked his brain for ways to make her smile or to shake her out of the doldrums, but nothing he did seemed to matter. He tried reaching out to the Minister, but even the Minister wasn't able to get through her funk. She was dead to the world.

1864 gave way to 1865 and the news of the end of the war was all over the Medford Mercury for months. Celebrations formed in the streets and squares of Medford, and there were daily reunions at the train station of the town's men and boys. The assassination of President Lincoln rocked the country, and many in Medford came into the store to ask if another war was coming. William didn't think the country had the tolerance for more loss of life. He was happy for the end of the war but upset that Lincoln wouldn't be around to see the new Union prosper. Abigail seemed to barely register the news.

July 2nd marked the second anniversary of Ben's death. The Smith family had a somber breakfast and then all walked to the church to light a candle and join a service with the other members of Medford that had lost someone in the woods of Pennsylvania at Gettysburg. After the short service, they all walked back. William reached over to Abi as they left the church and squeezed her hand. She looked up at him, tears in her eyes, and muttered "Don't."

William dropped her hand, and they proceeded back to the store. When they arrived, Abigail retreated upstairs while William and Charlie spent the rest of the day working in the store. The town must have known this day was hard for the Smiths, because there were fewer than normal customers. William didn't mind, though, and spent his time with Charlie in a silent vigil. He had hoped that Abigail would join them to mourn as a family, but also knew that he should give her the space she clearly desired. Lizzie vanished somewhere down the High Street, not wanting to be under the rain cloud of the day. William didn't pry – girls were a mystery to him.

When William finished his day, he was exhausted from the emotion. He stood at the bottom of the stairs and yelled up to Abigail.

"Any thoughts on what you want for dinner tonight, Abi?" he yelled.

She didn't respond, but these days she rarely did. Charlie usually came up about an hour after William as he finished the books, the cleaning and generally worked to get ready for the next day's customers.

William turned to Charlie who stood behind the counter. "What about you, Charlie? Any requests?"

"The salt pork needs to be eaten," was all that Charlie stated in response.

As William lumbered his way up the stairs to start dinner for the three of them, he called out again to Abigail. He was hoping to hear something from her. Anything.

Chapter 10

July 2, 1865 – Medford

William was exhausted from trying to keep it together that day. As he slowly climbed the stairs, he decided he was done avoiding Abi. He needed to get through to her. He was hurting too. Despite her drift into depression, she was still his anchor to this world. Maybe he would join her in Ben's bed tonight, for he could barely contain his grief and wanted someone with which to share it. He needed his partner back.

"Abi?" he called out. "Sweetie, we need to start doing something different. I need you back."

There was no answer. He reached the top of the stairs and still didn't hear any noise from Abigail. He figured maybe she was asleep, so he stepped down the hall and glanced in Ben's room. The bed was empty, and everything was tidy – Abigail had made the bed and cleaned it up. This was a promising start, William thought, and suddenly he had hope that she was starting up the other side of the mountain of her depression. Maybe she had decided that two years was enough. William hoped she would move back into their room and share a bed again. William drifted down the hallway towards their room and saw that the door was pulled shut.

"She's probably asleep in our bed. Maybe I can join her for a short nap before making dinner," he thought.

He pushed the door to their room with his cane and it swung open. William wasn't ready for the scene that he saw before him. The shock of it all caused him to drop his cane and let out a low wail as his world fractured and fell apart.

Abigail hung from the ceiling, motionless. Her neck was tilted unnaturally to the side and her body was suspended from a solid length of rope from one of the exposed rafters in the room. She twirled slowly in place, some unseen force causing her to rotate slowly. She had put on her wedding dress – a simple, floor length white dress with lace trim. Abigail's favorite part of her wedding dress was the train, which today hung beyond her feet to the overturned chair below. The dress was accented with bright red spots of blood, which William noticed as he scanned upwards to find her face. For some reason his mind couldn't help but think that the drops of red didn't belong on the white dress and in his shock, he wondered where they came from.

His mind drew blank, and a chill set in over his entire body. This couldn't be real. She would be ok. This wasn't real.

His gaze slowly traveled up and reached her face. What he saw barely even looked like Abigail anymore. Her eyes bugged out of their sockets and a trail of drool trickled from the corner of her mouth and down her chin. Blood trailed from her nose and down the front of her dress where the white fabric had caught the red. The rigors had not yet set in, but it was clear she had done this early in the day after they got back from church. William didn't have his cane, but he ran to her as fast as he could, ignoring the pain in his leg.

She had to be ok. She had to still be alive. This wasn't real.

He grabbed her legs and pressed himself into her. He braced her with his good leg and raised her up, hoping he'd get some sign that she was ok. All he had to do was take the pressure off the rope around her neck. That was the first problem he had to solve. He stood there, holding her legs, while he listened for a cough, a rasp, a choke. Anything at all.

This couldn't be real. She wasn't really dead. This was a dream. Why couldn't he wake up? This wasn't real.

He held her legs, trying to will air back into her lungs. 20 minutes later as the hall clock struck 6:30, every muscle within William was on fire. He had reached the end of his strength, and he finally let go. This wasn't real. He sat on the edge of the bed, restoring some strength in his legs and trying to overcome the shock.

Every minute that passed convinced William that this wasn't a cork you could put back in a bottle. The love of his life had gone. No. She couldn't be gone. He jumped back up and grabbed her legs again, trying to will air back into her lungs again. He couldn't let go. She would be ok. The denial gave way to grief, and as he kept holding onto her legs, he started sobbing. The grief came in jagged waves, as William abandoned his frantic attempt to rescue the love of his life. The noises that came with the jagged waves of grief were inhuman as his heart broke again and again.

What was he going to do now? How could he go on? Somewhere in the back of his mind he heard Charlie or Lizzie coming down the hall to see what had put his father into such a state.

"Stop! Don't come in!" William yelled through the tears.

They didn't listen. They both burst through the doorway and took in the scene. It was their mother, hanging from the rafters and their father, completely beside himself in grief, holding her legs while sobbing.

"Jesus," Charlie said, and ran back out. Lizzie collapsed in the doorway and didn't move.

Charlie reappeared with the police chief a little while later.

"Heaven help me," was the chief's reaction when he saw the scene, but snapped into action with an admirable sense of duty. William was still in the same spot, but his ragged wails had turned into quiet sobs. He had cried all his tears, and he was exhausted. The flame had gone out of his life, and his sobs echoed the emptiness he felt. William knew that when he let go, his heart would never be full again. He knew there was never anyone else who could fill that void she had left. He would never be happy again.

The police chief stepped over Lizzie and eventually separated William from Abigail's legs. William and Lizzie were directed to sit on the bed while the chief started the process of cutting her body down. Charlie left the room, unable to watch anymore. Lizzie buried her face in William's chest when Abigail's body fell to the floor with a thud. By then William refused to believe that the thing that fell was his Abigail and he completely detached from the scene, just like he had in all those battles during the war. He was merely watching a scene unfold, perhaps like the play that Lincoln had seen at Ford's Theater. William wished there was another Booth to come and end his misery so he wouldn't have to watch the rest of this play.

He saw the police chief leave the room again, presumably to get the undertaker. William knew that there would be no investigation. The scene was clearly a suicide, and the chief spared them all the pain of having to answer any questions about her death.

As he sat there, William knew that his Abi had finally decided the pain was too much. He was stupid for leaving her for two and a half years to chase justice and glory in the army. Those were two and a half years he would never have back. Two and a half years of missed kisses. Two and a half years of mornings he didn't wake up next to her. Two and a half years of goodnights and good mornings and good days. Two and a half years of laughter and joy. It was two and a half years he would never forgive himself for missing. He hadn't gotten to live with her long enough. He sat on the bed and his body was wracked with wave after wave of sadness. Although he knew he would never see her living face again, it was still too painful to admit she was gone. Lizzie crept out of the room, leaving William alone. Just like he would be for the rest of his life.

William looked around the room, looking for something to remind him of her that he could hold. As his eyes scanned the room, they noticed a piece of paper on the dressing table. He got up from the bed and stepped over the shape that was no longer his Abigail to get to it. It was a single piece of paper, folded in half with his name on the outside in her graceful, slanting script. The script that had kept him going all those years in war. The script that had signed their marriage certificate and balanced the store books. He raised the letter to his nose and sniffed. It smelled of lilac. She had used her perfume on the letter one last time. He brought the letter back to the bed and sat, motionless, while he breathed in the scent that would always remind him of her. The scent of a thousand nights and countless moments for two that were in deep love. The scent he hadn't smelled for these last two years. Breathing it in on the edge of that bed, a lifetime of memories came rushing back and for a moment William thought this was some metaphor. Abi wasn't dead, she had just metaphorically hung her old self from the rafters. The lilac was proof that she wanted to be with him again. Forever.

It was not to be. His eyes eventually opened, and he saw her lifeless form again, sprawled out on the floor. He set his jaw in a tight grip, and, for the last time, he opened a letter addressed to him from his wife. He opened it, hoping for an insight to her last thoughts and hoping that the message would be one of eternal love and longing. A message he could use to remember her. The words within left William without any question why she ended her life.

> *Damn you for losing him. It should have been you in Gettysburg. I can't be here with you or without him.*

She hadn't even signed her name.

Chapter 11
1865 to 1888 – Medford

Things continued to fall apart for William Smith after Abi's funeral. In the spring of 1866, Charlie told William he was leaving to make his fortune in Boston. He would close out April at the store, but after that William would have to find help or convince Emma to pull her weight. He wanted to work in finance, and the Boston Stock Exchange was looking for people after the war had decimated their ranks. William knew that Charlie's knack for numbers made this a perfect fit for him, but it was another loss he didn't expect.

Charlie moved out and found work trading Lake Superior copper. He visited regularly at the start, but as the years passed his visits back to Medford became fewer and fewer. In 1880 they stopped altogether. William didn't fault him for that. There was no joy in visiting an empty old, broken man. The last time William ever heard from Charlie was a half-hearted Christmas card in 1882.

Abigail's and Ben's deaths had also hardened Emma. After Abigail's body was found, she refused to let William call her Elizabeth or Lizzie. She stayed out late most nights and developed an untoward reputation as a woman of loose morals. When William tried to intervene, it drove a wedge further between the two of them. Emma clearly blamed William for Abigail's death and would let him know it. It came to a head in 1870, and they yelled at each other into the night and the early hours of morning. She left the next day.

Just like Ben had predicted, Emma boarded a steamer and

headed across the Atlantic to London. She left a letter letting him know she would find work in London, minding a store. She sent him a single letter after she left, giving him the address where she was staying. For the first few years, he tried to reconcile with her, by pouring out his heart in letters to the address she had given. He told her details from his life had never told anyone except Abigail. He wrote about his time in the war and the pain of the Bromine. He wrote about what he missed about Abigail. All the words just poured out of his pen, and it was cathartic for William.

His letters to her were never returned. He gave up in 1878 and figured that it was her turn to respond. He had tried for 8 years and was willing to wait for her to take the lead. He didn't realize he would never see her again. Much like Ben and Abigail, William never got the chance to say goodbye.

After Lizzie left, William thought about following Abigail into death. For some unknown reason, William could never be brave enough to go through with it. He didn't mind the after part, it was just getting there that held him back. He didn't think his broken body or spirit could accommodate the pain it would take to get to death. And so he plodded on with a life without purpose or direction.

William couldn't run the store by himself due to his leg. After Abigail's death, he had a regular rotation of younger people helping. He paid them a decent wage and the store still managed to turn a small profit. It was not nearly as lucrative as it had been when his parents bought it, but William didn't care. His heart wasn't in it, and he had no one to share money with. The only things he bought were food and whisky. He continued to use the whisky as a salve for his pain, and soon he was up to 3 or 4 bottles per week. He stopped going to church, feeling abandoned by his

God. He felt no guilt in abandoning that God right back.

He sold the store in 1875 to a young couple from Delaware named Thomas and Clara Foster who were looking to start a new life on their own. They had recently married, and Clara was already pregnant. William moved out of the residence above the General Store and shortly after the couple had their baby – a cute little girl that they named Elizabeth. It was another knife into a broken heart, but the Fosters did it without malice. There was no way they could have known.

William became the police chief's deputy and moved into a small apartment near town hall, which housed the police station. The apartment was on the ground floor of a building on High Street, which meant that William no longer had to walk up and down stairs. It had very limited amenities, and William took very few things from the house above the General Store. It was a simple life, and one William didn't really care about.

The police work was rewarding, and William's history as a seasoned veteran allowed him a certain level of respect among the townsfolk. Nothing seemed to bother him as a police deputy, as William had lost most of his emotion with the endless losses in his life. He developed a reputation as a grizzled loner in the town, and he was fine with that. He couldn't let anyone else get close to him. Everyone who was close to him just ended up leaving, one way or another.

He didn't even pretend to be religious anymore – that was Abigail's thing – and spent most nights quietly sitting in the front room of his apartment drinking from a whisky bottle. He would drink and talk to Abigail. He would tell her about his day and tell him all that was within his mind. He gave her updates on his police cases and updates on the General Store that was now under the stewardship of the Fosters. He gave her updates on the town, and he even told her more about his time in the war. He even told her about the time in that gulley and his role in it. He needed her to know all of his regrets and all of his pain. If he had shared this when he was still alive, she might still be his.

In the small moments before he blacked out drunk, he swore he could hear Abigail talking back. He wouldn't let go of her memory.

Chapter 12

April 1888 – Whitechapel, London

It was dark, but Elizabeth knew she had to get home to see her son. She had to make sure he knew what to do.

The day had started peacefully enough. It was the Easter bank holiday, and the rain clouds had hung low in the sky, giving London a dreamy feeling that reminded her of childhood winters in Massachusetts. She awoke to her son making breakfast. He made breakfast for her every morning, always before the bells of St. Mary Matfelon struck 10.

Elizabeth's son was the reason she kept this life. A divorced woman in her 40s was only eligible for so many things to put food on the table, and whoring was the only thing that paid enough to keep his belly full. She was also really good at it, and even enjoyed most of her clients. This morning, he had made her eggs over toast and a strong cup of cheap dredge water that passed for tea. She marveled that he was able to make such good food over a small open flame and a grill. It had taken her three months to save enough coins for the setup. He set aside an added slice of toast for himself, but he gave her the eggs. All he would ever say was "You need your strength" when she tried to get him to eat her share.

Elizabeth and her son never talked about what she did at night, but somewhere deep within, she knew that he was wiser than he let on.

They spent the better part of the morning doing mundane chores and cleaning their small space at the lodging house. She marveled as she watched him. He had so much poise and control that belied a maturity double of his 15 years. She also had a daughter, Sarah, 9, in Finsbury Park, but they hadn't spoken in the 18 months since Elizabeth walked out on her husband and took up her current position. It was a blessing that the boy still wanted to be with his mother. Elizabeth was worried that her ex-husband would soon start to cross the lines with Sarah that had forced Elizabeth to the street. Elizabeth had to figure out how to make more money in case she needed a bigger space for her, Sarah, and her son.

After chores, Elizabeth and her son had gone to a service at St. Mary's to donate a hay penny for the orphans. It wasn't something they could always afford to give, but Elizabeth knew that there were others even less fortunate than her. Her mother had always taught her the value of charity. They returned to the lodging house shortly before supper and decided to splurge on the group meal. There was a stew that promised beef, although Elizabeth was sure that it was probably horse meat. The food was fortifying all the same.

Mistress Mary, the keeper of her lodging house, was a mountain of a lady who didn't take any guff. The lodging house at number 18 George's Street was safer than most, and thievery was almost unheard of. Thieves who found themselves on the wrong end of Mistress Mary were kicked to the street without their belongings and with a broken hand for their trouble. The resultant reputation of the lodging house was one of security and family. Elizabeth had always been prompt with payment, and Mistress Mary would ensure her son didn't get into any trouble while Elizabeth was out working in return. She took a shine to him and would even sometimes slip him some extra food. Mistress Mary was aware of the Whitechapel gangs that specialized in intimidation, racketeering, and pickpocketing. She was also aware that the gangs loved to recruit boys in lodging homes with the promise of a quick payday. As long as she was in charge, though, they wouldn't dare recruit Elizabeth's son. He didn't avoid the gangs altogether, but he managed to stay on the edge of trouble. Mistress Mary would comment to Elizabeth some mornings that she saw him observing, as if he was absorbing the behavior of the other boys but never acting on the impulse to steal, cheat, or pickpocket.

Around 7 pm, Elizabeth started to get ready for her night. She knew that the Easter holiday meant the crowd was likely going to be rough and chose a dress she didn't mind getting a little torn. The kind of men that visit whores on bank holidays don't like to be at home with their wives and families all day, so by the time they're able to get to the pubs, their moods are dark. Combined with ale, it usually means higher prices but a rougher "transaction." It was almost certain that Elizabeth would need to rest and recover tomorrow.

The most important part of any whore's dress are the hidden pockets used to store earnings, and Elizabeth ensured that these were intact and strong. She began her night by walking down George's Street and waiting in the local pubs. She was known to several local inn keepers, who would look the other way as she serviced her customers in the back alleys in exchange for her fee. Her presence was beneficial for these inn keepers, as the men who came to Whitechapel wanted to both drink and whore.

She worked this evening like any other, pausing to freshen up between clients and then heading back on the prowl for another John or Jack. The payment was good tonight. She may be able to afford a rasher of bacon or some sausages.

Well after midnight, Elizabeth decided to find one more client for the night. She left George's Street and crossed over to Osborn. She noticed another whore named Margaret coming back up Osborn, likely done for the night. Margaret lived in the same lodging house as her and was an extra set of eyes to help watch over her son when she could. Elizabeth gave her a wave and a smile, but Margaret looked shaken. Elizabeth started to cross the street to try to talk with her, but Margaret kept going, her expression caught somewhere between shock and distress. That happened some nights, especially bank holidays. Sometimes a John was too aggressive and sometimes there was little choice in what he would do to you. Margaret seemed to have unusually bad luck tonight, and Elizabeth was glad it wasn't her.

As Elizabeth moved further down Osborn Street she set her sights on a pub near the cocoa factory, hoping to find one last client. It was late enough that the men would be in their cups, which meant 5 minutes of work for a high return. Then she could head home to join her son, asleep in their shared bed. She had pocketed enough money tonight to take tomorrow off and add some to the stash they kept under their bed in an old lye tin. She hoped she'd be able to dream of winter tonight and be awakened by the smell of breakfast before the bells struck 10 again. Tomorrow, if the weather got better, they could go to the park, maybe even all the way to Tower Green to watch the boats go by on the Thames.

Elizabeth was distracted in this daydream and didn't hear the swiftly approaching footsteps. Seemingly out of nowhere, something hard struck her across the face, and she immediately fell into the street.

"Why do you whores always crumble so easily" a high-pitched voice rasped at her.

As she fell, she struck the back of her head on the pavement. Elizabeth felt a warm rush at the point of impact, and was pretty sure the back of her skull was bleeding. She tried to cover her face, but another strike hit her across the nose before she could. It cracked and Elizabeth knew it was broken. A third blow struck her in the mouth and Elizabeth felt at least two teeth fracture.

"That's right," the voice snarled, "whores need to keep quiet. Talking isn't what you get paid for."

Panic started to creep into Elizabeth's mind, but now she focused on preventing more damage. She turned her head to prevent the blood from her nose draining back into her throat. Choking would not do her any good. Her hands were finally able to cover her face. The blows had stopped, but Elizabeth dared not move in case she angered the attacker further.

"What do you want?" Elizabeth pleaded through the blood, "Money? Sex?"

The only reply was a single word. "Pain" the man said, almost too quietly to be heard.

Perhaps this John was why Margaret looked so shaken just minutes before. Had he tried the same with her? Elizabeth had thought she was the lucky one tonight, though the hubris of it all was proving the irony of hindsight. She had to survive. She had to make it home. She started to think of ways through the problem, one step at a time, just like her da taught her. She didn't give him credit for much, but she shared a brain and a thought process with him. She wondered what he was doing right now.

Identifying her attacker could be a bonus. If the police

weren't interested, maybe the gangs would be. Elizabeth cracked her eyes slightly and saw a pair of men's boots. The boots were much too nice for this part of town, with nicely worn-in leather, calfskin laces and even some brogues around the toe. Elizabeth realized that her attacker clearly didn't need the money. This thought brought a new wave of terror, as a man who attacked a whore without the intent to rob was usually after only one other thing. Even though her mind was still reeling from the three strikes to her face, she thought of pressing her luck – maybe she could find one more identifying feature without giving up too much.

She started to turn her head upwards to try and identify the man, but as she did, she felt a searing pain in her right ear and a resistance that wouldn't let her turn.

"This clip of your ear will be what I send to the police," the man continued, letting out a peel of maniacal laughter. She had assumed he had attacked her to rape her, but this sentence made Elizabeth think she was in mortal danger. Elizabeth knew she had to get away.

She mustered up all the energy she could spare and let out a scream that sounded more like a gurgle through her bloody mouth and broken teeth. The pain started to recede, as it seemed that the man stopped cutting. She used that break to throw her hands over her head and curl her knees into her stomach, trying to protect herself as best she could. She was waiting for an opening to lash out and take this man unawares with a swift kick to the groin or the stomach. She had to time it just right.

"It seems we have a fighter here. I respect that. Maybe you didn't crumble as easily as I thought."

It was silent for a moment, and Elizabeth hoped that the

attack was done. Without warning, there was a flurry of motion below Elizabeth's waist, and the man rasped at her again.

"Out of respect for your fight, I'll not cut your throat. Tell the doctors to look for the rip."

Although her eyes were shut, she heard laughter as a pair of hands probed through her clothes. Her attacker tore at her dress, and she heard coins striking the pavement as the hidden pockets finally gave up their bounty. She laid there, letting the man take his prize and thought that the worst was over. She figured she had read the situation wrong. He was just a petty thief. His last phrase rolled around in her head, though. Was he referring to the ripped clothes? Was her ear ripped in two? What did it mean?

Just then, the world was brought into sharp focus and her pain was redoubled by a blinding pressure between her legs. She felt something tear, deep inside of her.

"I shan't stop ripping until my truncheon finds its most deserving target," the man whispered in Elizabeth's tattered right ear. Then he was gone. She finally let the pain overwhelm her, and unconsciousness was the only respite Elizabeth's body would allow.

Chapter 13

April 1888 – Whitechapel, London

Elizabeth awoke, disoriented and confused. Her clothes were torn, and she was sure her money was gone. She scrabbled around on the pavement, looking for some coins the man had missed – something she could keep from the night to afford her place in the lodging house and some food in their bellies. Her vision was blurry, so she groped the cobblestones, looking for the familiar shape of coins. She found nothing. She still didn't understand why he would rob her. She replayed all he had said in her head, trying to understand what he had meant. Tears mixed with the blood on her face as she cursed her luck. She would have to dip into the lye tin to keep their spot in the lodging house. She hoped they could afford food while she recovered, but she knew the pain between her legs put the timeline for recovery in question. Maybe Mistress Mary would allow her to fall behind a little on payment while she recovered. The pain was still unlike anything in her life, but she knew she could not remain in the gutter on Osborn Street.

She tried to stand, but the world would not stop spinning. Her face and head ached worse than they ever had, but the worst pain was still between her legs. She had been raped before in her line of work, and the force of that always left her tender and sore. This felt different and more permanent. She tentatively reached her hand down between her legs and pulled it away bloody. She had to get home. It would all make sense when she got home.

Tears and blood flowed from her face like the rain in the pre-dawn silence as she reached George Street. The last half mile had been a new fresh torture as she half-walked, half-crawled one painful step after the other. It was so dark, but Elizabeth couldn't tell if that darkness was from the rain-soaked streets or her blurry periphery as she tried to keep the pain at bay. She stumbled and fell again, face-down, as she came to the lodging house at number 18 and cried out for help. Elizabeth was hoping it was loud enough, but it was still a gurgle as her nose continued to bleed into her mouth. She hoped someone in the lodging house would be awake for an early factory shift. She was guessing it was around 4, but the weather may have skewed that as well. Someone would come and help her. They had to. She wouldn't give up. What would she tell her son? Would they finally be forced to move back with her monster of an ex-husband?

Elizabeth felt the movement before she heard it. Her ear was likely also filled with blood, but she was afraid to reach up and check how much of it remained. It was Mistress Mary who found her.

"Blessed Jesus" the woman said in her thick Irish brogue, and Elizabeth heard the door close behind her again. Elizabeth rolled over onto her side and looked at the door. The light from within the lodging house shone as Mistress Mary reopened the door and came back out, tailed by Margaret and what looked like Annie Lee. Annie was a whore who still had her innocence, as if this dark underworld wouldn't ever taint her. Annie believed that eventually one of the men she serviced would turn out to be her true love, whisking her away from this life and to a better place. Elizabeth and Margaret tolerated the fantasy because she was sometimes the light they needed in their own dark lives.

Annie took one look at Elizabeth and screamed a piercing, unholy scream.

"What is it, Annie?" said Margaret, who hadn't yet seen

Elizabeth in the street.

Annie pointed, and Margaret saw Elizabeth there in the street, blood streaming down her legs and face, pooling into the gutter to be washed away by the steady rain. It was to Margaret's stammering and crying that Elizabeth lost consciousness for a second time.

Elizabeth came to and watched the world pass by slowly. The sky was lighter now, but the rain persisted. She thought to herself that she really should be getting out of her wet clothes. Something about the way it popped into her head brought the evening rushing back and with it, the pain. Elizabeth was confused now, too. She was moving through the streets, but she couldn't register her own legs moving.

"What happened," Elizabeth cried out. "Where am I?"

"Oh dear, you've been attacked. We're taking you to the hospital to get you cleaned up." Mistress Mary responded. She was doing her best to remove the fear from her voice, but Elizabeth could tell that not all was right.

"That's nice," she replied. "I hope they have comfortable beds. Do you know where my son is?"

"He'll be along shortly," he heard Annie say.

Elizabeth couldn't see Annie, but that had to be Annie, she thought. Annie was such a sweet friend. Elizabeth realized she couldn't remember her son's name. He was the light of her life. She knew that his name was a word that needed to be formed and that she should be able to speak, but there was something wrong. Her brain wouldn't connect his name to her mouth. There was just so much pain. She had to concentrate and make her words precious and important. She couldn't let the pain win.

She suddenly became vaguely aware that Mistress Mary, Margaret, and Annie had to be carrying her. That's why her legs weren't moving.

"Where am I?" Elizabeth asked.

Mistress Mary exchanged worried glances with Margaret, and they picked up their pace.

Elizabeth realized that it was rare for Mistress Mary to leave the lodging house. Elizabeth vaguely wondered what had been so important.

"Why did you leave the house, Mistress Mary? Was someone hurt?" Elizabeth asked.

"Don't you worry about that right now, child," Mistress Mary responded. More worried glances.

As they headed back towards where Elizabeth had just come, she pointed down Osborn Street.

"That's where the man ripped me." Elizabeth blurted. "He said whores should be quiet and not talk. I didn't talk, but he talked a lot. He had nice shoes."

Margaret and Annie seemed to grasp what Elizabeth was trying to say, but something with the way Elizabeth was phrasing this didn't make sense.

"What do you mean you were ripped?" Margaret asked. Then, more to Mistress Mary than Elizabeth, Margaret continued. "I was on Osborn Street earlier tonight. There was a John there in dark clothing wearing a nice white handkerchief. He tried to bring me over for a go, but there had been some rough work during the night, and I was ready to be home. As I walked away from him, I thought he was following me."

Elizabeth was about to answer, but she heard Mistress Mary

tell Annie to run back to the lodging house and wake Elizabeth's son to meet them at the London Hospital. She was still so confused. Why did they need to go to the hospital?

Mary and Margaret continued to carry Elizabeth towards a white building adorned with a red cross. As they entered the London Hospital, the nurses rushed into motion. Elizabeth could barely keep up with the exchange of information between Mistress Mary and the nurses.

"What do we have here?" one of the nurses asked.

"Her name is Emma Smith, and she's been attacked on Osborn Street, near the cocoa factory" replied Mistress Mary.

Elizabeth heard the name. Emma Smith. No one called her that here. That was the name her husband used and the name she used with her Johns if they ever bothered to ask. To her friends, though, she was Elizabeth. Elizabeth was what her da used to call her. She saw so much of William in her son. Elizabeth was worried about William. All alone in Massachusetts after she left. She felt bad for leaving. She knew she had to, but she couldn't remember why. He had written her so many deeply personal things in those letters. She had read them aloud to her son when he was younger, and she hoped he would have a relationship with him some day. Some day he could return to Medford and be part of a family. Her son would be able to take joy and love from other people. That was his birthright as a Smith. The life Elizabeth led didn't provide that.

"What are her symptoms" another nurse asked.

"She seems to be confused. She keeps asking the same questions of us and she's blubbering like a child in primary school. From the look of her face, she's been beaten up, and I think a bit of her ear is missing." This time it was Margaret responding to the nurse.

Elizabeth knew she had to contribute. "Charlie and mom left my da. He's all alone. I don't know where they went, though. There was another one, too. What was his name? He left my da too. I punched Charlie once because he called me Lizzie."

They nodded at her politely, and Mistress Mary turned to the nurse, lowered her voice, and Elizabeth couldn't hear the words. She thought she heard something about a passage and a rip. That didn't make any sense to her. Why was there so much pain?

Elizabeth was brought back to the examination room. Her torn clothes were removed, and the initial examination was completed. The nurses did their best to stop the bleeding on her ear and her face. There was a moment where one of the nurses cracked her nose back in place, which caused another wave of pain to wash over an already overloaded mind. At that point, the nurses started looking at the wound between her legs. She looked around, and Margaret and Annie were next to the bed, crying.

Elizabeth asked, directing the words towards Annie. "What happened? Why are you crying? Is someone hurt?"

Elizabeth then felt the chill of the air and realized she was naked. "Why am I naked? Where is my son?"

Annie replied quietly, "He'll meet you after they cover you up, dear."

Elizabeth's mind was trying to tell her something important, but she just couldn't figure out what that was.

She was moved to a bed with scratchy white sheets and a kind-eyed man in a white coat stood over her with a needle. She couldn't understand why his fancy white coat said Haslip on it. What kind of a word was Haslip? Her mind drifted.

Was it Hay-slip? Or Has-lip? Has lip. That's funny. Of course he has lip. Everyone has two! The man with lips spoke to her.

"I'm going to give you something for the pain. Just enough to take the edge off. I want to get as much information out of you before it's too late," he said to Elizabeth.

Elizabeth tried to figure out the last two words he had said, but then she felt the warm bliss that only Morphine could provide. The warmth of the Morphine provided clarity, and she realized she could form her words more easily now that the pain wasn't as bad. She smiled then as her son came to her bedside. He would get a family in Medford. She had to tell him to go find his family.

"Ok, Emma. I need you to tell me everything you remember from tonight," the doctor began.

The doctor and her son listened as Elizabeth recounted what she remembered. Blood. Pain. Theft. Nice shoes. More pain. A promise to send her ear to the police. Ripping. Laughter. Darkness.

"Thank you, Emma" the doctor said, his kind eyes unwavering. "I'm going to give you the rest of this Morphine dose so you can rest now. We need to do surgery on your abdomen. That man caused a lot of damage."

Elizabeth became aware of the warmth of Morphine again. She wasn't sure how much longer she could stay awake, so she had to make this count. She had to tell her son to go and be part of a loving family. She called to her son and stared into his face. She managed two short sentences before the darkness took her. She would not escape the embrace of the darkness ever again.

"Go to Medford. Take what is yours."

Chapter 14

October 22, 1892 – Medford

William dreamed a wonderful dream. This same dream had visited him many times before, but that didn't make it any less wonderful to him. He was chasing Elizabeth through a snow-capped pine forest near the small cottage in the woods where they used to live. This must have been before they moved into the General Store and before the war. Before it all fell apart. He doesn't know why he's chasing her, but he's running freely with two working legs, and he knows he needs to find her. Elizabeth's peals of laughter come filtering through the forest, and he redoubles his efforts to get closer to her. He gets where he can almost grab at her scarf, and then she pulls away, laughing again. He glances back over his shoulder and sees Abigail chasing them both, her face red with effort in the cold winter air. She is happy.

"Come back, Elizabeth!" he yells after her, playfully.

"You have to catch me first!" Elizabeth yells to him, the joy cascading through her voice. "You have to catch Ben as well!"

"When I catch you, I'm going to tackle you!" William responds.

Her laughter is the only response he hears. William puts his head down and tries to get his legs to move faster and faster, but his legs won't move. They're just so heavy, and it feels like his feet are tethered to the ground. He knows he can run faster than this, but something won't let him. Is it the snow? If only he could fly! He jumps to try and take off. Suddenly William jerks himself awake. Pain cascades through his bad knee and all memory of the delicious dream fades.

All is dark and the clock on the wall shows that it's 3:47 in the morning. There's a flash of lightning and a peel of thunder, and the lightning illuminates his small bedroom and the scattered whisky bottles that are strewn about on the end-table and the floor. William's head hurts so much. The realization of his life comes flooding back to him, and the joy within the dream quickly fades. As he sits up in bed and throws both legs over the side, he realizes that today was the early hours of Saturday, the 22nd of October. It was his 67th birthday.

"How many more of these will I have to suffer," he wonders aloud.

It had been quiet the last few years, but his heart had been walled off with the final brick when he received a letter in July of 1888. It came to the store, and Thomas Foster walked it to his apartment. They talked about the store for a while, Thomas asking for his opinion on which spring crops he should stock for the next spring planting season. After Thomas left, William looked down at the letter and noticed it was postmarked by the London branch of the Universal Postal Union and came from some place called 18 George's Street. Hoping it was news from Lizzie, he tore it open. Instead, it was from a woman he had never heard of named Mary.

Mr. William Smith-

Emma Elizabeth Smith was hurt in Whitechapel. There was a man with nice shoes and Elizabeth was hurt real bad. She was ripped open and died in the hospital. We went through her things and found letters from you. Thought you should know.

Elizabeth was real nice - shame that bastard killed her. Her son moved out, but I don't know where he is. Her daughter is still with her ex-husband.

Regards, Mary

There was a lot to unpack in the short letter. This was how he learned he was a grandfather by Lizzie, but didn't know the names of his grandkids. He didn't even know that Lizzie had gotten married. Apparently, she had also been divorced. In the end, it didn't really matter. William had lost another person in his life. That night William drank harder than he had in years. He wanted to find the bottom of the whisky bottle and tell Abigail the news about their daughter. He would still talk to her when he was drunk, but it was rarer and rarer for him to think he heard her respond. He needed her tonight.

The loss of another family member was probably all God's revenge for what he did to those 11 other men on that day in 1863. This was just part of his punishment. He resigned himself to write to Charlie to let him know. He didn't know if he'd hear back, but a son had a right to hear that his only sister was dead.

William spent some time trying to find news of Lizzie's two kids, but his attempts went unanswered. He abandoned his quest to find his family and sunk himself into his work. By 1892, William was the Police Chief. The old chief had retired in 1890 and had moved to Hartford to be with his grandkids.

William had built the Medford police department and had a deputy named George at his disposal. There was also a bailiff related to the courthouse, but that bailiff reported to the judge. Medford had continued to grow and had around 18,000 people in

1892, and William was trying to add another precinct to support the growth. Truth be told, William had George do most of the work, because William was slow to get anywhere with his knee. George's physical fitness couldn't replace William's mind though, as William was still able to see crimes and intent better than anyone else in the town. William had a very high conviction rate, which discouraged crime and made Medford a safe place.

The pension from the army and the job as Chief paid more than enough to fund his whisky habit and pay the apartment rent. William had no other spending habits but had no one to share it with. He had briefly hoped he could find and bring his grandkids to Medford with his savings and provide for them to go to Tuft's college and perhaps join Charlie in Boston, but without being able to reach them, there was no other way to have that plan move forward.

William assumed that when he died, all his wealth would pass to Charlie, even though William didn't have a will. Charlie doesn't need the money. He still lived in Boston and still works in the copper trading industry at the stock exchange. He lives in a big house close to the exchange with a pretty wife and two children of his own. William gets a card in the mail from his grandchildren about once a year, but they never come to visit. William is pretty sure that they would be scared away by the smell of stale whisky and the sight of a hobbled war vet, anyways.

He snaps back to reality. The pain in his leg is nearly constant now, so he uses his hands to knead the sore muscles into submission. The pain is worse when it rains and when it's cold. He should have moved somewhere a little warmer, like Texas or Oklahoma. Deep down he knows he'd be just as miserable there as here. The drinking and the constant pain meant William was a very light sleeper. The punctuation of the night by the bolts of lightning and cracks of thunder guaranteed that he won't get any more rest tonight.

His self-pity is interrupted by a knock on the door. William isn't sure if he heard it, but just as he's considering laying back down, he hears the knock again. William grabs his belt and laces up his shoes. He grabs his cane as he opens the door wearing his most waterproof coat. Standing in front of him is a rain-soaked tall young man with bushy blonde hair and a rugged look.

"You ok, Jack?" William asked the young man standing in front of him.

"No, Chief," Jack replied. "You need to come with me to the butcher's house. Edna was in a right state about something, but she wouldn't tell me what. Want me to tag along?"

"I would appreciate that," William responded. "If the scene is bad, help from the church is very effective crowd control."

Jack was the assistant minister at the Universalist church but had only been in Medford for about 6 months. It felt like he had been in Medford for years. The head minister was a man named Henry DeLong and was about William's age. He had been a beacon of the Universalist church, but his father had been the more formative DeLong in William's life. Henry's father had been the minister that Abi and William had heard when they were kids and the one that married them. William was also pretty sure it was Henry's father's oratory that convinced Abi to let William leave for war. When Henry took over his father's pulpit, he had actively worked to grow the congregation of the Universalist church through more modern thinking and a less rigid interpretation of the scripture.

Even though Henry and William had grown up together, Henry's life had taken a massively different pathway. Henry never volunteered for the war and always lived in a loving household. He had a good relationship with his parents up to the day they died and was living out his twilight years doing something he loved. William was jealous of the man's life. If there was one consolation, it was that Henry moved around even slower than William. It was Henry's slowdown that had caused the rest of the congregation to put out an open call for an assistant minister's position, and Jack had shown up. He had gotten the job almost at once, as he had an incredible mind with a modern grasp of scripture.

In the first month that Jack was in Medford, he had picked up a very good grasp of names and locations and realized the way to the heart of the congregation was through the elderly ladies. After the sermons on Sunday, William had seen him playfully flirting with the older ladies outside the front of the church. Jack was still single, as far as William could tell, but he also knew that the Universalists didn't restrict their clergy from marriage. It was only a matter of time before one of the locals snapped him up. Jack had a good relationship with Henry and seemed to look up to the older man for guidance and wisdom. William watched Jack for several weeks after he arrived, and William had decided Jack was a decent kid. As the months went on, William started to trust Jack.

The thunderstorm tapered to a light rain as William walked past the Universalist church. This is the same church where he used to sit each Sunday and try to get the attention of Abigail. This is the same church where he lit a candle to Ben on that day when his life fell apart. William typically takes any road he can to avoid the church and its memories, but tonight there is an urgency so he put his feelings aside.

Jack started off towards the butcher's quickly but realized his mistake and dropped his pace to match William's. William was happy for the company on this wet, dark night.

"What keeps you up this late, Jack?" William asked.

"Minister DeLong wanted me to replace all the candles on the altar and check the hymn books for missing pages. We think some of the local kids have been ripping out pages of the hymn books during the Sunday services. I'll be honest, I took a nap instead but woke around 1 and set about my task." Jack hung his head and managed to look sheepish, even in the low light.

"Well, I'm sure Henry won't mind as long as it's done by tomorrow morning's service."

"That's the idea," Jack finished. The men walked in silence for a bit, until Jack posed a question. "Any ideas what this is all about?"

"Nope. At this time of night, it could be something bad or some misunderstanding," William responded. "I'm betting it's the latter. About 5 years ago little James Foster at the general store had me out of bed about once a month with his night terrors. The neighbors thought he was getting murdered in his bed and kept asking me to check it out. It got better after about three months, but I didn't sleep a lot those nights."

"Hope you're right. Seems like this town doesn't see a lot of bad," Jack continued. "Henry says that's thanks to you."

This last comment made him blush, and William was thankful for the dark. They continued in silence and walked up to the Butcher's shop to see that the oil lamps within were lit. Medford was laying electrical lines for all the shops on High Street, but it was likely a few years away from completion. The street had electric lights, but the city made the individual houses pay to connect to the supply lines, so it was rare for any of the houses to be connected to the grid. It was too much of an expense for the average storekeeper. William did know that the General Store had connected to the street lines, so the Fosters were either forward thinking or doing well financially. He hoped it was the latter.

John the butcher and his wife Edna were usually up before dawn to start their daily prep, but this seemed a little too early for them. William splashed through the rain-soaked gutter and knocked on the door. He was greeted in a hurry by Edna, who looked pale and distraught.

"Oh my God," she said as she recognized William. Her voice quaked while she invited him in. "Come in quickly, Chief. It's terrible. I've never seen anything like it."

"I'll stay out here," said Jack, correctly reading the situation. "You don't need me messing up the scene."

"Thanks, Jack." William looked around and saw people spilling into the street and heading towards the Butcher shop. The fanfare had woken up half the High Street, and curiosity was getting the better of people.

William turned to Jack, "Keep these people outside. I'm treating this as an active crime scene, even though I don't know what's in there." William saw the young man nod, and then turned and walked into the butcher's shop.

Chapter 15

October 22, 1892 – Medford

John and Edna kept a tidy butcher shop. Every morning, they would get up early and start preparing for the day's business. They started with the counters, scrubbing the butcher blocks until they shined. If they were too stained, they would scrape away the top layer of wood. After scraping or scrubbing the counters, they would apply fresh beeswax to seal the block. After the counters were prepped, they cleaned the floors from the previous day. The floors of the butcher shop were dusted with a light layer of sawdust to catch and absorb the errant drops of blood through the day, so they would sweep the old sawdust out, give the floors a good scrubbing, and sprinkle a light coat of fresh sawdust on the ground. John believed the sign of a good butcher shop was its cleanliness.

After the counters and floors were clean, John would start bringing out and hanging up the cuts of meat he intended to sell. At the end of the day, anything that was past its prime would be expertly deboned by John and added to a bin to make into sausage. He would sell the sausages for a discount and then cook those that remained the day after. He sold the cooked sausages cheap, as he figured that selling them for cheap was better than not selling them at all. A hot, cooked sausage was always a popular treat for anyone who happened upon High Street around 3 pm when the factory shift bell rang. That meant the butcher shop was a cavalcade of delicious smells of tallow, fat, cooked sausages, beeswax and sawdust. William liked visiting the shop, even if it were just for the smell.

John and Edna did not have any children of their own, but they employed a boy of 19 named Luke to help them around the shop. No one knew where Luke came from before he lived in Medford, but when he arrived, he found John and Edna's "Help Wanted" sign in the window and instantly applied. Luke lived in the cellar of the butcher's shop, and John took the price of the room from Luke's wages. John and Edna were kind and charged a below-market price, which meant Luke still made enough to save up for the next chapter of his life. Everyone in the town believed that Luke was happy with this arrangement.

William stepped through the door into the main sales room of the butcher shop on high alert. William was instantly aware that the smell was off. Instead of the normal smell of beeswax, sawdust and tallow, it was a smell that instantly brought him back to the surgeon's tent at Gettysburg. He knew it had to be Bromine. William frowned, knowing that Bromine would ruin any meat it touched. Whoever had been in here was not a seasoned butcher. Or wanted William to believe they weren't a seasoned butcher. William looked around in the dim light of the oil lamp, looking for what had caused Edna to scream.

At one end of the main counter, John and Edna used a beam scale that hung across the main display table. It was a primitive design but highly effective. On one side of the beam scale was a tri-hook where John would hook the cut of meat. There was also a tray attachment for top cuts of meat that weren't meant for piercing. John would slide a counterweight on the beam until an exact weight was recorded and a price was calculated. If the customer didn't want what was weighed, John would take his razor-sharp deboning knife and expertly carve away some of the meat until the weight was right and the customer was happy.

These shavings would be added to the sausage bin, for waste was a luxury that the butchers would not abide.

As William's gaze turned towards the beam scale, what he saw made his blood run cold. Someone had used the beam scale for another purpose. Both the tri-hook and the tray were attached to the large overhead beam. In the tray was something circular that William couldn't quite make out. Was it perhaps a pig shoulder socket? He couldn't tell. However, there was no mistake as to what was on the tri-hook. He paused to avoid retching.

It was Luke's severed head.

William breathed deeply, shocked by the grisly sight before him. He took a moment to compose himself and glanced around to see if he was alone in the shop. John stood in the doorway between the back office and the front display room, a look of sadness on his face.

"It's really him," John said. It wasn't a question.

"Looks that way," William responded, knowing who John meant at once.

John continued. "I saw him before we went to bed tonight. He said that he was going to be up for a bit, but likely go light a candle in the church for his mother and then get in bed before 10. You know how early we get up here."

William nodded his head, listening, but analyzing at the same time. Luke's mother died right before Luke came to Medford, so that part made sense. William's well-practiced mind started taking over, disassociating the severed head from the person it was before. There was potential the answer lay in the story John was telling him, and there was likely a lead buried in his words.

"Do me a favor, John, don't come back here. Not until I can

collect some evidence," William said.

John nodded in return as William passed to the back of the counter. He was looking for two things – the rest of Luke's body and the bromine. As he passed closer to the counter, he had a chance to examine Luke's head a little more. William examined the cut that had severed Luke's head from his body. William paused.

"The body. Not his body. Keep it together," William muttered to himself. He smiled and said to himself, "Happy Birthday, old man."

The cut was clean, without marks of hesitation or sawing. A sharp knife made this cut. A very sharp knife held by an expert hand. That made three things he needed. Murder weapon, body, bromine.

William looked around behind the counter and saw John's collection of knives. He saw a breaking knife, a skinning knife, a cleaver, and a paring knife. The deboning knife was missing. He glanced back up and finally identified the object that was in the meat tray. It was one of Luke's eyes, gouged out of his head with the optical nerve trimmed closely to the eyeball. The optical nerve was coiled at the base of the tray, serving as a resting point for the spherical eye. The eye was perched in the center of the coil with the pupil facing the door. The placement didn't seem accidental. It was signaling something to William, but he couldn't quite figure it out. Not yet. He'd get there. William tucked this detail away for later and went back to the search for the missing knife. There were three important things. Those had to be the focus.

"Where is your deboning knife, John?" William asked, cautiously.

"It should be back there behind the counter," John

responded.

William nodded his head and looked around some more. No knife was found. No bromine or rags either. He looked in the bin where John stored the scraps he made into sausages. It was full of something that William hoped was meat.

"When's the last time you made sausages, John?" William asked.

"Last night. The bin should be empty," John responded.

William nodded, knowing that the full bin identified one of the three things he was looking for. He approached the sausage bin to confirm his suspicion. He looked in the bin and saw what looked like the rest of Luke's body. William grabbed the wooden push stick used to unclog the meat grinder and sifted around, looking for all the parts that used to make up Luke. He counted two legs, two arms, and a quartered torso. No organs that he could see. All the pieces still had their bones, though, so there were limits to the killer's insanity. William continued to the other side of the sausage machine and saw that the killer had taken a severed end of Luke's intestine and rammed it onto the casement holder. The killer was inviting someone to make human sausage.

William turned around toward the entrance of the butcher shop and saw the organs displayed on the counter. It appeared the killer had removed the heart, the kidney, and the liver and placed them on the counter very carefully, as if the killer was treating them with reverence. Like he was showing off his prized cuts of meat. William examined them as closely as he could in the dim light. There were no stray cuts. William saw steady, quick movements from a sharp knife. The killer had an expert hand, and this wasn't the first thing they had butchered.

William realized something else was missing from Luke's body. William could not find Luke's genitals anywhere. The fact that they were missing hinted to William that they were removed prior to Luke's death. William tucked that tidbit away for later as well. That was two messages being sent to him from a killer. Eyes and penis.

He didn't say anything to John but glanced down at the floor and found it to be completely clean of any sawdust. The floor looked like it had been swept and scrubbed after the murder. The killer had time. Somehow, they had killed Luke, drained the corpse of blood, butchered it, placed the body in the sausage machine, placed the eyeball in the meat tray and mounted a head to a hook without being detected. That probably meant that the killer had operated in the dark and had not lit any lamps. William looked back to the clean floor. It smelled of bromine, but it was not completely clean. William looked closer and saw that where he had stepped, there was a faint pathway of red shoe prints. William had tracked in blood from somewhere.

William turned to retrace his steps. The tracks got bolder as William approached the door. The blood came from outside. He started to open the door to go back out to the street, but stopped when he saw a crowd of 20 people that were trying to see in. William drew the blinds and closed his eyes to mentally retrace his steps.

He had splashed through the gutter on his way here. That was the only place he could have stepped in that much blood. Whoever had killed Luke had drained the blood into the gutter with the rain, using the thunderstorm to mask the disposal.

A picture of the incident formed in William's mind. Luke was coming home and heading into the front door of the shop.

Maybe he was heading to finish some chores or just lock the door. The killer had been waiting for Luke, knowing which pathway Luke would take. The killer had crept up behind Luke and likely slit his throat. That was the logical move because the heart would help drain the body quickly and would prevent Luke from crying out for help. Luke would have gurgled helplessly and bled out in the gutter while the thunderstorm raged to help mask the sound and the sight. Luke was likely butchered outside, with parts of the body brought into the store and placed in the sausage maker. The killer had probably mounted the head on the meat hook last, gouged out Luke's eye, and set it in the meat tray right before they vanished into the darkness. An involuntary shiver went down William's spine. This was not a crime of passion. This was planned and then executed without emotion. It was surgical.

"Take me to Luke's room," William said to John.

"Through here," John said as he turned his back and started heading down the stairs. William followed slowly, carefully planting his cane in the right spots and not putting too much weight on his bad leg.

John pushed open the door and stepped in to light an oil lamp. As the light started to illuminate the room, John backed out to allow William entrance to the small space. It was small and looked like it was typically kept tidy. However, it was clear there had been a struggle here. William frowned – that didn't fit with the timeline that he had just constructed. He was missing something.

The only chair and a candle were knocked over. An empty lockbox was splayed open on the floor next to the upturned chair. William turned to look at the bed and saw a splash of blood on the white sheets. William would bet his salary that blood belonged to Luke. He approached the bed and used his cane to turn back the top sheet. Laying in the bed was Luke's missing, dismembered manhood. This part, William saw, was not cleanly removed. The cut was sloppy here – the edge of the skin was ragged like it had been moving during the cut. The killer had rushed this stroke, or it was when Luke was still alive. An interesting message. William turned to go.

"See what you needed to?" John asked.

"Yes, John. More than I needed to. More than I wanted to." William responded, "I hope I never see something like this ever again."

William had to regain composure and force his calm demeanor to resurface. He was supposed to be in control here. He needed to compartmentalize the horrors he had seen to avoid spooking John. Although he knew the man quite well after all these years, a boy living under his roof was expertly butchered and one of John's knives was missing. He had to be a suspect.

William started back upstairs, momentarily glad that his body was slow. It allowed him time to process the facts he had seen and update his theory. The killer likely severed Luke's manhood while Luke lay in the gutter with his throat cut, bleeding out. The killer had run inside, down here, looked for something in the lockbox, and then back outside to find the corpse waiting for him. Then the killer butchered the boy in the street under the cover of the storm and arranged the macabre scene in the store. Then everything was cleaned and scrubbed with bromine.

Whatever the killer had taken from Luke's room, they had taken it and the deboning knife somewhere else. By the time William got back to the butcher shop's main floor, a theory had started to form in his mind. He was still missing some key evidence, but William bet that he knew where to find it.

The door to the butcher shop opened, and William turned around to see his deputy come into the shop. That was good. William would need help for this next part.

"Good to see you, George," William said, nodding at his deputy.

William didn't know George's exact age, but he was likely around 18. He was beyond the phase of his life when he was awkward in his new frame but not to the point where everything hurt. George stood at least 6 foot 2 inches, had tufted brown hair, and sunken facial features. No matter how much the man slept, there were always bags under his eyes. George was strong though, and he stood as a physical contradiction to his sallow face.

The way George told it, he had come to America on a steamer ship from Liverpool by himself when he was 15. He had joined the police academy in Boston on his 16th birthday and worked for two years. William could never figure out why George stopped being a policeman in Boston, and George would always change the subject when it was brought up. He had moved from Boston to Medford and started working in the brick factory. The long hours of shoveling heavy things had built a solid, muscular core. When an opening was posted as a deputy, he was one of the first people to apply, and the physical size and previous police experience had made him a logical selection as William's deputy. Despite his size, the man was exceedingly kind and would help you without question. There was also something strangely familiar about George's mannerisms that drew William to the man.

William turned to John. "I need to see your rooms, John." John opened his mouth to protest, but then just dropped his shoulders and nodded in quiet agreement.

Chapter 16

1888 – London

Benjamin Smith was born in 1873 in London. His mother had named him Benjamin after her brother who died in the stupid American Civil War. Son of Tom and Emma Smith, he grew up in the streets of Finsbury Park and Whitechapel. There was no relation between the two Smiths, but his mother would always joke to Ben that it was a lot easier not having to change her last name. Ben showed a propensity for maths in his schoolwork and his teachers believed he may have a future at Cambridge or Oxford. However, Ben wasn't sure he wanted a future that involved staring into space and doing maths on a chalkboard. Luckily or unluckily for him, he never had that chance because of where and to whom he was born.

His father, Tom, was the owner of a pub named The Tailor's Tape in Finsbury Park. He had met Ben's mother while Emma worked as a clerk in the neighboring cloth shop, and they started flirting. Flirting led to kissing and kissing led to rushed, late night back-alley sex. When Emma told him she was pregnant, Tom responded in the only way he knew how.

"How can you be certain it's mine?"

Tom had beat Emma for the first time that night, telling her it was her fault that she was pregnant. Tom made it very clear Emma wasn't the only person he was with, but the others had the decency not to get pregnant. Emma went to bed with sore ribs and Tom didn't come home that night. The next morning, Tom came back smelling of booze and smoke. He apologized for his outburst and blamed it on the financial pressure another mouth would mean to the pub. Emma just believed he didn't want to be tied down.

"Don't worry, love, you can still bend over whomever you want, just come back to me and the babe afterwards. I won't control you," she assured him.

This assurance helped keep the peace between the two of them, and as soon as Emma started to show signs of pregnancy, they were married. Ben was born 4 months later, and Tom was decent with little Ben. There was never real happiness, even though Emma held true to her word and let Tom get away with having whoever he wanted. She figured it was better to have a good roof over her head than be homeless.

Tom was bad at business but paid the serving girls so poorly he still ended up turning a profit through marketing and volume. He hired young serving girls just above school age and required them to wear scandalously inappropriate clothes to bring in more customers. He saw the serving girls as disposable and one step above whores. If a customer was too handsy and the girls complained, Tom usually fired the serving girl, unless they took Tom into the back alley for a blow or some sex in exchange for a second chance. If the serving girl was particularly pretty and didn't ask for a second chance, Tom came home and beat Emma. During the violence he said at least once that he blamed Emma for his "missed opportunity." His penchant for the younger girls made Emma truly sick and would eventually be the reason she left him.

Somehow Emma stayed with this terrible man, and even more remarkably Sarah was born 6 years later. Ben knew his father didn't believe Sarah was his, but Emma was very convincing. Ben didn't believe that his mother ever strayed from her wedding vows, even in the face of Tom's abuse and adultery. Regardless, his father was a little happier when Ben's mother bore him a daughter.

Tom groomed Sarah to be his little pet from the moment she could walk and talk. His mother saw the way that Tom leered at Sarah and divorced him as soon as she could. Emma had to protect her daughter from the evil that lived within her husband. In a travesty of legal rulings, the London courts would only let her take her older child because of her lack of income. She tried to find a job as a clerk at a local store, but London was reeling from the Long Depression and Great Depression of British Agriculture. Jobs were scarce, so Emma had to turn to whoring to make ends meet. She moved to Whitechapel to get enough money to hire a barrister and get Sarah out from under the clutches of Tom before she was of an age he fancied. The clock was ticking.

Ben loved his mother but saw within her a weakness of character and a willingness to give up too easily when her own happiness was involved. He believed she internalized pain too readily and refused to fight back against the source of that pain. When he moved to Whitechapel with his mother, he started working with some of the street gangs, running pickpocketing and protection schemes for the Odessians, a Jewish gang. He hid all of this from his mother and the house matron, but by the time she was murdered, he had managed to acquire close to 2000 pounds sterling, hidden across several bank accounts. He would need that money to plot his revenge for his mother's murder.

He knew that Medford was the ultimate destination. Those were the last words she had said to him, and he owed her that. Before he made that journey, though, Ben needed his vengeance. The police were completely incompetent, and they missed the obvious pattern of violence that developed in the weeks and months after his mother's death. It wasn't difficult for Ben to find the murderer, and one night in early September, Ben tracked him down.

Ben watched the killer through the back half of September 1888 as the killer stalked new prey. The killer was stalking whores that followed a pattern, and so all Ben had to do was find the same whores faster. Finally, on the night of September 30, Ben knew that the killer was going to strike. Something was different about the night. He tracked the killer into the heart of London's poor neighborhoods and followed him onto Berner Street and watched from a distance near Dutfield's Yard as a woman's life was ended, much in the same manner as his own mother's. Ben had bought a cheap folding knife and a cudgel, and he was planning on knocking this man out and then stabbing him. It would look like successful self-defense and no one would be wiser to Ben's existence.

Something spooked the killer in Dutfield's Yard, and the killer left before Ben could get close. Ben didn't think this man's hunger had been quenched for the night, so he followed. The killer shifted east to the familiar hunting grounds of Whitechapel, and Ben watched from the bushes near Mitre Square as the killer selected and ended another victim. It appeared he had selected another whore, and Ben watched as the killer slit the whore's throat. Panic rose within Ben, but he swallowed it down and set his resolve.

Ben crept up behind the killer as quietly as he could.

He was five feet from the killer's back and thought to himself, "It would just take one good smack across the back of the head and the killer would be unconscious."

As he raised the cudgel to prepare to deliver the blow, he

glanced at what the killer was doing. The man was crouched over the whore's lifeless body, ripping her open from groin to ribcage. A steady stream of blood had pulsated out of her slashed neck, and the pavement was creating channels to allow for the slow drainage of the red liquid into the city sewers. It danced through the cracks, and Ben couldn't help but watch. He was paused with his cudgel raised overhead, still ready to strike this man that had taken his mother from him. Ben glanced back towards the body and saw the miracle of life reduced to a pile of inanimate flesh. The innate complexity of the human body was all undone with a few simple strokes of a knife.

Ben lowered his cudgel as he felt an electric rush of excitement wash over him. His body tingled and a warmth spread through his chest and legs. He was captivated by the surge of power that he felt, knowing that this woman's entire being had just been extinguished before his eyes. He understood the rush killing must give this man, and he knew the reasons why the killer didn't stop. In that moment, a whole new pathway of possibilities opened in Ben's mind, and he shifted the entire trajectory of his night. He would become a better version of this creature.

Still, there was one lingering thought that nagged at his subconscious. How could he reconcile this new pathway with his need for vengeance? A voice from within answered him instantly.

Don't abandon vengeance. Learn from this man. When he has taught you all you need, set things right in this world and take your power.

He was still perched 5 feet behind the killer. He prepared himself to run, just in case this went poorly. He could always help the police find this man if this plan didn't work. Or he could find another night and go back to his original plan.

"Life is wasted on those who are unwilling to take chances," the voice within prodded. He said a silent prayer to an unknown god and cleared his throat.

"If you've already murdered her, why take the time to mutilate her?" The man jumped. He clearly hadn't heard Ben approaching.

"What did you say to me, boy?" the man hissed at him.

"Look, you have a real knack for this work. I want you to teach me," Ben responded.

"I don't take apprentices."

"You murdered my mother, Emma Smith. Over by the cocoa factory on Osborn Street. You owe me."

"I remember your whore mum. She never screamed when I ripped her open. Impressive death, that one. Still, she had it coming with every cock she serviced. That makes you a whoreson, so why don't I just murder you right here and now, then? You probably don't even know who your father is with how many men your mom serviced." He spat the word 'serviced' with hatred and malice and spittle flew from his mouth as he enunciated. "The world seems like it would be better without you in it."

Ben realized that this man couldn't control his urge to kill. That was the first weakness Ben saw. He wasn't calculating, he was emotional. Whether it was sexual repression or suppressed abuse from an earlier life, it seemed he needed to punish harlots to make the world purer in his eyes. Ben realized the way forward was to make sure this ripper didn't confuse him for his mother. Ben realized that the man was waiting for a response.

"You can't kill me because I'm protected. I'm with the Odessians, and your life will get a LOT harder if you take out one of their favorite numbers men. I may have started as the son of a whore, but I've changed into more than that. And I know who my father is. He was married to my mom when I was born." Ben let this sink in with his quarry, even if the part about his favor with the gang was a slight embellishment.

"Look. I don't want you to stop. I just want to learn your ways. If you say no, I'll make sure everyone knows how easy it is to find you."

"It hasn't been that easy for anyone to find me, especially those dirty coppers. You probably just got lucky." There was a pause as the dark man considered something. He swapped his knife between hands, clearly deciding what to say next. "You want me to teach you. Who is your target, kid?"

"My father," Ben said, with all the conviction he could muster. He couldn't let on that his true target was staring him down. Ben paused, waiting for the other man to do something. Truth was, Ben was still ready to flee, but he put on a brave face and stood his ground. He pushed his luck.

"By the way, it was easy to find you. You have a pattern that radiates out from a central point. I'm betting that you either live or work on the other side of the Thames closer to Greenwich. You focus on Whitechapel as it has enough people who won't be missed. I think you're driven by curiosity and an inner darkness. I'd also bet you work at a school or another learning institution that allows you to acquire the tools you need. Finally, I think you have a good knowledge of the law, as that allows you to understand police process and understand how they review crime scenes. I would wager that with an afternoon or two, I could probably find your name by comparing the list of teachers at private schools with the list of barristers in the Law List."

The man stayed silent and knelt to finish his work. Eventually he said, to no one in particular, "This whore was named Kate Eddowes. She had sex with more men than I could count since I've been watching her. She lives her life with only the guidance of lust for the bottle and for men. Lust is one of the deadly sins. I reminded her of her failure to the human race before I spilled her blood. The world is better off without her."

He took the victim's intestines and flung them over her right shoulder. He severed a portion of the intestines and placed the severed piece between the victim's torso and left arm. He stood up. He was well dressed in a salt and pepper suit, a cloth cap and a red neckerchief. He also wore a cloak that was finely tailored.

"I removed her uterus to remind all the other whores that they should never reproduce. I placed the intestines to tell the police they're shit at investigating. I doubt they'll understand, though. They really are quite stupid. You're the first thing that has impressed me in quite some time."

The man leaned down one last time and with a quick slice of the knife severed the dead woman's ear clean off. He quickly and expertly sheathed the knife somewhere within his cloak and extended his gloved hand.

"Montague Druitt, at your service. But the police call me Jack the Ripper."

Ben noticed a wry smile as Druitt said this last part. He was proud of this second identity more than his first, thought Ben. Another weakness – pride. "Let's get out of here before the patrolman comes back. I'm done with this whore." Druitt kicked the dead woman in the ribs and turned to go.

"Teach me everything." Ben said.

Chapter 17

October 22, 1892 – Medford

It had already been a long day for William. He sat back in his chair at the police station within the town hall and started the process of mentally recapping his day.

Earlier that morning, John the butcher had led William and George up to the room he shared with his wife, Edna. As they pushed open the door, everything looked normal. It was a modest room, but well-tended and orderly. The head of the four-poster bed was centered in the middle of the wall that it rested against, with the foot pointed into the room. A dresser adorned the opposite wall and was nestled between two windows. A small carpet lay at the foot of the bed to tie the room together. The bed sheets were ruffled as if someone had left them in a hurry but nothing else seemed out of place. If his hunch was right, William knew he was looking for something that would be designed to be overlooked.

William motioned to George to stay near the door and started pacing around the outside of the room. William walked on both sides of the bed, looking and listening for anything out of place, intermittently probing at things with his cane. He stepped towards the door and George naturally shifted to give William some room. George walked over next to the bed and William heard what he was looking for. One board made a different noise than the others. Hollower.

"Whose side of the bed is this, John?" he asked the butcher.

"That's mine, Chief Smith," John replied.

William motioned George to stand back in front of the

door. The large man obliged, and William reached down and tapped the floorboards where he had heard the different sound.

"Hollow," he said, out loud, mostly to himself.

John looked nervous and took a step towards William. George closed the distance to John, placing a hand on John's arm. It wasn't threatening, but a clear sign that George was watching him. William was happy for his deputy's raw strength, as John stopped moving. The tension in the room rose as the three men watched each other, waiting to see what would happen next.

William trusted his deputy and broke eye contact first. He looked down at the floor. The floorboard in question looked just like all the other boards, but as William looked closer, he saw an inset slot in the middle of the board right at the top. There were no other distinguishing features. He removed a knife from his belt while glancing up at John. The butcher seemed tense but didn't resist. William saw George's grip tighten preemptively. A simple twist of the blade of William's knife brought up the board.

His hunch from downstairs was right. In the cubby beneath the floor, William saw a stack of money, a jar of bromine, and a bloody deboning knife.

William glanced at George and then at the butcher. "John, I'm placing you under arrest for the suspected murder of Luke," William said as he rose to his feet. "George, please restrain him and take him to the station. Put him in the jail cell."

William raised his knife, hoping that he wouldn't need to say anymore. John was a big man but had always come across as a gentle giant. Sometimes giants woke up. William knew he didn't have any speed with which to dodge any attacks from the butcher, so he was relying on the knife as a visual deterrent.

"It wasn't me. I loved that kid, Chief," was all John said, his entire body collapsing as the last energy went out of his body.

George led John out of the room and down the stairs. William stayed behind to place all the things he found in the cubby inside of a bag. He made his way back to the police station and to his desk. He was tired. Not the way he wanted to spend his birthday, and it was barely even light. George was nearby, watching William with a look of something on his face. Concern, William decided. William was thankful for that. Something about those mannerisms was just so familiar. William placed the bag of belongings on his desk. He made sure John was secure and then told George he was going home for some rest. He'd talk with John later in the day.

He left the town hall and noticed a small crowd gathered outside. "Curiosity always wins over common sense," he thought to himself. Reporters were there from the Medford Mercury asking him for a quote. Terrified people looked to him for an answer. Some guy named Bill started yelling at him about this being his fault. People in large crowds always seemed to devolve to their basest forms, looking for someone to blame.

He slowly hobbled back to his apartment, all the while taking abuse from the crowd. He knew they were scared, and he knew they weren't smart enough to know the reasons they should be terrified. Everything about this murder showed a cold, calculating hand. The precision. The planning. The ability to cover their tracks. The messages. There was someone in Medford who was really good at murder. William had to find them before they struck again.

"Happy birthday to me," William thought, sardonically.

Chapter 18

October 22, 1892 – Medford

Elizabeth Foster woke up to a bright and sunny morning. It had rained hard the night before, but she was greeted by blue skies and chirping birds. She had slept very well and felt ready to greet the day. She got out of bed and dressed in her small room above the Foster's General Store. She selected a brown wool dress that flowed to the top of her ankles and black, thick leather boots. She completed the ensemble with a wool half-jacket. She admired herself in the mirror, thankful that her generation had decided to forego daily corsets and petticoats. They just weren't practical for a woman anymore. She wanted to do anything that her brother James could do.

Medium height and slender, Elizabeth had long, wavy sandy hair to compliment her green eyes. She loved her eyes. She thought the atypical color gave her an air of mystery and a touch of the supernatural. When people noticed her eyes, they always commented. As she peered at herself in the mirror and ran her hands down her front to smooth a stubborn wrinkle out of her dress, she smiled as she thought of the night before. She grabbed a mother-of-pearl hair pin from her dresser, wrapped her hair into a loose bun, and used the pin to secure the bun. She finished the bun with a blue calico ribbon. As she left her room, her mind drifted back to last night. What a feeling that was. What a rush.

Last night started when she met up with Luke after dinner and walked the High Street. Her stomach fluttered the entire time, and the conversation flowed so easily and naturally. He knew how to ask the right questions and how to wait to listen for an answer.

He spent the last portion of their night talking about the future. He wanted to find someone who was an equal – he thought everything else would fall into place after that. They walked the High Street, and she even let him hold her hand. His hands felt strong and rough, but capable of being gentle and loving. As the dark rolled in, Luke walked her back to the general store. He leaned in and gave her the briefest of kisses on the cheek.

"Do you want to meet up later tonight?" he had asked. This was the seemingly hundredth time he had asked her to break curfew, and she had rejected his advances every other time.

"Not tonight, Luke," she responded, just as she had a hundred times before. "I have to be up to help father with the store tomorrow morning and so I need my beauty sleep."

"It won't do any good, you know." Luke replied, playfully forlorn.

"What won't? Helping with my father's shop? I need to learn the ropes if I'm ever going to take a larger role there," Elizabeth responded, equally playfully, a smile creeping over her face.

"No. Beauty sleep. You are already perfectly beautiful." Luke's saddened face had suddenly brightened as he waited for the corny comment to land. She hit him lightly on the shoulder with a balled-up fist, playfully, and had no response. He reached over and brushed a strand of hair off her face and tucked it behind her ear.

"Will I at least see you at John's shop tomorrow?" Luke asked.

"Yes. Probably in the afternoon when father lets me have a break," Elizabeth replied.

"I may lose my head before then," Luke joked. "I cannot

seem to spend more than 3 hours without you, Elizabeth Foster."

"You're too much, Luke." She hit him again, still playfully. She was beaming.

"Around 10 tonight I'll wait for you behind the tailors. If you're not there by 10:15, I'll know you haven't changed your mind."

"Goodnight, Luke," she insisted firmly. "I'll see you tomorrow." Her wry grin as she went in the door let him know that she wasn't actually mad.

Her wonderful night had ended as she climbed the stairs to her room, smiling at her luck. She had her eye on him for quite some time and was quite taken with the man he was becoming. She had made regular trips to the butcher store for as long as she could remember, and since he had moved in, there had been silent flirting between the two of them. One day he had finally mustered up the courage to ask her for a date. He had been so nervous, and John the butcher suppressed laughter, seeing the boy's misery. She put him out of that misery quickly, though, and agreed before he could get all of the words out.

Given his tentative nature, she was nervous about his ability to carry his end of the conversation during their first date, but he showed up on time, took her out for a nice picnic, and they had wonderful conversations about Medford. In a one-on-one setting, he was talkative and engaging. He listened well and had this cute habit of brushing hair behind his ear, even though his hair was too short for the motion to do him any good. He spoke passionately about the butcher's shop and his role in making it a success. He was hoping to either take over John's role or start his own shop someday. He spoke of how he was saving money to make that a reality. That was 2 months ago.

Her daydream snapped back to reality as she descended the stairs, freshly dressed, to see a group of men huddled around the front counter, talking in hushed tones to her father. Portions of the conversation drifted to her on the staircase.

"It's obscene, Thomas, that something like this would happen in Medford," one of them said. "What is Chief Smith going to do to solve this?"

Thomas Foster had become a middle-aged man without realizing it, but he still had an energy within that made hard work one of his defining attributes. He had great endurance when it came to running the General Store. Elizabeth admired this in her father, even if neither she nor her younger brother James shared the same attribute. Truth be told, Elizabeth worried about the future of the store. She wasn't sure if she had the skills to take over the business. She liked the idea of running the business and felt she could do a really good job taking the General Store into the new century. She just doubted her ability to maintain generational ownership.

She knew the last owner, William, didn't have children to pass the store to, and that was one of the major reasons her parents had been able to buy the store. Although from what she had been told, the situation with William's children was very different.

"I know what you mean, Bill, but we have to let the process work," Thomas responded. He looked up to see Elizabeth finish descending the stairs and hushed the man who was speaking. He gestured in Elizabeth's direction, and she saw all of their eyes briefly glance to her and then watched their gaze find something interesting on the floor. Within the next 3 minutes, they all amazingly professed another pressing appointment, and soon Elizabeth found herself alone with her father.

"Good morning, father," Elizabeth said cheerily. "How did you sleep?"

"I suppose I slept all right, Elizabeth," her father responded. "Elizabeth, I need to..."

"Ohhhh, are those this year's Christmas ornaments from Boston?" Elizabeth enquired, seeing an open box of bright baubles behind Thomas.

"Yes, but..."her father started.

"I must look at them and buy one for Luke," Elizabeth continued, excitedly. "He adores Christmas so much."

"Elizabeth. Stop." Thomas raised his voice to make his point. "I need you to listen to me for a second. I have to tell you something terrible."

Elizabeth stopped in stunned silence. This tone was unlike her father. Thomas took a deep, quiet breath with his eyes closed and started again in hushed tones.

"Last night something happened to Luke. Someone attacked him, and..." Thomas trailed off, choking off something unsaid.

The color drained from Elizabeth's face. Her smile that was impenetrable just a moment before had vanished. She couldn't speak and her stomach rose to her throat. She urged him to continue with pleading eyes.

"Elizabeth, honey. He's dead," he finally finished.

Elizabeth heard the news, but it didn't register for several seconds. She stood there, waiting for her father to say that it was some cruel joke. Some prank. It had to be. This was a man she could see herself spending the rest of her life with. She was excited about being a butcher's wife. She thought that Luke could help her take over the General Store and they could expand into the butcher business. That couldn't have changed this quickly. Her father had to be telling her a lie. She stared at him blankly, tears filling her eyes.

As the silence built between them, Elizabeth started to realize that her father wasn't going to take it back. He wasn't going to tell her that it was a joke. Luke wasn't going to pop out from behind the counter and rush to her, taking her into his arms and holding her tightly. The knot in her chest finally burst, and she started to cry.

She ignored Thomas' outstretched arms and ran back up the stairs to her room. She threw herself on the bed in a fit and sobbed into the pillow. Maybe if she got back into bed, this cruel joke would be over.

As she threw herself on the bed, the sudden rush of air blew something from her nightstand onto the floor. She lifted her head briefly from the bed and saw a letter addressed to her. She hadn't remembered receiving any letters yesterday, and she hadn't remembered putting anything on her nightstand the night before. How had this gotten here? It didn't matter. Her grief had overwhelmed her, and she didn't care. Not right now. She sobbed herself into a fitful sleep.

She was vaguely aware of Thomas coming to check on her, but she pretended to be asleep so he would leave her alone. Thomas rested his hand on her back in a gentle, protective way, making it clear to her that he was there if she needed him. She didn't move, though, and eventually he withdrew his hand and left her alone. She noticed that he didn't close the door and smiled through her tears. He was clearly telling her that she could come find him when she needed the help.

Several hours later, she rolled over and woke up for the second time that morning. She lay there as the events of the day came rushing back. She still felt hollow inside but had cried all the tears she had for now. The only emotion left was a growing curiosity about the mysterious letter. Her curiosity finally won, and she reached down and grabbed the letter off of the floor. She looked down through blurry eyes at the short, stunted script. She had to re-read it three or four times, as it didn't make any sense.

I watched the two of you last night and I couldn't let him get in my way. He thought he had gotten a-head of me, but he had to be separated from you. You will be mine before I'm done.

Chapter 19

October 22, 1892 – Medford

William had slept for about 3 more hours. He had a hard time getting back to sleep. Every time he closed his eyes, the images from his morning haunted him. The eyeball peering at the doorway. The dismembered manhood left in the bed. The invitation to make sausage. The precision. All of these images danced in his head and made his sleep fitful and unrewarding. The clock struck 11 am and William knew that any more sleep was folly. He got back out of bed, redressed, and made his way slowly to the police station. He hoped the crowd had dispersed by then, and to his surprise it had. Only about 5 people remained, and he saw the familiar face of Thomas Foster in the crowd. William was surprised. Thomas didn't strike William as someone who was part of a herd. William put this thought aside and opened the door to the town hall. As he went through the door, he heard Thomas call out to him.

"Chief – I have something you need to see," the shopkeeper said.

"We're kind of busy today, Thomas. Can we do it another time?" William responded.

"You need to see this. It'll help you with what happened last night."

This tidbit changed everything, and William turned to look at Thomas. The other people standing outside the town hall leaned in, craning to hear some juicy gossip. William looked around nervously, wondering how much the crowd knew of the grisly scene in the butcher shop.

"Ok..." William started slowly. "But not here."

Thomas nodded in agreement and followed William into the police station. Once inside, William turned around and locked the door before anyone else would think about following. George looked up from his desk, exhaustion showing on his face. William stopped at the big man's desk.

"You ok, George? Get any sleep?"

George looked up at William, his face blank. "I've seen this level of violence before, Chief. During my time as a kid in London I lived through Jack the Ripper. That level of violence was about the same."

The mention of the Ripper made William waver. He had to lean over and hold his desk. He had looked at all the papers from London after his Lizzie died, and although the police weren't sure, some people said that Lizzie was the first of the Ripper's victims. How did this creature follow him across an ocean? He shook the question out of his head. He would deal with that wave of emotion later. Or he'd swallow it down with a glass of whisky tonight. He couldn't reopen those scars. He hadn't told anyone in town about his connection to those murders, and he couldn't afford to bring it up now. William walked past George's desk with Thomas in tow and motioned Thomas to sit.

"What did you have to show me?" William asked.

Thomas slid a folded piece of paper across the desk to the older man and didn't say a word. William opened the flap of paper and stared at the words as a look of concern spread across his face.

"Where did this come from?" William asked slowly.

"My daughter found it in her bedroom," Thomas said

steadily. "Do you think it's from whoever killed Luke?"

"I don't know yet, Thomas, and we shouldn't speculate until we know a little more. It doesn't make any sense. This letter is mocking us. The weird phrasing about being a-head and the separation...do you think it's related to how Luke was displayed?" William wondered out loud.

"What do you mean, displayed?" Thomas asked.

William had forgotten that not everyone knew how Luke was found. It was a slip that William had to credit to fatigue.

"Nothing," William said, trying to cover Thomas' curiosity. "Just a poor turn of phrase."

"It's a sick person who would kill that boy," Thomas responded, his eyes darting towards the holding cell. John was pacing around the cell, and noticed Thomas look in his direction. John stopped pacing, freezing under Thomas' gaze.

"Thanks for bringing this by," William said, not engaging with Thomas any further.

William stood up, which was Thomas' signal to do the same. William limped over to the main door and unlocked it, ushering Thomas out. William closed the door and relocked it after Thomas had disappeared.

"George, can you put a chair by the cell? I think it's time I talked to our guest, and I don't think my leg will let me stand for very long today," William said.

George nodded silently, and took a chair over to the cell, about four feet back from the steel bars. George felt protective of his boss and didn't want anything to go wrong. William slowly walked from his desk towards the cell and moved the chair closer to the bars. He leaned his cane up against the cell and sat down.

"Need some water, John?" he asked the man in the cage.

"I'd like that, Chief," John replied.

William looked at George and then pointed at the small sink in the corner of the police station. George went to the sink and grabbed a glass, filled it, and walked back to William. William pointed at the bars, and George set it on the crossbar in the gap between two of the cell bars. As George stepped back, John stepped up and accepted the gift. He drained the glass in two quick swallows and placed it back from where it had come. He wiped his lips.

"Thank you, George," John said. The deputy walked away, not responding or acknowledging John's statement.

William had interrogated enough people to know that kindness usually won in the end, and convincing the accused you were on their side was a powerful tool to finding the truth. That's all William ultimately cared about – the truth.

"We've got a real problem, here, John," William started. "I have a person in your employ that stays on your property that has been cut up by a hand that knows their way around a knife. I also found a likely murder weapon in your room with chemicals that were likely used to clean up blood. Finally, I have a pile of money from an unknown origin that was found with the weapon and the chemicals. Help me understand what I see. Let's start with the money. Is that yours?"

"No, Chief," John said. "We keep our money in the bank, and I won't say it's that much. The shop scrapes by, but Edna has a sick sister in Boston that she sends money when we can. That doesn't leave much for us. In fact, money has been tight this last year. The price of meat is going up, but we can't seem to sell it at fair price anymore. We're basically kept afloat by the sausages."

"Any idea whose it could be?" William continued.

"No."

The sausages being such a large portion of John's income didn't fit with the scene. If John killed Luke, why would he have tainted the equipment that was keeping him afloat? William poked at another piece of evidence.

William kept the questions coming at rapid fire, without any pause. He found that stringing questions together gave suspects less time to lie. The truth was easier. "Ok, how about the chemicals in the jar. Tell me what you know about them."

"I've never seen that jar before in my life," John pleaded. "I don't use bromine in the shop. It spoils the meat. Even the smell of it can taint the high-quality cuts and then I get customers who demand replacement without paying."

"That is your deboning knife, though, right?" William asked.

"Yessir. That is definitely my knife. I'd know it anywhere." John replied, almost instantly. "It's the sharpest knife I have, and I use it as an extension of my arm all day."

John realized his mistake and tried to take the words back out of the air. He cut off what he was going to say next and lapsed back into silence.

"Ok, so if you say you haven't seen the money, nor the chemicals, but you know that's your knife, walk me through your version of the night you just had. Make sure to tell me as well if you saw or talked to Edna or Luke as part of your story." William felt there was still something missing to John's story. Something he wasn't telling William.

John sighed and sat down on the bunk in the cell. If it was possible, his shoulders belied defeat even more. William motioned again to George, who came and retrieved the glass, filled it back up, and set it back between the bars again.

"Ok, Chief," John started. He reached for the refilled glass and took a sip of water. "But this isn't going to make me look less guilty."

Chapter 20

October 22, 1892 – Medford

"I think the best place to start would be in the evening, the last time I saw Luke alive. He had just come home from spending time with Elizabeth Foster. It was probably around 9 pm. Luke was in a good mood. He always was after spending time with her."

"Huh," William interjected. "This morning in the shop you said he went to church to light a candle and didn't mention anything about Ms. Foster."

William couldn't bring himself to say her first name.

"Now chief, give me a break. You wanted to know the last time I saw him, which was after he came from the church. He went with Elizabeth until around 9, came back, and then left again. That's what I'm trying to tell you."

"Sorry, John. I'll be quiet," William said, sheepishly. "Continue."

"We do most of our prep work in the morning, so there wasn't much for him to do. Nevertheless, he looked around, making sure everything was in order. He is a good apprentice."

John paused at this point, trying to figure out the next words.

"That was when he asked me how much money someone would need to start a butcher shop. This caught me a bit off guard. He's young – only 19. Lordy. I should have said was young. He's gone now, isn't he. I can't believe that. I figured he'll walk in the door at any moment."

John paused, trying to compose himself. William gave him

time to gather his thoughts, knowing that pushing at this point would cause John to shut down. The butcher continued.

"We had talked a little over the years about his future and about how one day he could take a larger and larger role in running the shop as I got older. Edna and I didn't want to stop, but we knew we couldn't continue at this pace forever. We're getting up there in age, you see. Not old like you. Sorry. Not old. But, you know, seasoned. I won't be able to butcher a pig or a cow much longer without help. Back in my day I used to be able to quarter a cow in a flash, all by myself! My da said my cuts were clean and precise and I knew what I was doing. He was a butcher too, you know."

John was rambling again. It was a habit that all butchers had to have, to keep their customers engaged while they plied their craft. He seemed to realize he was rambling, as he brought the conversation back to the original story. "Anyways, I asked him why he needed to know."

John paused at this point, looking up at William to see if there was any change in the Chief's demeanor. William sat in the chair with a face hard to read, giving John the space to tell his story. William was good at this. He hoped that George was watching, in case the deputy ever took his job someday.

"Luke then told me about how he'd been saving pretty much all of his wages since he got here, and he figured he had about a thousand dollars saved up. I was dumbstruck. That's more money than Edna and I have saved, and about twice as much money as we used to start the store. My first thought was keeping him safe from thieves, though, so I asked him if he kept it in a safe place. He told me he kept it in a lockbox in his room under his bed. I told him I could keep it for him somewhere safer in my room if he wanted. He didn't know about the hollow board – only Edna did until you found it. Honestly, I was shocked you found it so easily, Chief."

William interjected. "I hear George walk around every day. I can recognize his steps and when something sounds off. It's also a very logical place to hide things. You'd be amazed how many people want their most precious things in reach of them when they sleep. I may be old like you said, but that doesn't mean my mind is slipping." William paused here and shot the man a smile before continuing. William needed to keep John at ease.

"What did Luke say when you offered him a place to store his money?"

"He didn't like it at all. Got really defensive. Started accusing me of trying to steal his money. I told him I was just trying to help keep him safe." John stopped at this point, eyes darting between George and William.

"Go on, John." William prodded.

"At this point he and I were yelling at each other. He told me that he thought I should stop trying to be his father and I should focus on just being his boss. Told me that if I didn't loosen my control over him, he was going to leave. I yelled back that there's no way I would let him open a shop in the same town, and him opening a butcher's shop in Medford would drive me out of business. Then he. He..."

George opened his mouth to prod John to keep talking but closed it again as William shot him a glare. William knew that this was it – the turning point in an interrogation where the suspect was about ready to slip up. This was the point where the key evidence was going to come to light. William knew it had to be on the prisoner's terms, so he waited, silently.

John continued, his voice barely over a whisper. "He said that if I wanted to prevent him from opening a shop in Medford, I'd have to kill him and take his money. Then he ran out the door."

John hung his head. William knew that was the whole story and wasn't going to hear any more.

"Get some rest, John," William said, standing up and heading back to his desk.

William sat at his desk for a long while, writing notes about what he had heard, then signing and dating them. He found it was best to write things down as soon as possible, including a date. The act of signing made him believe that he was swearing to someone that he was telling the truth. William knew he needed to hear another set of facts. Too many things were unknown about the night before Luke was murdered. He knew the next person he'd have to talk to was Elizabeth for two major reasons. First, she may have been the last to see Luke alive and second, he needed to find out about that note.

I watched the two of you last night and I couldn't let him get in my way. He thought he had gotten a-head of me, but he had to be separated from you. You will be mine before I'm done.

The words and the phrasing reminded William of the ripper. The papers over there had come up with silly names for them like the 'Saucy Jacky letter', the 'From Hell letter,' and the 'Dear Boss letter.' William didn't like that his daughter's murder had been reduced to a tabloid fantasy. William wished they would have caught the bastard and avenged his Lizzie.

His mind drifting again, William grabbed a piece of paper and scrawled on it quickly a short note.

Elizabeth-
Please come to the police station when you can.
We need to talk about Luke.
-Chief William Smith

He folded the paper over once and handed it to George. "Take this to the Fosters. Don't let anyone else but Thomas Foster or Elizabeth read it."

"Elizabeth Foster?" George asked. "The pretty one?"

William nodded his ascent and George slipped out the front door and through the crowd. William wasn't sure why Elizabeth's looks had anything to do with it, but watched George vanish and settled in to wait. He hoped he wouldn't have to wait long for one of the Fosters to return.

Chapter 21

October 22, 1892 – Medford

It was two hours later when Thomas and Elizabeth came pushing through the crowd that had reformed outside of the town hall. William looked up from a late lunch as they knocked on the door. Elizabeth looked as though she had been crying nonstop, and Thomas looked as though he was trying to shield his daughter from the world. Another wave of emotion washed over William, reminding him of the failures to shield Ben, Abi, and Lizzie from the world.

"Happy birthday to me," William thought to himself. "Here's some more emotional trauma!"

At William's behest, George let them into the station, and William gestured to two empty seats that were out of the sightline of John. It was better if they didn't see him.

"Thanks for coming in. I know this won't be an easy task, but I need to talk a little about what happened last night. Is it ok, Elizabeth, if I ask some questions?"

Elizabeth glanced at her father, who nodded slightly. Elizabeth turned back to William and nodded in more perceptibly. Thomas and William got along well, so William was hoping that Thomas knew he would be gentle.

"Do you want a glass of water, Miss Foster?" George interjected.

"No thank you, George," Elizabeth responded. "You are being so kind to me, and I thank you for that. Stay near me, please, George. I may change my mind."

George turned bright red but did as she asked, and Elizabeth turned her attention back to William.

William noticed how easily Elizabeth controlled the room. Everyone's attention was drawn into her orbit and pulled in by her presence. The corners of his mouth turned up in a half-smile. It reminded him of his Lizzie. "Ok, when did you last see Luke?" William started.

"It was last night around 9. We had spent a few hours walking the High Street and hanging out on the Winthrop bridge, talking." Elizabeth replied. Her voice was monotone and lifeless.

The Winthrop bridge crossed over the Mystic River at the West End of the High Street. The current was slower there, and the trees hung over the Mystic River, giving the night a magical quality. A lot of young couples would walk the High Street and end up on the Winthrop bridge and pause for a while, looking up at the moon and watching its reflection in the still surface of the river. William had taken Abigail there a few times during their courtship. It was one of his favorite spots in Medford, but it was an area he couldn't visit anymore. The memories were too strong, especially in spring when the natural lilac bushes bloomed, and their scents erupted on the wind.

William shook himself out of a pleasant memory, drawing his mind back to the task at hand. He was investigating a murder, and he needed to be serious. He realized he was going to have to play a more active role getting a story out of her than he had out of John. Her fragile state of mind had to be protected, but there was a truth he needed to find. He wasn't sure if this was a byproduct of grief or just who Elizabeth was, but he prepared to be more active in his interrogation.

"Ok, when you two were done with your date, did he seem

scared to go back home? Did he seem like he was afraid of anything?" William asked.

"No," replied Elizabeth.

Well, thought William, let's try a different track. "When you two had been spending time together previously, did Luke talk about his future plans?"

"Yes, he did. He said he wanted to take over from HIM or start his own shop," Elizabeth replied. The way she nearly spat the word 'him' made William believe that her mind was already made up as to where the guilt lay. He would have to tread carefully with this next question.

"Ok, that's good to know that you two talked about that. Do you know if Luke had ever mentioned his plans to Edna or John?" William purposely used Edna's name first to soften the blow of the second name.

"He said he had mentioned it, and he mentioned that he wasn't clear if he would be taking over the shop or starting a new one. I kind of hoped he'd start a new one and we could run the general store together with a butcher's store in the back. He always seemed to think John was a little controlling." Elizabeth started.

She quickly stopped talking as Thomas squirmed when she mentioned taking over the shop. It was clearly a sore subject between the two of them. William's mind drifted back to that day in the tent near Gettysburg when Ben had told him the same.

"Thomas, you ok if we keep going?" William turned to him, pausing more than asking. He needed a moment again to clear his mind. Ben. He had failed to protect Ben. John had failed to protect Luke. But John was the suspect here. William couldn't get emotional about this.

Thomas nodded his head, and William continued. "Ok, I have two more questions, Elizabeth." William started tentatively. "And these are a little harder to answer. First, did Luke ever talk to you about his relationship with John?"

"Yes, he did," Elizabeth responded, then continued after a small pause. "Luke always looked up to John. Luke said that John was a master of his craft and had such accurate precision with his cuts that if he ever needed surgery, he'd insist John did the work. He admired Edna's balancing of the books and her control over the financing. He saw them as surrogate parents. He never talked about his dad, but he loved his mom. I think that's why he was always closer to John, though. John filled a void in Luke's heart where a dad should be."

William asked a follow-up. "You just mentioned John's need to control, though. Was this something Luke talked about too?"

"I think that's the worst part. I think Luke was of the age where he wanted the relationship to change. This last year he was looking for guidance instead of a parent, so he had started to resent them. But at the end of the day, Luke was indebted to these two. They took him in after his mom died. They raised him to be the man he is. And that man is someone I wanted to get to know better and maybe even marry. Now he's gone."

Sobs retook Elizabeth as she uttered this last sentence. George was there in an instant at her shoulder with a glass of water and his handkerchief. William realized that George was picking up some good habits after all. He'd need to make sure he complimented him once the Fosters had left. William waited patiently until it seemed Elizabeth could continue.

William sighed. "Last question and then we're done. The

note you got in your room. Do you have any idea who may have written it or what it was about? Do you know how someone got into your room or when?"

When William mentioned the note, George looked at him with an intense gaze. William swore this was the same gaze Abi used on him when he came upstairs after whisky. Half contempt, half curiosity. William realized that he hadn't told George about the letter or its contents. George's outrage would have to wait. He needed to focus on this answer. William could feel that so much hinged on this answer.

Elizabeth paused for a bit, pondering the question. Her eyes were still laden with tears, but she was clearly thinking through possibilities. She shook her head gently. William let out a breath he didn't know he was holding. A dead end.

"Thank you for your time. Thomas, you should take her home and keep her out of sight. Many people will want a word with her but let her come to terms with this for a while."

Thomas nodded in agreement, stood up, and walked with his arm around Elizabeth out the door and back towards the shop.

Chapter 22

October 22, 1892 – Medford

Elizabeth left the police station under the cover of her father. They pushed through the crowd that was still milling outside of the town hall and headed back towards the General Store. She was grateful for his presence and his protection at that moment. She felt the crowd silently judge every emotion and felt their eyes peer into her soul, looking for answers as to what made her special.

She didn't know why her beau was murdered and didn't know why someone was targeting her. Something about her seemed to attract people and she didn't want that anymore. She wanted to scream and hide under her bed. She wanted to be alone forever. She was 18, but she felt like a child that day. Her future that had started to form so nicely in front of her had come crashing down in less than 24 hours.

She got back to the store and immediately retreated to her room upstairs and lay on the bed, facedown, covering her head with her pillow and hiding from the world. Her father hovered near her bedroom door to ask if she needed anything. She didn't respond, and she eventually felt his presence recede down the hallway. She appreciated him but didn't really have the patience to deal with people. She couldn't sit here, cooped up in this house anymore.

She needed air.

She rose from her bed and walked down the stairs and through the store. She yelled in the direction of her dad that she was going on a walk, and then, before he could respond, she drifted out of the back door. She walked behind two buildings and then cut into the High Street right near the Universalist church. She wanted to blend into people and be an unknown and unseen anonymous person. There weren't enough people around for that, so she resigned herself to staying off the road as much as possible. As she rounded behind the church, she saw Jack come out of the back of the parish house and empty a pot of steaming water into the gutter. He threw a half wave in her direction, but she dropped her gaze and redoubled her pace. She and Jack had made small talk after the church services, but she really knew nothing about him. His defining feature was his faith, and although he seemed intelligent and kind, she just didn't want to hear anything about "God's will" or "divine plan" or anything else from the church. Right now, it all felt like disingenuous crap. She wanted her grief and her rage to get her through this day.

She turned onto Winthrop Street and headed towards the bridge over the Mystic River where she and Luke had walked just last night. She paused on the bridge overlooking the river and stared into the meandering current. Her eyes teared up again as she thought of her time with Luke on this bridge. They had looked at the city lights flickering and talked about a future where electricity was in every house. They had talked about their life together here or somewhere else. She wanted to relive every one of those moments. She wanted to fall into his arms and be enveloped by his strong butcher's hands. She had known his kiss when she was able to steal it from him, but little else. She thought she had felt a stirring in his loins when they embraced, but she was never sure. She didn't even really know about that side of life. It wasn't a topic that her mother or her father would ever discuss with her. She wished she had known everything about his body. She yearned for someone to make her feel whole. Someone to take her and lay her down and tell her everything was going to be all right. She wanted to be caressed and have the moments drift away underneath the pleasure of another's touch. That was supposed to be Luke, but it would never be him, not ever again.

A stiff October wind tore through her light coat, and she shivered. She wasn't prepared for the temperature drop an October evening in Massachusetts can bring. She had worried more about getting out of the General Store than staying out in the cold. She considered heading back home when she felt the weight of a thick coat drop onto her shoulders. She froze, not sure what had happened. She must have been completely lost in the pleasant daydream that the thought of Luke's caress had inspired, as she hadn't heard anyone approaching.

"Thought you looked a little underdressed," a voice said to her.

Elizabeth spun around and saw Jack backing away quietly from her, both hands up in an apology. His eyebrows were raised as if in alarm. He had the collar of his thick coat turned up against the wind, and he looked very warm.

"I'm sorry, Elizabeth, I wasn't trying to scare you, just help you. We had this extra coat in the alms box, and I saw you tear by the parish house underdressed. I ran back into the church, grabbed the coat and followed you as quickly as I could. I didn't want you to catch cold. I know you've had a hard day, and I don't want it to get worse. I'll be on my way now," Jack continued. "Unless…" he paused, "you want me to stay and walk you home."

"Thank you, Jack. I'll return it on Sunday," was all Elizabeth muttered in response, leaving the last question unanswered. Elizabeth returned to her thoughts, hoping that Jack would get the hint that she wanted to be alone.

Jack took the hint and started back towards the church with a polite nod.

Elizabeth stared back across the gentle water of the Mystic River and felt empty again. Why did it have to be Luke? He was so kind, generous, and he had such a wonderful soul. She should have snuck out and met him behind the tailor's shop that night. She may have been able to save him. Yes, she decided, if he was with her, this wouldn't have happened. Her last words to him were that she would see him today. Now she would never see him again. The emptiness redoubled and she stared down at her feet, bracing against another gust of wind.

Her eyes were drawn back to the dark water. A nice dive to the bottom of the river didn't sound so bad right now. She thought of how quickly it could all be over. She could join the void where Luke was. They could walk together, wrapped forever in emptiness. She would be able to see him today, just like she promised.

The logical part of her brain reminded her that the water would be cold, so she wouldn't just drift off into the void, but would have to journey through a freezing cold struggle to get there. That didn't sound so nice.

Her eyes looked to the middle of the river for some sharp rocks, thinking maybe she would be able to dash her head against one, allowing unconsciousness to take away the bite of the cold. Then that irritating part of her that wanted to survive reminded her that the chance of getting it just right was very low. She'd likely just make the struggle and the pain worse.

It wasn't worth it, she decided. She had to keep moving – both through life and away from this bridge. Although she didn't know what she was going to do with her life anymore, she formulated a plan to talk with someone to help get this emptiness out of her.

Adrenaline suddenly coursed through her veins, and she came to an epiphany. This would not be the defining moment of her life. She would rise above this. She would not be a victim. Her life required her to be the victor.

"I promise, right now, that this will not define me," Elizabeth said to the river. The river gurgled in return.

She shook her head defiantly, turned on her heel, and started back towards High Street. She pulled her new, borrowed, heavy coat around her, and walked briskly towards home. She got there just before dark settled in.

Her parents were both upstairs, and she could tell they had been worrying. Before they could ask, she said, "I had to clear my head. I'm doing better now. What happened to Luke isn't ok and I won't be in a good head space for a long time. I feel empty and like I missed out on a great love in my life. But neither of you need to worry about me. I am stronger than this. I am not a quitter."

They ran to her and embraced her tightly. She felt their love flow through her, and it made her feel better. No matter what happened in her life, she would always have the unconditional love of her family. That, she knew, she should not take for granted.

The embrace came to a natural and comfortable ending, and they all sat down to dinner. Elizabeth ate the first meal she could stomach of the day. She didn't know what the next days would bring, but she knew that she needed to be in control of her destiny. That night she was rewarded with a dreamless sleep.

Chapter 23

October 23, 1892 – Medford

Forward progress starts with a first step, but sometimes you have to stumble a bit to find your bearings. The morning after Elizabeth stared into the Mystic, she woke to a renewed wave of grief. She paused for a while in her room, putting together the pieces of her heart and telling herself it was going to be ok.

"This does not define me," she repeated over and over to herself.

The mantra helped, and she was able to get her emotions under control, dress herself, and head out for breakfast. She chose a plain wool dress with long sleeves and put her hair into a tightly braided ponytail. She kept the blue calico ribbon from the day before as a bit of a reminder of rock bottom. The only way to go from here was up. As she left her room, she grabbed her winter coat, hat, and gloves, making sure she would not repeat the same mistake from last night.

It was nearly 9 by the time she got herself together, and thankfully her parents had left her a plate of food for breakfast. She sat down at the table to pick through it and was thankful for her support system. Her parents were giving her the right balance of emotional support and space to process. It was quiet as she chewed on her cold eggs and toast, and the quiet was both a blessing and a curse. She didn't have to speak with anyone else, but the only person left in the room were the thoughts in her head.

Thoughts of inadequacy.

Thoughts of loneliness.

Thoughts of hopelessness.

"Stop it," Elizabeth thought, slamming her fist down to the table to remind herself that this behavior would not be tolerated. "This does not define me."

She cleaned up and put her dishes away. She descended the stairs into the store to see both of her parents working. They looked up as she descended and took turns coming over to give her a hug. Her father enveloped her in his arms, making her feel safe and warm for a moment. Her mother's embrace was less welcoming, but that was her way. Clara Foster grew up in a house that frowned on showing emotion, where Thomas was the opposite. Elizabeth knew her mother loved her dearly; she just wasn't capable of outwardly showing it. Clara's love manifested itself in small acts, like the breakfast plate left for her that morning.

"Good morning, Elizabeth," her mother said with a touch of forced optimism. "What do you want to do today?"

"I am going to church to light a candle for Luke," Elizabeth replied instantly. She had thought about this a lot and figured that the lighting of the candle was a good first step to healing. This was how she moved forward – one step at a time.

She repeated her mantra for what felt like the hundredth time that morning. "This does not define me."

"That sounds wonderful, Elizabeth," her father interjected. "Do you want one of us to go with you?"

"No thank you. I'd like to be alone."

Elizabeth left the through the front door and turned towards the church. The general store was not far from the Universalist church – all she had to do is take the High Street across Forest Street, past the high school and then wind away from the Mystic River until she reached the church. The walk gave her time to take nice, healing, deep breaths of the cold October air. What had been a shock last night was invigorating today.

"It probably helps that I'm dressed appropriately," she thought. Cold air was great at clearing her head, and one of her favorite noises was the wind through the dead leaves that hadn't yet been shed from the oaks and maples that lined the Mystic River. It had a magical quality – a quality that was good for the soul. This was what she needed today. Things that were good for the soul.

The Universalist Church was an easy to see landmark on the High Street, with an imposing square bell tower and a peaked roof making the front façade of the church. Elizabeth held the coat that Jack had draped over her shoulders last night. She had every intention of returning it to the alms box before she lit a candle and said a brief prayer, but she didn't really want to talk to Jack or to Minister DeLong. She walked into the church through the main entrance, centered under the square bell tower. Once inside, she then turned left to enter the nave near the altar. The layout was a little weird this way, where the congregants walked into the front of the church and had to walk past the altar in the nave to get to the pews.

The candle stand was in a small narthex at the back of the church and candles adorned the three-tiered cast iron stand under a backdrop of a seasonal tapestry. It was the end of October, so the church was in the season of 'After Pentecost,' which meant the backdrop was a nice red, white, and green banner inset with an embroidered crucifix. Elizabeth looked forward to the hanging of the Advent banner, which was a beautiful violet tapestry inset with a large white candle. Advent and Christmas always made the church seem more beautiful and austere.

As she walked towards the narthex, she saw Jack and Minister DeLong talking in hushed tones near the altar. She would have to make this quick before they came and joined her. She really didn't want to deal with any questions today. She dipped the candelabrum into a lit candle and used it to light an honorarium candle. She closed her eyes, bowed her head, and tried to come up with the appropriate words. What do you say to the dead soul of a boy you knew pretty well and maybe wanted to marry in the future?

"Sorry someone killed you," she started. That didn't feel right. She'd have to try again.

"I miss you" was all she added before opening her eyes.

She turned to go but saw Jack standing between her and the door. So much for the quick escape, she thought. Determined not to stay, she bowed her head to avoid making eye contact and soldiered towards the door. As she passed him, he slipped her a piece of paper, squeezed her hand gently, and then went back to Minister DeLong at the altar. She passed back through the door of the church and was on the High Street again. She unfolded the note and saw a flowery script scrawled on the paper.

Matthew 5:4

She hadn't seen Jack's writing before. It was beautiful, almost calligraphy. He had clearly been instructed in the art of writing, and she spent more time looking at the letters instead of just reading the words. On a whim she smelled the paper, half expecting it to be scented. It smelled of candle wax and paper, but little else. She read the note again, and realized she didn't know this verse, even though it was from her favorite gospel. She resolved to look it up in the family bible when she was able to get back home. She had one more stop to make.

Elizabeth made her way towards Purchase Street, which was past Winthrop Street where she gazed into the dark waters the night before and then a right at the fork in the High Street. It was still a short walk, which gave her time to think more about her silly prayer. She'd need to figure out how to talk to someone who was dead. A thought came into the back of her mind without unbidden.

"What if my difficulty coming up with the right words to say was a sign of something? Have I already started to not let this define me?"

She arrived at a small building and stepped through the door. As she entered the offices of Dr. Ferguson a bell above the door rang, notifying someone in the back room to her presence. Like so many other buildings in Medford, the business was on the ground floor and a staircase adjoined the business that went up to the residence. This allowed Dr. Ferguson and his wife to live and work in the same place. Elizabeth looked around, admiring the clean and sterile office that they kept. A short moment later Dr. Ferguson's wife Eunice came waddling through the door. She was as large as Dr. Ferguson was thin, and they made a nearly comical couple. Nevertheless, Dr. Ferguson was kind and always listened. His methods were not modern, but Elizabeth had never had complaints. She just needed someone to talk to.

"Elizabeth!" Eunice greeted her warmly. "I didn't know you had an appointment today."

Elizabeth was both glad and disappointed that Eunice didn't treat her with the same soft gloves that the rest of the town seemed to. Maybe she didn't know what had happened last night.

Elizabeth gathered her courage. Progress forward starts with a first step.

"Hey, Eunice. Does Doc have a couple minutes? I need to talk to him about something."

"Sure, honey, just give me a minute to let him know you're here," the portly woman responded.

Eunice disappeared through the door where she had emerged just seconds earlier and returned with the doctor in tow. Dr. Ferguson was a tall and skinny older man, who always wore a white doctor's coat with pockets bursting with the tools of his trade. His best qualities were kind eyes and soft hands, so all his patients felt comfortable in his care. Dr. Ferguson had clearly told Eunice something, as her earlier demeanor had completely changed. Eunice seemed guarded and reserved and had difficulty looking Elizabeth in the eye.

"Come on back, Elizabeth," the doctor said.

Elizabeth followed the doctor back to the small exam room which was little else but a table, two chairs, and a sink. She had been in this room many times over the years, but as she grew the room started to feel smaller and smaller. Today it felt almost like a coffin.

No, not a coffin, she quickly corrected herself, a closet. Don't think of coffins. Luke is the one in the coffin. The walls started to feel like they were pressing against her, trapping her. She felt her heart rate increase, and her breathing did as well.

"No. This does not define me," she said to herself. Luckily, Dr. Ferguson chose that moment to speak.

"First, Elizabeth, let me say how sorry I am about what happened yesterday," Dr. Ferguson said as he sat in the chair and gestured at Elizabeth to sit in the other. Elizabeth remained standing.

"Thanks, Doc. It hasn't been good," Elizabeth responded, fighting back another wave of tears. There was the grief, she thought to herself. Where was that in the church?

"So what brings you in. Feeling sick from the change in weather?" the doctor continued.

"Doc, this is hard to say and a little bit of a strange request. I want to…" she paused. He waited patiently for her to continue. "…not feel the world so much."

The doctor looked at her with a concerned look on his face. He leaned in on his chair and studied Elizabeth for a while. Elizabeth felt exposed and embarrassed.

"Tell me why."

"Look, I know this is very recent, and I thought about this a lot last night and this morning. I almost threw myself off of the Winthrop Bridge last night, but I didn't because I figured it'd be too cold and too painful. But here's the truth – there was a murderer in my room two nights ago. Chief Smith probably doesn't want you to know that, but I need to tell you everything, so you believe me. I was sleeping and the person who murdered Luke crept into my room somehow and left me a note on my nightstand. Can you imagine how afraid I am to close my eyes at night? I know that I was only dating Luke for about two months, but I knew he was special. I knew that he was worth marrying and starting a family with. And right now, I just can't go through that again. I need to feel less so I don't feel more. I need to matter in this world. I need to be bigger than this town. I need to make an impact. I can't let this loss define me. I can't do that if I'm hung up on someone that won't be back with me ever again. I know I'm rambling and I know I shouldn't tell you all this because you're probably going to think I have hysteria or something and you want to commit me to an asylum, and maybe that's where I'm headed right now, but my feelings are too much and my life is too important to be stuck with my feelings all the time and…"

Dr. Ferguson had raised a hand to interject. "I understand. Give me a second."

He walked out of the room. Elizabeth didn't know if she was done and her eyes darted around the room, trying figure out what to do next. Should she stay there? Should she leave? Was he going to get her dad or mom to take her to an asylum? Would she have to lie to them and tell them that she hadn't said all that? Her mind was racing as Dr. Ferguson walked back into the room. He wasn't with anyone else and held something in his hand.

"This is a very small vial of laudanum, Elizabeth. Find a way to put one or two drops in your morning tea. Not on Sundays, though. Your body needs to have a break once a week from this."

She nodded at his instructions, taking them in. He handed the vial over to Elizabeth but didn't let go.

"No more than two drops, do you understand? I need to hear you say it." His kind demeanor vanished, and Elizabeth could tell he was serious.

"No more than two drops." Elizabeth repeated back to him.

"Good. I'm not going to tell your parents about this, and I'm not letting Eunice know either. This is our secret, and when this vial is gone, there will be no more refills. I've lost my fair share of important people. Grief is a room with an oil lamp on the wall. The oil burns strongly at first, but as the oil fades, the grief gets dimmer. It will never run out, but the light will be so dim you may not be able to see it. Sometimes something comes along and fills the oil lamp with fresh oil, and the grief is bright again. This laudanum is like tinted glasses. It helps you when the light is the brightest, but you need to get used to the light with your own eyes."

She nodded and absorbed this parable. This made sense to her. She saw a tear form in the corner of one of his eyes. Something about this conversation had filled one of his lamps with a little oil. She wanted to hug him and tell him it was ok. She wanted to comfort him and be there for him. Her empathy took over and she forgot about her own problems for a little while.

"Maybe that's what I need," she thought. "I need someone to take care of. Maybe then I won't worry so much about caring for myself."

She resisted the urge to comfort him and rose from the chair. She thanked him, left the small examination room, tucked the vial into one of the pockets in her coat and stepped back onto Purchase Street.

She looked back when she was about 15 feet from the door. She saw Dr. Ferguson hugging his wife tightly. She would ask him someday about his oil lamps, but not today.

Chapter 24

October 23, 1892 – Medford

Elizabeth walked back towards her house. It was around lunch time, and she was hungry. She walked past the high school again and saw kids out on their lunch break. She had graduated the previous May at the top of her class and was considering enrolling in some courses at Tufts. There had even been a story in the paper about it, which had identified her with a misogynistic headline.

'Local girl bests boys to be top of class.'

The university had just allowed women to enroll that previous July, and the first female enrollees were starting this fall. She had missed the application deadline for this year but planned to enroll next year. She had a knack for school, with a special propensity for debate. She liked convincing people that her opinion was right and theirs was wrong.

As she walked down High Street, an idea came to her on a whim. Without any foresight or planning, she walked towards the town hall and the police station within. The crowd that was hanging around outside yesterday had dispersed, so the door was unlocked. She turned the knob and entered the station.

William and George both looked up from their desk, registered who it was, and rose to stop her. Elizabeth knew them to be kind and caring officers who really wanted to make Medford safe, and both of them were clearly exhausted from a long few days. She'd need her skills in debate for this one but knew she would eventually get her way.

"Whoa, Miss Foster. Just hold on," started George. "I'm not

sure you should be here."

"Why did you come?" William added, more forcefully.

"I want to look John in the eyes," Elizabeth responded. "I need to know something."

George and William looked at each other, a worried look still on their faces. They didn't seem sure this was a good idea, and, frankly, Elizabeth didn't blame them. While they were looking at each other, Elizabeth just walked past the two of them, explaining herself as she went.

"Look," Elizabeth stated, trotting on with a confidence she wasn't sure she felt. "I've known John a long time. I will keep calm and stay back from the bars."

William grabbed his cane and nodded at George. "Ok, just for a moment though. And I'm going with you."

The holding cell was towards the back of the station, and they walked in that direction. As they approached the cell, Elizabeth heard John stand up, trying to find out why people were coming to see him. He froze when he saw Elizabeth.

Elizabeth looked at him and saw nothing but a man in grief. There were dark bags under his red, puffy eyes, and he looked defeated. Elizabeth realized that he had lost Luke as well. Elizabeth had an advantage, as her grief was able to be shared and reduced by her family around her. John had no one and was locked in a cell. He was truly alone, and it showed.

"Hey, John," Elizabeth began, brightly. "Do you need anything from Edna or from home?"

John looked shocked that Elizabeth was talking to him. After the last two days, he figured that she would be the last one to talk to him. It was clear he blamed himself for Luke's death, even if he wasn't the one holding the knife. It wasn't too far-fetched to assume that John blamed himself for a portion of Elizabeth's emptiness.

The big man sputtered a request. "Can you have Edna bring a blanket? This one is terribly scratchy. With the Chief's permission, of course."

Elizabeth and John both glanced at William. He mulled this request over in his mind and nodded his head. Elizabeth would have to delay her return home as she went to retrieve the blanket. She suddenly realized this means she'd have to return to the butcher shop. The scene of Luke's last moments. Her act of kindness had thrust her back into grief, and the brightness of her grief lamp flared. A wave of shock and sadness swept over her.

No. She couldn't do that.

Thankfully, William watched Elizabeth freeze up and understood what had just happened. He mercifully interjected.

"The undertaker is finishing up this afternoon," William said, not sure if he was talking to Elizabeth or John. "George can go after that."

Elizabeth slowly approached the bars and reached a hand through, offering it to John. He stepped up and lightly grabbed it. Elizabeth squeezed.

She looked him dead in the eye, and holding all emotion back that she felt, said "If you're innocent, I hope they let you out soon." His eyes softened.

"If you're not, I hope you rot in hell, you monster."

She grabbed her hand out of John's and walked out of the police station and into the street. For the first time in two days, she smiled. That had felt good.

Chapter 25

October 1888 – London

The month of October in 1888 was a crash course in murder for Ben Smith. Montague Druitt was not a patient teacher, nor incredibly forthcoming about his methods. It made him a frustrating tutor and Ben often wondered if he was being set up to be a patsy for Druitt. On their first night together, Druitt reduced the training to five simple rules for Ben to keep in mind:

1. Be as stealthy as the night
2. Send a message with your crime
3. Don't kill for sport
4. Have a day job above reproach
5. The best alibi is someone else's obvious guilt

Druitt reminded Ben that there was an unspoken rule that superseded all. Don't get caught. That was the only unbreakable rule. The other rules were guides, but they could flex to meet the needs of each situation.

Ben fell into a routine and found it exhilarating. Although he hardly ever slept, he felt energized and alive with all the things he was learning. Ben would run numbers for the Odessians during the day, and at night Druitt spent time teaching Ben the intricacies of his craft, boiled down into three categories.

It started with knife-craft. The older man was so fast with the knife, Ben could barely keep up. Druitt ran him through drills on how to hold the knife and how to attack with it. His focus was on balance and explosion through his arm, as these two skills set the foundation of all other knife work. He spent hours on the difference between a slash and a stab and which type of knife was optimal for each motion. Druitt had Ben run drills to hone his knife skills on straw dummies in the small flat Ben had moved into after his mother's death. Soon every surface in the apartment was covered with a light dusting of straw particles. Ben realized he would have to keep it clean to ensure he was above reproach. Nevertheless, he drilled and made mistakes until he was as confident with the knife as he was with his own hands. The blade became an extension of his arm.

The second topic Druitt taught was anatomy. Knowing the body was vital in disarming it. Druitt and Ben spent time on pressure points, ways to effectively maim someone, and the general makeup of the body. Druitt lent him textbooks to study, as acquiring live samples for dissection wasn't as easy.

Druitt also taught Ben about basic chemicals and how to obtain them. He reviewed laudanum, chlorodyne, camphorated tincture of opium, foxglove and hemlock. Ben knew where to find them and how to dose them. Ben knew the pharmacists in London who would provide chemicals for cash, all the while forgetting the faces of those that paid. To help increase the speed of Ben's medical knowledge, Druitt would jab his finger into random spots on Ben and quiz him which organs were beneath his finger and where the closest arteries were located. If Ben got it right, he was rewarded with a poke in a different spot. If he got it wrong, it was a smack across the back of the head and then a poke in a different spot. Bruises started to form on Ben's stomach and back and he was grateful when Druitt moved on to his third topic – stealth.

One night in mid-October, a note waited for Ben at his small flat. Within it was a silver coin and an address.

You have until the bells strike 11 to slip this into my pocket without getting caught. Good luck.

The address was St. Mary's Matfelon, the same church bells that Ben listened to with his mother when they lived on George's Street. Ben was pretty sure this was a reminder from Druitt that Ben could be "cut off" from training at any time.

As Ben made his way into Whitechapel, he passed the Royal London Hospital where his mother had died just 7 months ago. A lot had changed in his life, but he found that the reminder didn't make him sad. It only motivated him to do even better than he was. The other thing he felt was rage. It was a blinding, white hot rage that fueled him on cold nights. It made him angry at the man who had taken his mother from him. A son needs his mother's love.

The rage took away his calm, and people who lose their calm get caught. Ben paused across from the church, resetting his emotions and looking around for the best way to get inside and find Druitt. He didn't hear the footsteps behind him.

"You lose, Smith." Druitt said, walking out of the shadows. He smacked Ben across the back of his head. Ben surrendered the silver coin back to Druitt, who then vanished into the night. Ben was ashamed. He had forgotten the simple words Druitt had taught him about stealth – know your surroundings better than everyone else. It appeared to Ben that calm was equally important.

From then on, this same charade repeated itself. A letter would show up under Ben's door, with a silver coin and an address. For the next two weeks, Ben tried and failed. Druitt always had the upper hand. He would see Ben coming, and was usually behind him before Ben even knew he was there.

Ben noticed that the address on the paper Druitt gave was always a church. He realized that two men hanging around a church a night wouldn't be seen as suspicious. Lots of men who worked all day would pop into a church at night to pay their respects. Druitt had developed an alibi that was above question. Ben marveled at the forethought and chided himself for not thinking of it sooner. Druitt really was a master at stealth. No wonder he saw the police with such disdain.

On the last day of the fortnight, the note changed. It was delivered with just the address of St. Mary's Matfelon and no silver coin. Ben arrived at the church and expected Druitt to jump out and surprise him. Druitt didn't appear, so Ben walked into the church. He noticed the shape of Druitt sitting in the pews and went to join him. As he sat next to Druitt, the older man leaned over to speak.

"You've done well these last two weeks," Druitt said quietly.

"You caught me each night, though."

"Never in the same way twice. You learn. You adapt. You'd have me if there were two more days. Besides – I am very good at this, and your target will likely be that drunken fool you call a father."

"So why end the game before I get a chance to find you?"

"It's time to move on. The clock is ticking."

"Ticking for what?" Ben urged.

"It is nearly time to take your final exam. But first, the thesis," Druitt said. "Combine stealth and knives and hunt the mongrels of London. If you can out stealth a mutt, a whore has no chance."

Ben nodded. He was ready to end something's life. Ready to watch the light go out of their eyes, even if it was a dog. He wanted to feel that same rush he felt when he stumbled upon Druitt in Mitre Square. Druitt continued, delivering his orders to Ben.

"Bring me 8 dog's tails by Halloween night. If you don't, you won't see November."

Chapter 26

October 1888 – London

Ben found he couldn't do it. He couldn't corner a dog and murder it. It wasn't right and seemed a lot like hunting for sport, which violated one of the rules. He didn't feel the same rush when he thought about killing a dog that he did when considering killing a human. He had tried a few times, but ultimately, he stood over the dog, looking into its eyes, and seeing empathy and kindness. It wasn't benevolent to deprive the world of dogs, even though London was overrun with mutts and strays. He knew that Druitt wouldn't tolerate this morality, so Ben had to do something to prove to his mentor that he was ready for his "final exam."

Salvation came in the form of the Battersea home in South London. The Battersea home had opened its doors to stray dogs. The police in London had sent tons of dogs there, not all of which were able to find new homes. Disease and injury sometimes required a graceful end to the life of a stray. A simple night-time break-in to the Battersea's morgue, and Ben became the proud owner of 8 tails, just as his mission required. He wrapped them tightly in cloth and hid them in a loose floorboard in his apartment, waiting for Halloween night.

He spent the rest of his time until Halloween working on his stealth and his tracking. He chose to focus on stalking whores, assuming Druitt would have him pick out a whore for his final exam. At Druitt's insistence he never practiced in Whitechapel. Druitt saw Whitechapel as his sacred hunting ground.

The stalking and tracking gave Ben a glimpse into the life

of Druitt as well as what he presumed to be the life of his mother. It was amazing how quickly Ben was able to disassociate the person from their soul. He was worried during his training that he'd blink at the time of murder, not able to finish the job because of the morality of murder. He found more and more he was able to see the woman as a thing and see her as the symptom of a putrid underbelly of London. Soon Ben started to think like Druitt – that everyone was a whore, and ridding the city of this underbelly would make life better for the rest of the populace.

On Halloween night, Ben stayed in his small apartment, ready for a note under the door. Instead of a note, he heard a light rapping on the door around 10 pm. Ben threw open the door to see Druitt, dressed in a full-length cloak and gloves. Ben watched Druitt's hand flash under his coat and knew that Druitt held a knife. Trust was still not established between the two of them.

"Show me the tails," Druitt whispered, almost too quiet for Ben to hear.

Ben calmly walked backwards towards his bed and bent down near the false floorboard, never taking his eyes off of Druitt. Trust was a two-way street. As Ben reached into the well, he saw the glint of a knife being removed from Druitt's coat. The older man was protecting against a double cross. Ben withdrew the wrapped tails and set them on the bed. With a silent raise of the eyebrows, Ben waited for Druitt before unwrapping them. Druitt nodded slightly, and Ben unwrapped the cloth and laid his acquisition out on the bed. Druitt counted the 8 shriveled dogs' tails, sheathed his knife and quickly retreated from the room. Ben rushed after him into the hallway, but Druitt was already gone.

Ben had apparently passed the test.

He heard nothing from his mentor until the 2nd of

November, when a note slid under Ben's door. Ben opened it nervously, trying to guess what it would say. Maybe Druitt didn't like the way that Ben had found a loophole for the dogs. Maybe Druitt wanted nothing more to do with him. So many possibilities went through Ben's head. He looked down at the letter and read it twice before realizing what it said.

Next week is your final test. You will kill a whore for me in Whitechapel. It will look like my work, but you will do it. This will be your initiation. If you mess this up, I will pin all my murders on you or gut you like a fish. Either way, you will just be another whore, led by me to slaughter. This isn't for sport. This is how you send your message. This is your coming out party. After this, you will do great things in homage to me, your teacher. You will mimic me.

-Saucy Jacky

He slipped the note into the small potbelly stove that sat burning in the corner of the apartment. Ben cracked a smile. He felt ready.

The next week, Ben prowled the streets of Whitechapel at night. He dressed like a factory worker and hunted when the second shift ended. This allowed him to blend in and be as stealthy as the night. This also happened to be the time of the night when the most whores were out, selling their bodies to the men who were tired from their shift. After three nights he had his mark. Her name was Mary Kelly. He followed her up Fashion Street and down White's Row and figured out she lived on Dorset Street in a small lodging house on Miller's court.

Ben selected Mary as his target for a few primary reasons, but the most obvious was that her door lock was broken. It allowed him easy entrance to her room, away from prying eyes in case the nerves got the better of him. She also had a steady man in her life, who worked as a fish porter. As Ben bought a fish knife from a vendor across town he smiled again.

Murders only need two things: a victim and a scapegoat. Once you've found the person to blame, the rest is easy.

Chapter 27

October 23, 1892 – Medford

William stood by the jail cell, mouth agape, as Elizabeth walked out of the front door and headed down the High Street. He had always seen Elizabeth as an innocent soul. Someone who wasn't aware of the darkness in this world. The outburst condemning John to hell had shattered that impression. He shook his head quickly to get that last exchange out of his mind. He noticed John and George doing the same. William knew that Elizabeth likely wasn't the only person who felt like John deserved to 'go to hell,' so there was an urgency to solve this crime and send John to the hangman's noose or back to his wife.

The interviews of John and of Elizabeth in the last day had left a couple of holes in the story. He would go with George to the butcher shop and see if he could ask Edna some questions while George retrieved the blanket that John had requested. A couple of hours later, William saw the undertaker drive his horse-drawn cart past the police station. The cleanup work was done at the butcher shop.

"Alright, George, I think it's time that you got John that blanket," William said, a little louder than normal so that John would hear. William wanted John to realize they were treating him kindly, but also that if he was guilty, this was another chance for them to find evidence at his home.

George stood up from his desk and grabbed his belt. He slid his truncheon into his belt and quietly moved towards the door. William called out to him.

"Hold up, George, just a second."

The big man paused and slowly pivoted to watch William stand up from his desk, grab his cane, and trod over to where George was standing.

"I'm going to walk over there with you. I would like to ask Edna a couple questions," William continued.

William said this quietly so that John would not hear. William was being cautious. Probably too cautious, but it was his job to work on the best leads they had, which was currently a man with the murder weapon and motive stashed beneath his floorboards. George nodded silently and they both pushed open the police station door and turned towards the butcher shop.

They walked for a bit in silence, the noise of William's cane on the cobblestones providing a metronomic background noise that was soothing and calming. It was George who spoke first. "So tell me what you think happened, boss."

"Honestly?" William responded. George nodded, and William continued.

"I've thought about this a lot over the past two days. I don't think it was John. Whoever did kill that young man really wanted us to think that it was John. Everything was planned to make it look like him, but there are two things that aren't right."

William paused as a couple passed them on the street, arm in arm. He tipped an imaginary cap in their direction before continuing his monologue.

"The first oddity is that the person who has the most to gain from John going to jail is actually the one who was killed. I hardly believe that Luke cut off his own head."

William paused here, thinking of the visual of a man taking

a deboning knife and slicing clean through their own head.

"And the second?" George asked. William looked back at him blankly, still distracted by the image in his head. George continued, too kind to get upset at William's apparent short-term memory, "What's the second odd situation in this case?"

"The note." William said. "There's one part I keep coming back to."

William watched as George nodded, but it was clear that the deputy didn't yet grasp what William was trying to say. William would need to cite some examples. William started with a reminder of the note:

> I watched the two of you last night and I couldn't let him get in my way. He thought he had gotten a-head of me, but he had to be separated from you. You will be mine before I'm done.

"I think the killer spelled ahead as 'a-head' in the note to indicate the first thing we would find. That's why I think the eyeball was in the tray, too. The killer was telling us that he was watching us discover his crime. I would bet that the killer was in the crowd outside of the butcher shop. It's the perfect cover," William explained.

"The second bit was the word 'separated'," William started again. "I think that obvious implication here is the way that Luke was found – separated into his parts. But I think that's a ruse. I think the killer was more referring to the romantic connection between Luke and Elizabeth. It had to be. The cuts on Luke's genitals were rushed. Hurried. Frantic. They were done when Luke was still alive. Then it was left in Luke's bed. The killer is trying to romantically separate Luke and Elizabeth as well."

William paused for a moment so George would be able to follow.

"This is where I figured it out and started to look at the case differently. This is also one of the reasons I think the killer is a man. It isn't likely it's an old man, either. I think that anyone under 30 better watch themselves, though."

George knew enough not to interrupt when the chief got going, but gently prodded William along with a subtle "How" inserted in the correct part of the conversation.

"Elizabeth is very important to this killer. I think that the killer wants to be with Elizabeth, and he'll go after anyone that tries to get in the way. That logically makes it a young man. Someone who isn't married and thinks of her purity first. I'd like to think that means it isn't an older man, but I also know that some people are just…" William couldn't bring himself to use the word perverse. He found it a little funny he was assessing the perversions of a murderer.

George looked shocked. "If he's going to going after anyone Elizabeth is nice to, the killer may murder half the town. He'll fill the graveyard with love notes. That girl is very kind to everyone she meets, and you can't help but watch her when she walks into the room."

William found George's turn of phrase a little odd. Why

would a dead body be a love note? William shook this off, nodded silently in George's direction, and continued with his analysis.

"The last part I can't figure out is the way that the killer closes the note. 'Before I'm done.' That part is bothering me, because there are only really two basic explanations of what it could mean. The first is that the killer will be done if he's able to be with Elizabeth, and anyone else that stands in the way will be eliminated. There's an underlying insecurity in this thought process, as who can honestly think that they can ever hold the complete attention of someone?"

William's mind drifted to his time with Abigail. He thought he had captured her complete attention before they had kids, but knew that as soon as Ben was born, he started to slide down the priority list in her mind.

George interjected again, shaking William out of his thoughts. "And the second?"

"The other possibility is that the killer isn't done killing and I'm wrong about his connection to Elizabeth."

They walked in troubled silence the rest of the way to the butcher shop.

Chapter 28

October 23, 1892 – Medford

There were still a few people milling around outside the butcher shop as George and William walked up to the front door. William was betting the novelty of a small-town murder would be a good source of gossip for more than a few weeks. He hoped, for Edna's sake, that the town would get over it and move onto something different as quickly as possible. The crowd saw the two policemen approaching and moved out of the way to accommodate their passage. William and George stepped into the shop and saw that the undertaker had done a good job cleaning. Even though William was in this room two nights ago, it seemed like everything was brand new.

Edna heard the door open and came out from the back rooms, ready to shoo away anyone looking for some gossip. Her hair was disheveled and there were dark bags under her eyes. She looked like she hadn't slept in two nights. She wore a thick sweater over her nightgown, and dirty leather slippers poked from underneath the gown.

As she saw the two of them coming towards her, she quickly put something wooden and solid behind her back. William thought it looked like the wooden stick that John would use to de-clog the meat machine. William wondered if she had to use it as a threat to some gossip seekers who were a little less than polite.

"Oh, it's you, Chief. What can I do for you?" Edna asked.

"George here has been tasked with bringing John a more comfortable blanket. Seems he doesn't like our accommodations as much as yours." William said. He was trying to defuse the situation and show Edna that they were on her side. "I thought I'd tag along and keep George company."

"That sounds wonderful, Chief. George, let me go get the one from our bed. I have been sleeping upright in the chair by our small fireplace, and I have an Afghan that keeps me warm enough," Edna replied.

She turned around and headed for the stairs, but William quickly interjected. "How about we send George upstairs and you and I can have a quick talk about some things, Edna?"

Edna looked back to see if William had truly asked that as a question. Edna turned around and started back towards William. She didn't believe that his request was optional. Good. That would make this a little easier. He had to figure out how to ask this carefully, though. George disappeared up the stairs, headed to get the blanket. William looked after him and judged when he was out of ear shot.

"Edna, there's a few things in the story I need to understand. First is about where Luke was going after him and John got in a fight," William began.

Edna looked around nervously, trying to see if anyone was listening.

"What do you mean, Chief?" she asked.

"Edna, I'd like to know where Luke went after he left here. It was around 9 pm as John tells it, and I want to know if Luke said anything about where he was going."

William left out that 9 pm was a common theme between Elizabeth and John. That made it a solid, corroborated point in the timeline. However, John had said two nights ago that Luke went to church. Then he said during his interrogation that he didn't know where Luke went. Elizabeth had said nothing about his destination after she saw him. This means that there was some way that John knew that Luke went to church.

Edna looked up at William and said, "We don't know where he went, Chief. They were both mad with each other, and usually the best way to get over that is to give them some space. They have argued like this before. It started about 6 months ago when he told us that we couldn't make him work in the butcher shop anymore and he wanted to leave to find his dad. No one knows where he is, though. He doesn't talk about where he came from. His mom died when he was so young, and then we took him in when he got here. We wouldn't know where to start or what he did in between. We don't even know why he came to Medford."

"We got through it by assuring him we knew he wasn't here forever. After those fights, Luke would go to the church and light a candle for his mom. I was surprised when John said that was where Luke went two nights ago. We don't know where he went, and I think John just assumed."

"That's ok, Edna," William said. "There was a good enough reason to say that, since that was Luke's pattern. You're sure you didn't see or hear him after that?"

"Promise, Chief," Edna insisted. "We should have heard the floor. This thing creaks like the Dickens. Whoever did this must know where all the creaks are."

Edna looked surprised at this admission. She realized she had just painted her husband with a guilty light. No one would know the creaks and cracks of the floor better than the person who spent most of his time there. William let this simmer for a bit. He wanted her to trust him and tell him the truth.

"One more question, Edna. Why were you up at nearly 4 in the morning to discover Luke?"

"Well, Chief, it's a little embarrassing." Edna flushed.

"It's ok, Edna, take your time. It's just a pretty odd coincidence that you were up to find him before John."

"It's nothing bad, Chief," Edna started. She still seemed embarrassed, so William waited, quietly.

"I'm not sleeping like I used to. I wake up in the middle of the night five or six times a week. I just jolt awake and I'm burning up, like I'm in the middle of summer. I usually come down to the shop floor and sit for a while in the chair by the door. The cool air of the night makes the windows cooler, and I'll lean against them in my nightgown. This helps me feel cool. Sometimes, if it's really bad, I'll head to the ice box where we keep the meat and just stick my head in it for a while. Doc Ferguson says it's something all women my age go through, but I still don't like to talk about it."

"What happened when you came down that night?"

"I lit the oil lamp and that's when I saw Luke's head on the spike. I ran out the back door, but I didn't know where to go. I don't know why I didn't go back upstairs to John. I just couldn't think clearly. It was so gruesome I didn't know what to do. I ran to the one spot I could think of that was safe, and that's the church. I knocked on the side door and Jack came right out with a hand full of candles. I barely got two or three words out and then he told me to go into the church pews and he ran to get you. I'm so glad he was up."

"Do you remember what you told him?"

"I think I said. 'Luke is dead, blood everywhere,'" Edna said. "You'll have to ask him."

William nodded. George returned then with a blanket over his arm.

"What will you do now, Edna?" George asked.

"Well, I'm going to have to start by selling a few things." Edna said. "I don't think I'll ever be able to use the sausage machine or the beam scale again. I'll have to take them to Boston, out of reach of the gossip. After that, hopefully my John will be back to me. Then we'll probably have to get our things together and move out of Medford, maybe to the West. John has family in Ohio, and we may go start a new shop in Cincinnati. Lots of pork flows through there from the Ohio River, and there's always a need for butchers. The money should be good, and I hear the town is nice."

"Thanks for the time today, Edna. We'll take this to John." William said, pointing at the blanket that George held.

As they left to head back towards the police station, William mentioned to George that it looked more and more like someone was trying to frame John. George only quietly nodded in return. William couldn't help but notice George's silence.

Chapter 29

October 23, 1892 – Medford

William needed to write this down to make sense. As he got back to the police station, he made for his desk and pulled out his notebook. He scrawled the date across the top and started writing.

Unknown time – Luke goes on date with Elizabeth. They walk on the High Street and by the Mystic River. I assume that the killer knew about this date. He either saw them out walking or, if it was John, had seen Luke leave the butcher shop.

9 pm (estimated) – Luke gets home from his date in a good mood. He asks John about what it would take to start a new shop and mentions he has around $1000 saved. Luke gets into an argument with John about money and the future. Luke leaves and heads somewhere unknown. Edna believes that Luke went to the church to light a candle for his mom. John assumed the same and mentioned this to me during the night of the crime.

3:30 am (estimated) – Edna discovers the body and runs to the church. Edna alerts Jack, who is up replacing the candles. Jack runs and wakes me. I make my way over to the butcher shop and am first on the scene.

4 am (approximate) – I investigate the butcher shop and John is in the back door. Jack stays outside in the crowd. Unknown where Edna is or how John was alerted to Luke's body. I discover Luke's body, dismembered with the eye in the weight tray, the head on the meat spike, and the separated body in the sausage machine. Luke's genitals are missing. The floor and counters are scrubbed with bromine (note: my assessment, based on the smell). At this point, George has joined the investigation.

I visit the victim's room and see an apparent robbery and discover the missing genitals in Luke's bed. I examine John and Edna's room. I find a false floorboard with a cubby underneath that contains money, the likely murder weapon, and an empty jar of bromine.

I place John under arrest and take him back to the station.

Later that morning, 10 am (approximate): I obtain John's side of the story, who mentions that he fought with Luke about opening a new store. No more details in the timeline between 9 pm and 3:30 am.

Noon (approximate): Elizabeth and Thomas Foster visit and offer their side of the story. No more details are added to the timeline between 9 pm and 3:30 am.

October 23rd, 1 pm (approximate): Elizabeth Foster returns to the police station to talk with John. They exchange words, but no more details.

3 pm (approximate): Deputy George and I head over to the butcher shop to retrieve a blanket for John. Edna greets us and confirms the fight and the suspicion that John's statement about going to the church was an assumption. Edna also details how she found the body. She reported this to Jack, who came and summoned me.

Suspects:

John (under arrest) – motive was money and not letting Luke open competition, opportunity was Luke living under his roof, means was the deboning knife. Cuts to the victim were surgical in precision and reflected a high level of knowledge of the workings of both knives and butchering.

Edna – motive, opportunity and means are all the same as John's.

However, my theory about the involvement of Elizabeth Foster would rule out both John and Edna. No other suspects at this time.

Open areas of investigation:

Talk with Jack to see if he can fill in any gaps of the night.

William put the notebook down at this point. It had been enough of a day. He wanted to go home, eat a small dinner, and then drink his second meal. He craved some whisky right now. He was planning on getting pretty drunk.

Drunk enough to tell Abigail about the last two days and hopefully get a response.

Chapter 30

November 8, 1888 – Whitechapel, London

Ben was nervous. He had checked in with Druitt and confirmed that tonight was the night. He had prepared his clothing to blend in. A dark overcoat, a fish knife stashed in a custom made pocket, and various tools to help him make a quick getaway. Fabric wraps for his feet, laudanum to spike someone's drink, thick belts to tie them up, cyanide if they got rowdy. All of this fit within his cloak, but each piece of equipment was wrapped in lamb's wool so there was no chance of it making an errant noise.

Druitt looked him over. He nodded his approval and then gave one final, stern warning.

"You'll end tonight my disciple or my whore. There is no other choice."

Ben proceeded into Whitechapel to wait for his opportunity. Mary Kelly started the night with her boyfriend, and he heard them get into another one of their arguments about the rent. Ben had only been stalking Mary for 5 nights, and each night they had yelled at each other about the share of rent that the other owed. Ben was hoping the argument tonight would be long and loud, giving all the neighbors the idea that things were not well between them. The argument lasted only around 15 minutes, after which the boyfriend stormed out. Mary left her house a short time later and headed to a local pub, the Ten Bells. Ben walked into the pub five minutes later, sat in a back corner, and watched.

Mary had a drink with a friend, and they were both jovial and happy. Mary's happiness attracted men, and Ben watched as she negotiated. She was good at her craft, pitting multiple men against each other to maximize price for her affection. It was amazing to Ben how primitive these men were, chasing after their lust right out in the open, letting everyone in the bar see their sin. He empathized a little with Druitt, understanding why the man wanted to free the world of this vice. Ben remained lost in this thought but watched Mary eventually settle on a partner. Money exchanged hands and Mary made her way out the backdoor where Ben knew there was a dark alley for dark deeds. Ben got up and pretended to stumble from too much booze and asked a serving girl where he could relieve himself. She pointed out the same way, and Ben headed back to the alley but vanished into the bushes. He crouched, motionless, and observed Mary, who was waiting for her customer. She hadn't seen nor heard Ben come out after her. Druitt was right – stalking drunken fools was a lot easier than stalking serial killers.

A short time later the man came into the alley as well, alone and without some of the bravado he had demonstrated in the bar. Ben wondered if he had a family at home. Ben wondered if his wife ever fornicated with him, or if the man just needed his release. Ben watched as the man made himself ready to take what he had bought. Mary dropped to her knees and freed his manhood from his breeches. She bobbed up and down with her mouth, warming up her client. The man's eyes rolled in the back of his head, a combination of drunkenness and pleasure. Ben felt a flutter between his legs at this moment, knowing that watching this unfold was another crime. He couldn't take his eyes away from the scene, and found himself wondering what her mouth would feel like on his own member. Wondering if the bliss was as fantastic as the man was portraying. Ben felt himself get hard and was ashamed.

Mary stopped sucking as the man let out a guttural moan. The man looked disappointed and started to open his mouth to complain. Mary laughed as she stood up, slipping her knickers down to her ankles. Disappointment turned into raw, uncontrolled passion, and Ben watched as the man tore Mary's breasts from her shirt while lifting her skirts. He inserted himself into Mary and reached around with his hands to cup Mary's breasts. Mary played her part, but Ben was enough of a study of people to understand when someone was acting. In and out the man thrusted and in under a minute it was over. The final spasms from the man were the signal Mary needed to disconnect, leaving the man standing there in the breeze. The man slid himself back in his pants and vanished back into the pub. As he left, he flipped a coin to Mary, who caught it in mid-air and pocketed it. She tucked her breasts back into her shirt, pulled up her knickers, looked around to see if anyone was watching, and walked out of the dark alley.

When it was over, Ben didn't understand how this was desirable. Sure, it had caused a new reaction within his body, but there was no love. No passion. No fire. Ben wanted intimacy. To stare into the soul of his partner, watching their pleasure come to a head. To reach the climax together and to fall beside each other on a soft bed, exhausted and satisfied. It was what he imagined murder would be: an intimate event between two people. He stayed in the bushes for a short while after Mary left and then followed her silently.

Mary went to a second pub, but Ben did not follow her inside. She stayed longer at this one, the Horn of Plenty, and even found herself a partner to take home. This complicated the situation for Ben, but this was a puzzle he would figure out. By the time she left with her new partner, it was nearly midnight, and Ben was tired. He needed another shot of adrenaline to keep him going. As Ben left his post near the Horn of Plenty, he thought he saw a quick movement across the street. He guessed it was Druitt, keeping tabs on his apprentice, but the movement was the shot of adrenaline that Ben needed. He was back in the hunt and his heart rate quickened.

Mary stumbled home, arm in arm with her quarry, singing Irish drinking songs at a volume too loud for nearly midnight. They slipped into her small flat and Ben found another hiding spot on Dorset Street, within view of Mary's apartment. Ben hoped the gentleman caller would be as quick to finish as the first man at the Ten Bells. Mary needed to be on time for her appointment with Ben's knife. Sounds of another performance from Mary wafted to Ben's hiding spot and Ben's wish was granted. The gentleman left Mary's apartment around 12:30 am, still singing the Irish drinking songs. Ben knew it was time. Excitement rose within as his pace quickened again and Ben felt a tingle of anticipation all over his body. This was it. The moment he had been waiting for. Time to kill.

An oil streetlamp hung directly across from the apartment where Mary lived. Ben knew he had to be quick, which was easier since he knew that the door lock was broken. He covered the distance from his hiding place to the threshold of the door in the span of seconds, and before he knew it, he was inside the apartment. It was smaller than he thought, and he looked around to see Mary passed out in the bed directly across from the door. This would have gone differently if she was still awake. The small stove was stoked in the corner, and it gave off a strong heat against the cold of the November night.

His heart thundered in his ears. Was he really about to do this? Was he going to be able to end someone's life? Even if she was a whore, she was still a person. Someone's daughter. Someone's friend. Someone's lover. Was he about to condemn his soul to an eternity of hell and damnation? Was this the path that he needed to walk? He could still turn around and leave. His cloak provided enough cover in the dimly lit room that she would never identify him. He could be gone from London within 2 hours and on the next steamer to America. Druitt would never find him. Druitt knew nothing about him or his plans beyond a desire to kill his father.

He shook his head and thought of his mother. She was also someone's mother, someone's daughter and someone's friend. Life is fleeting. People beyond saving needed an appointment with the reaper, and that was his role in this cold, cruel world. He was their end. This was his destiny. He was doing Mary a favor, freeing her from a life of pain and sin.

As the anticipation turned into excitement, his nerves got the better of him. He stepped towards the bed and the floorboards let out a loud creak. Mary's eyes popped open in response to the noise.

"Shit," Ben said.

His nerves broke. He let out a high-pitched, nervous peel of laughter and sprung towards the bed. In one motion, he jumped on top of Mary, straddling her chest, and removed his fishmonger's knife from his coat. He had spent so much time sharpening that knife. It was so sharp it sang through the air and with a quick, deft slash, blood started to pulse from Mary's neck onto the bed. There was panic in her eyes as she gurgled and tried to call out. He reached his other hand up and with an index finger he gently called to her.

"Shhhh. It's over now. Shhhh."

She had already lost so much blood she didn't have the strength to resist, and Ben watched the light fade from her eyes. He was surprised how quickly someone's life could be extinguished. It was so quick. It was the most intimate moment Ben had ever experienced. It was so fast. Seconds. He had done it. He had taken a life. Whatever else he did with his life, he would never be the same. He felt…

Joy.

Ben basked in this feeling for a short while, enjoying the afterglow. He couldn't help but smile. He looked down at Mary's dead eyes where life had been just minutes ago. He remembered her laugh at the Ten Bells as she pitted her potential customers against each other, knowing she wouldn't be able to do that again. She had no kids – he had ended her line. Such power flowed through his veins.

"If sex has a release that is anything like this," he thought, "I can see why people pay for it."

He sat there, listening to the street outside. He wanted to be sure that no one was coming before he started on Druitt's second rule.

Send a message.

Ben noticed that he had been overzealous in the slash to Mary's throat, and it had severed her neck all the way down to her spine. He could see the musculature, the arteries, and the bone.

"It was a work of art, the human body," he thought. He fell into a trance looking at all the little details exposed by his knife.

His mind drifted to that night in the London Hospital with

his mother and Dr. Haslip. The doctor had taken the time to give Ben an account of everything Druitt had done to his mother. Before he knew it, rage took over and Ben found himself slashing open Mary's abdomen and cutting out organs, one by one. He started the night staring at her breasts, bouncing out of her shirt while that unnamed man fondled them and thrusted in her. He cut off one of her breasts as well. He placed the uterus and kidneys beneath her head and wedged her neck with the removed breast. There. A smile crept across his face. A perfect pillow for a drunken whore.

The rest of her organs he removed and put at the foot of the bed. He didn't know why he did this, he just didn't want them in her body anymore. He ran out of room by her feet and just started placing the liver and the lungs on the bedside table. For the last cut he needed light.

He quickly stripped off Mary's clothing with his knife and pulled them from underneath her lifeless body. They were stained red, but the fire would cleanse them. He walked over to the stove and added Mary's clothing. The fire was at a low roar but with plenty of hot embers, so the additions caught quickly, casting a dancing light onto the woman's naked body. Ben stared for a while at the bloody form, focused on the remaining breast.

"Life can be given from those," he thought. "So why is it that a grown man wishes to return to them? Is it a desire for a simpler time?"

He didn't know. The foundations of a plan started to form.

"…a victim and a scapegoat," he thought.

Ben returned his focus to the body and very carefully severed the vena cava and removed Mary's heart from her body.

He drained it and wrapped it in lamb's wool. He'd need it for later. He placed it in his coat and turned to leave.

He glanced back at his work one last time, nodded with a sense of pride, and left the room.

Chapter 31

October 29, 1892 – Medford

Elizabeth was six days into the doses of laudanum that Dr. Ferguson had given her. She had been good about sticking to only two drops in her tea in the evening, but it was amazing how it helped. As soon as the tea was completely consumed, a wave of joy and calm washed over her.

Time had a lovely way of dancing in and out of focus, and the future didn't seem so bad. Her senses were sharper, and specifically found that she enjoyed all the textures around her. The lace doily under her tea mug, the rough but comforting blanket she laid on her bed to protect from the October chill, the distant sounds of birds and nature through the open window, or even the general noise of her parents living their lives around her. Even her socks rubbing against the skin of her feet was a feeling and a texture she enjoyed. Elizabeth surrendered her mind and embraced the warm, amber rush that came over her each night. Her myriad of problems faded to the gentle background, but she still felt in control of her life. She would curl up in bed and feel attached to the mattress, with a heavy head absorbed into her pillow. She would lay there and feel the way her bed wrapped itself around her and the way the weight of her blankets allowed her to become part of the bed. It also helped her sleep nearly instantly, and the dreams were calm and warm like the world around her. With the help of the laudanum, she would be ok. Luke's death would not define her.

She estimated that Dr. Ferguson had given her less than a teaspoon of tincture in the vial, which meant that she probably only had a supply for about a month. She realized she'd have to face this world without the comfort of the liquid, but that was a problem she could put off for another week or two. Maybe she could decrease her dose to one drop and postpone the possibility of life without the magical liquid for another month. Maybe Dr. Ferguson would give her a refill. Maybe she could find another doctor who would. Maybe she could head to the streets near the brick factory and buy some from one of the dealers down there. The buzz of the laudanum hushed these problems and reminded her that they would be dealt with later. Not now. Now was the time for warmth and comfort.

The morning of the 29th, Elizabeth meandered out of bed and got dressed. She selected a plaid skirt that went down to her ankles. She matched that with a white blouse and complemented the blouse with a warm sweater. There was talk in the store that there may be light snow today, and she didn't want to get caught without the appropriate layers of clothing. After she was dressed, she went to the vanity to apply some blush, light lipstick, and give her hair a comb. That's when she saw it. Another note was left on her vanity, with the same cut-off, slanted writing from after Luke's murder. Her pulse quickened and she started to panic. She couldn't relive that morning. She hoped that this wasn't another murder. She couldn't hold another death on her consciousness, regardless of how much the laudanum helped. She would be lost!

Elizabeth could not calm down.

"No. This will not define me," she said out loud, sternly, to herself. She grabbed the note and sat on the bed, weighing in her mind if she wanted to open it or pitch it in the kitchen stove fire. She decided to open it.

My dearest Elizabeth—

Laudanum is the escape for the weak minded and soft-willed. You are neither of these, but perhaps you need a reminder. Just one more dose and I shall demonstrate to you the futility of medication. The only escape from your pain is me.

Always yours.

Elizabeth froze in panic again. How did this intruder know about the medication? Dr. Ferguson had been the only one in the room when he gave her the vial. He said it was off the record and wasn't written down. She took it each night in her tea when she was by herself. There were only two possibilities. One is that she wasn't as in control as she thought she was. The other was that someone was watching her.

She glanced around nervously in her room, looking for anything else out of place. Her eyes drifted over to the open window. Her room was positioned above the store's potbelly stove, and the heat radiated upwards in the winter months. It was usually sweltering in Elizabeth's room at the end of even the coldest of days. Elizabeth needed to leave the window open on most nights to let the heat out and allow her to have some sort of restful sleep.

That had to be the watcher's ingress point, she thought. She got up and drifted over to the open window. She looked out the window and down, looking for a possible way someone could get in. It was a sheer drop to the ground below, and where her window was positioned meant that there were no ledges, tree branches, drainpipes, or other roofs anywhere near the window. Elizabeth had no idea how someone was able to creep into her room, but she would absolutely start locking her window at night.

Starting tonight, she would also reduce her dose to one drop instead of two. That means she'd be in more control, and she wouldn't run out as quickly. She just wanted the sweet release of sleep that the liquid had granted her. She wouldn't quit. She wasn't ready to be told what to do by someone who wasn't even willing to show their face. The intruder was a coward, hiding behind notes and refusing to approach her.

She also knew that she couldn't take this note to the police or to her parents. The laudanum was a secret that was between her and Dr. Ferguson, and she didn't want any bad rumors impacting her or her family. She had heard the old ladies at church gossiping about people who were addicted to opium and knew the contempt with which they saw addicts. She had no plans of becoming addicted but knew that was a distinction that was too fine for the average church gossiper.

She headed downstairs and checked in with her dad to see if he needed any help in the store. It was Sunday, so those were usually slow mornings. Her dad said he did not, so she proclaimed she was going to head to the morning church service. She called out to her mom upstairs, who decided to join her at church.

They walked the short distance to the Universalist Church in the brisk October air. As they passed through the front doors,

Minister DeLong and Jack were there, greeting the worshipers.

"Ahh hell," Elizabeth exclaimed.

"Elizabeth," scolded her mother. "And even in the church. What has gotten into you, girl?"

"Sorry mother," Elizabeth responded, hanging her head in a sheepish manner.

Elizabeth hadn't looked up the bible verse that Jack had slipped into her hand. She didn't want him to think that his outreach was ignored, even if she wasn't sure why he had singled her out.

She and Clara settled into the pews and made small talk. Elizabeth noticed that there were bibles intermittently spread in the pew-back holders. She grabbed the nearest one and opened it to Matthew, Chapter 5. She used her finger to follow the text down to verse 4 and read to herself.

Blessed are they that mourn: for they shall be comforted.

Elizabeth screwed up her face in confusion. Why would Jack want her to know this? Was it some way of telling her that it was ok to be sad? Of course she could be sad. She didn't need an assistant minister to tell her how to feel. Was he trying to tell her to come to him for comfort? She barely knew him. They had barely exchanged more than one sentence at a time since he moved here. It was then she realized that her mom was trying to get her attention.

"Dear, where is your mind this morning?" Clara started. "I swear, you've had your head in the clouds these last few days."

Elizabeth blushed. Was this a sign that she couldn't hide the effects of the tincture like she thought she could?

"Sorry, mother. What were you saying?"

"I was telling Mrs. Thomas here about your plans to go to Tufts next year. She asked what you were thinking of studying," Clara recapped.

Mrs. Thomas was one of the teachers at the local high school, and Elizabeth had always thought that she was a tough teacher. She liked Mrs. Thomas.

"Oh, thanks for asking, Mrs. Thomas," Elizabeth turned to meet the gaze of the older woman. "They offer a liberal arts degree for women that can be done in as little as one year. I think that would be a really good thing to help me understand more about how to run a business. I don't know yet what I'm going to do with my life, but having a good baseline of skills will only help in the long run."

"That's wonderful, Elizabeth," Mrs. Thomas responded. "It's nice to hear that you won't just be tied down to a man, waiting to see what he would allow you to do. I want to see you continue to *'best those boys.'*" She said this last part with a mischievous glint in her eyes.

This statement caught Elizabeth off-guard. Elizabeth had no idea that Mrs. Thomas was such a radical suffragette. Secondly, the thought of Elizabeth in a married relationship brought her mind back to Luke. The impact must have been obvious, as Mrs. Thomas saw her mistake and quickly changed the topic.

"Are you planning on taking over the store from your father?" she asked, quickly recovering.

"I don't know yet. Honestly, we haven't talked about it as a family yet and I don't know what he will want from me as I grow up. There's also my brother James to consider. He's not far behind me in school," Elizabeth said.

Mrs. Thomas thought this looked like a good breaking point and backed out of the conversation into another one behind her pew. Elizabeth was thankful for the grace of the older woman to recognize when a conversation had run its course. She felt her mother's eyes boring into the side of her face, but Elizabeth couldn't turn to meet her gaze. The words Elizabeth had just used to describe her future weren't well known to Clara. The two of them just didn't really talk about the future and a woman's place in it.

Minister DeLong called them to order, and Elizabeth sat down next to her mother. She spent the rest of the service thinking about the future. Tufts, education, a store, something else? The possibilities honestly seemed to be very good right now for a young, educated, intelligent woman. Massachusetts had just abolished the poll tax for women, which meant that Elizabeth would be able to vote in the Medford elections. What after that?

Would she stay in Medford, even if it was James running the store? Would she find another man who made her excited? Would she get married? The thought of another man in her life made her sad, but not like it had on the day Luke had died.

"That was yesterday," Elizabeth said quietly to herself, shocked at how much she had grown in just over 24 hours.

"What's that, dear?" her mother asked.

"Oh, nothing, mother. Sorry, I was just thinking about something else. I should be paying attention to the service."

Elizabeth considered her feelings of sadness again and felt

like she had pinpointed the cause. It wasn't sadness of loss; it was sadness for a wasted life. Wasted ambition. Without knowing it, Elizabeth had become a suffragette herself. Any man she brought into her life would have to be able to be her equal. She would not only be bound to a man's ambitions.

The tincture took over Elizabeth's mind, and time ebbed and flowed while Henry gave the sermon. This one was something about caring for those in need and taking in those that are stranded in life. She wasn't really paying attention. It was over before she realized, and soon she was filing out of the church with Mrs. Thomas and her mom, headed back towards the store.

It snowed that night, but the ground wasn't yet frozen. By morning all this snow would be gone, but that night Elizabeth laid in bed with the window open listening to the snow falling through the dead leaves of the oak and maple trees on the banks of the Mystic River. Just before midnight she got up, closed, and locked the window. She didn't want any more visitors.

Chapter 32

November 1, 1892 – Medford

Snow has a wonderful way of dampening noise. He had heard the science behind this: sound traveled through the air but bounced off each snowflake and left part of its energy behind. That made sense to him, and he imagined the sounds from his soft footsteps careening towards the row of silent houses in the distance but bouncing off a particular snowflake and falling to the ground. He was trying to avoid getting too close to those houses, and the snow was helping that goal.

It was a good analogy for his conversations with Elizabeth. She was as pure as white snow, but each time he tried to say more than one line to her the energy bounced out of the air before it got to her. He couldn't figure out how to crack the code and ensure she heard him. He needed it to stop snowing in his brain.

As he crept through the night, he thought about how Elizabeth forced his hand. She didn't understand that he couldn't tolerate her poisoning her body with that awful stuff. He had seen so many people overdose in his time on the streets. It wasn't fair. He was just lucky that the snow tonight wouldn't be sticking, so he wouldn't leave any evidence. Chief Smith was a smart man and had a criminal's mind. A worthy nemesis worth watching.

He moved along the river and stuck to the woods to stay out of the streetlights. It made the going slower, but it ensured he wouldn't be seen. Nights like these are great for staying out of earshot, but terrible for staying out of sight. Everything glowed at night when the snow came down. London never had these problems.

He arrived behind his target house and crept towards the back door. He moved slower with the light, pausing every other step to listen to see if he had been discovered. He had enough authority in the town such that if he was discovered, he would be able to dismiss it as part of his duties, but he didn't want it to come to that. After murdering the butcher's boy the other week, he needed to be sure he maintained a low profile. Another killing this soon was risky. This was a risk his mentor would have taken and look at what happened to him. His mentor had always let emotion get the better of reason. That was an area he hoped he didn't mimic.

He just had to save Elizabeth from herself before it was too late. Everything about her was enrapturing, and he had appointed himself to be her protector.

This house was the second stop of the night, with the first being Elizabeth's room. She had tried locking the window, but that didn't matter to him. He had come in through the back door of the general store, through the main floor, up the stairs, past the living room, past the dining room, past the room where Thomas and Clara slept, and into Elizabeth's room. The hardest part had been opening the drawer where he knew she kept the laudanum. He had opened that drawer very slowly, keeping a constant eye on her to ensure she didn't move. The open window had provided more noise for his cover last time, but he eventually got the vial out. He had left how he arrived and doubled back towards the river. He unscrewed the cap of the vial and dumped the amber liquid on the ground. He had then tossed the vial into the Mystic, one piece at a time. The splash of the tiny vial was imperceptible, but it was a huge weight off of his chest. She wouldn't be tainted anymore.

He snapped back to reality. He figured it was around 4 am, a time when all normal people are asleep. People always seemed to sleep extra well after Halloween night. Nevertheless, he had to focus. The initial opening of any door was always the hardest and riskiest part. One creak could mean he was discovered. He reached into an internal pocket of his cloak where he retrieved a small vial of oil. He laughed to himself as he realized this container looked exactly like the one that the laudanum had been in. The symbol of the problem was the symbol of the first part of the solution. The hinges were on the inside of the door, but he had opened enough doors to know some tricks. He tried the knob to check if it was open. It was. The people in this town were so stupid, leaving their doors unlocked at night.

He pressed up on the door with his left hand while turning the knob, relieving some of the weight on the hinges. When the door was about a third of the way open, he paused. He kept his left hand on the door as he took out the vial of oil. He applied one drop to each of the three hinges, then let go of the door. As he let go, he put a foot against the door so it wouldn't move. Patience was a valuable tool to the intruder.

As he waited for the oil to penetrate the hinges, he thought about Elizabeth again. When he first arrived in Medford, he went to the General Store for some basic sundries. She had helped him, and he was instantly smitten. She completely commanded the room, and her poise was unlike any he had seen since his mother's. He missed his mother, but he knew this woman would care for him like she used to.

"I wonder what she smells like," he thought to himself, making a mental note to pay attention to that detail next time he was in her room.

He put the oil back into his cloak's pocket and reached into another, larger pocket. He retrieved two fabric wraps and held them in his right hand. He figured that by now the hinges were properly oiled, so he pulled up again on his left hand and opened the door the rest of the way. It was silent for the entire travel. He closed it gently behind him but did not secure the latch nor close the door all the way. He always figured the time saved in the escape outweighed the visual indication that the door was open.

Alone in the back room, he bent down and covered his shoes with the fabric wraps. He had sewn lambswool as a liner to the wraps, so they were very effective at deadening footfalls. He stood back up and walked quickly and silently down the hall. He stuck to the edges of the hall where the floorboards met the wall. Floor creaks come from the middle of floors. He had learned that the hard way in the bedroom of Mary Kelly.

He took a right through the first door and found himself inside Dr. Ferguson's makeshift pharmacy. The good doctor kept basic medicines here, filed and logged. He reached up and grabbed a bottle off the shelf. If there was time he'd put it back. He turned around to exit the room and paused. Something had caught his eye. Barbituric Acid. He turned back around, reached up, and grabbed the small bottle, which he placed into a pocket in his cloak. He may need that one later. He left the room in search of the stairs to get to the second floor where his target lay.

The logical layout of the house allowed him to find the upstairs very quickly. He ascended the stairs like a cat, taking two at a time, always placing his footfalls at the edge of the tread. He paused at the top, listening for signs of life. He heard the gentle snoring of the doctor in the next room. As he crept closer, he listened for signs from Eunice but heard none. This part was the riskiest. He thought back to 9 days ago when it had almost fallen apart in the butchers. Edna came downstairs while he was putting his finishing touches on his message. Luckily, he had been able to sneak out the back as he heard her coming down the stairs to cool off. Another minute and all would have been lost. He would have had to kill that innocent butcher's wife.

He placed his hand in his cloak and found his favorite knife, right in the sheath that he had sewn into the coat lining. It was small, fast, and sharp. He was pretty sure he would be able to cut snowflakes in two with that knife. He leaned around the corner and peered through the open door. One. Two. Two motionless lumps in the bed. Eunice was asleep.

Excellent.

His left hand still held the vial he had retrieved from the makeshift pharmacy. He placed it quietly down on the dresser and reached into his coat. He withdrew two syringes. Each of the barrels were made of glass, capped with metal. Instead of hollow needles, though, he had ensured he had bought a dropper tip. He had gone into Boston to buy these so no one in Medford could place them with him. They were too suspicious on their own. He filled each one with 4 tablespoons of laudanum. He was hoping he guessed the dose right.

He closed his eyes and focused on his hearing to ensure Dr. Ferguson and his wife didn't wake. He thought of his mother's broken body lying in the London Hospital and let all the rage within him bubble to the surface. He had to let the hate overwhelm him. Touching that well of hate within him was the only way he could do this to innocent people. It focused him, fed him, and made him a wall, immune from the morality of what he was doing. These two before him were not necessary deaths. Elizabeth had to stop poisoning herself, and this was the only way.

Standing in the middle of the room, holding one filled syringe in each hand, he raised both arms at ninety-degree angles and flexed his neck back and forth. Now or never. He took two quick steps and jumped from the floor onto the bed. He landed on his knees between the two sleeping figures, waking them both. That's fine, he needed them to see this happen. That was part of the intimacy.

He jammed a syringe into each of their mouths and depressed the plunger, releasing the fluid into their mouths. Their eyes alighted with shock and fear. He stared into their eyes in turn, using his gloved hands to hold the syringe in place and hold their nose, forcing them to swallow. They tried to open, tried to fight, tried to scream. He was too strong for them. He saw Eunice swallow. One down.

Dr. Ferguson tried to get up, but the man on top repositioned his knee on Dr. Ferguson's sternum, immobilizing him. Dr. Ferguson struggled, trying to hold his breath and avoid swallowing.

Eunice fell out of bed. She had tried to get up, but the laudanum was fast acting. Eunice likely couldn't feel her legs anymore. He heard her moan something, but he couldn't understand what she said. No matter. She would be dead soon anyways.

Dr. Ferguson continued to resist, trying to open his mouth to spit out the liquid. The man on top of him slapped him across the face, hard. Dr. Ferguson winced, but didn't give up. He reached his spare hand into his coat and withdrew a knife. This one was shorter. Stubbier. Just as sharp, though. He took it out and showed it to Dr. Ferguson. He held it right in front of Dr. Ferguson's face to be sure the older man saw it. He took the knife and ran it down the side of Dr. Ferguson's face slowly and rested the knife point on Dr. Ferguson's throat. The doctor would be impaled on the knife if he tried to get up, and the doctor knew enough anatomy to understand that would be quickly fatal. Dr. Ferguson's eyes still shone with panic as he looked frantically around the room for something. His eyes rested on Eunice's body half-out of the bed and the man saw the doctor register that his wife was gone. The man in the dark watched as Dr. Ferguson's throat finally swallowed the liquid, deciding life without his partner wasn't worth it.

The killer dismounted the bed and walked back to the dresser. He needed some insurance. He filled the syringe up again and brought it back to the bed. Dr. Ferguson was still conscious, but just barely. The man put the syringe in his mouth again and pressed the barrel, allowing Dr. Ferguson another 4 tablespoons of laudanum. Dr. Ferguson had no choice but to swallow. This would be more than enough to send the man to a permanent sleep. Ferguson swallowed willingly and then closed his eyes as the laudanum took over.

The man walked around the bed to Eunice and checked to see if she was still breathing. Her breath was short and ragged, so he put her back in bed next to her husband. He was pretty sure the laudanum had already taken effect, and his suspicions were confirmed about a minute later when Eunice's body shook in the spasms of death.

The killer stood at the foot of the bed, holding his knife, ready to plunge it into Dr. Ferguson's heart if he had to. It wouldn't be as artful, but death was the goal. The message was secondary. That's what his mentor had taught him.

The killer stood there for a shade over five minutes, then

finally heard the telltale gasping for air, indicating that Dr. Ferguson was dying. He looked at the clock next to the bed. 4:42. He had time.

The killer walked over to the bed and started to arrange the scene. He reached down with his smaller knife and severed the index finger of Dr. Ferguson, grabbed it off the bed and turned towards the door. He grabbed the bottle of laudanum on the way out and was gone ten minutes later, his clues left where he was sure they would be found. Eventually.

Chapter 33

November 1, 1892 – Medford

The nights of the last week had been rough on William. He had gone to bed beyond drunk each night, trying to get the image of Luke's dismembered corpse out of his mind. He had always been able to compartmentalize. What had happened to Luke was no worse than what he had seen during the war, but for some reason this stuck with him. His whisky habit had taken over his nights, but all that seemed to do was make the mornings come faster.

Abigail hadn't whispered to him lately, either, which means he started most days hungover and grouchy. He felt like his life was falling apart. Why wasn't she whispering to him anymore? Why did he keep having that stupid dream about Lizzie in the snow?

Each day he had tried to find more information about what happened to Luke between 9 pm and 3:30 am. He hadn't had any luck. Jack had told him that if Luke was at the church, that was when he was taking his ill-timed nap instead of the chores he was supposed to be doing. The streets were empty due to the incoming rainstorm and so no one was able to confirm any comings or goings.

The town was getting impatient, and William knew that he needed a breakthrough to either set John free or send him to trial. He woke the morning after the snow, determined to make a decision. If he didn't have any justifiable cause to let him go, he'd officially send John to trial.

He rolled out of bed and took a swig from the whisky bottle to help calm his hands from shaking. He rifled through the pantry and settled on a handful of peanuts from the bag in the corner. He put another handful into his pocket, not knowing if they'd help this morning.

William grabbed his cane and left his apartment to start the short walk to the police station. As he walked, he would occasionally grab a peanut from his coat pocket, crack it, and eat it. It was a nice distraction. He arrived at the station and said good morning to George and yelled down the hallway to the cell that held John. George looked as tired as William felt.

"Late night, George?" he asked the large man.

"Yes, Chief. I'm living in a shared living space right now while I try to find my own place. Some of the residents got into a fight. I decided to leave and walk around last night instead of listening to it, and I just couldn't get to sleep after that. Halloween night always brings out the worst in people."

"Yeah, that's what they said in Salem a couple hundred years ago, isn't it?" William responded, dryly.

William sat down at his desk. He was hoping it would be a quiet day. He needed time to think about the next steps in Luke's case. He was at a dead end. He took out his notebook and re-read all of his notes. Maybe there was something in here. Something he missed the first seven times he had read it. He also thought about his conversation with George on the way to see Edna, trying to jog his memory.

He realized George wasn't surprised at all when William told him about the connections to Elizabeth. He barely reacted with any emotion at all. George was also in the crowd that night at the butcher's shop. He was there right after William had explored Luke's room to help him detain John. Who had gotten him out of bed? How had he come to know that he was needed at the butcher's shop?

William's mind started racing, considering every detail and everything he knew of George. He was desperate for a lead.

William knew very little about his deputy. George had come to Medford and kept a low profile. He never talked about his time on the force in Boston or time before Boston in the UK. He was suspiciously good at not answering any questions about his past.

William found a sheet of paper, wrote a short note, and put it in an envelope. He addressed it to George's sergeant in the city, hoping that he could get some details about the big man. William knew he was probably grasping at straws. Nevertheless, William would watch George and see if anything came to pass. He mentally added George to the list of suspects.

That afternoon, Minister DeLong came into the police station. William registered him entering but didn't think much of it until George came over and rapped lightly on his desk. William noticed that George's knuckles were scraped, like he had been in a scuffle. That was curious. William looked up, expectantly, and waited for George to speak.

"Henry says we need to go check out Doc Ferguson's place," George said. "Wouldn't tell us why but said something was off."

William looked up at the minister and noticed the minister wouldn't meet his eyes.

"What's this about, Henry," William asked him.

"I'd rather not say what I saw, Chief," Henry responded. "I had an appointment this morning but when I got there the door was still locked. I looked in the window and saw... something. I think it's best if you go see it."

William was starting to get annoyed. "I can't walk all the way over there for a hunch. Can you tell me?"

Henry shook his head. "How about I get you a carriage, then. The local carriage company offers me free carriage rides because I'm a minister. It's the least I can do."

William relented, stood up, grabbed his cane, and headed towards the door. George rose to do the same, but William waved him back.

"I got this one, George. I'll send for help if I need it."

George nodded but didn't yet sit back down. William could tell the big man was uncomfortable with this arrangement, but right now William only trusted himself.

Chapter 34

November 1, 1892 – Medford

The carriage ride may have been short, but it was a blessing for William. On nights when he drank too much, he woke up with aches up and down his bad leg. Sometimes there was a burning pain in his kneecap where the bullet had torn through, and sometimes the pain was reflected higher or lower. The worst days were when it was all three. After multiple nights in a row of drinking too much, it had turned into all three for multiple days in a row. As William sat in the carriage, he tried to knead out the knots that had formed in his thigh, trying to coax some of the pain away. When he arrived at the doctor's office, William had brought the pain to a tolerable level. Maybe he'd ask the doc for something to help with the pain.

He arrived at the doctor's office and found it just as Henry had said. The front door was not typically locked this late in the morning. As William looked in through the window, though, he saw why Henry hadn't wanted to share this. William wouldn't have believed it. Scrawled in some material across the wall, someone had written:

This doctor kills patience.

The handwriting was very similar to the handwriting William had seen in the note Elizabeth brought in after Luke. Was it possible that William was walking into a second killing? Was it possible that he would be seeing someone else butchered like Luke was? He had the urge to call George for some backup but realized that his suspicions of his deputy weren't yet played out. Besides, he wanted this crime scene to himself. He knew his mind would find things that others would miss, and other people were always in the way.

William's mind drifted back to the note on the wall. The misspelling was obvious. It was clearly intentional, but what did it mean? William filed this question away for later. He reached down to try the door, but it was still locked.

"Doors don't magically open, dummy," he said to himself.

William hobbled around back and found that the backdoor was not locked. He turned the knob and pushed, and the door swung easily open. As William stepped into the house, the first thing he noticed was a smell. It smelled like lilac.

William wavered and was glad he had his cane for support. The smell instantly brought him back to Abigail. This wasn't fair. Why did it have to be lilac? His focus wavered, and he had to sit there and fight off a wave of grief as the smell brought him back to the day he found her hanging from the ceiling. First bromine, now Lilac. Was this coincidence? Was the killer playing with William? Who could know these details about his life?

Another set of questions he'd need to file for later. He had to pay attention. He could be walking into a trap.

William had been in this office a few times and had a general idea of the layout. Last time he was here, Doc Ferguson had yelled at William for his drinking problem. He used fancy words like cirrhosis to refer to William's liver, but William didn't care. William hadn't been back to the doctor since. He stepped through and checked the exam room. Nothing out of the ordinary.

William moved over to the wall where the cryptic message was found. The writing was from some sort of paste, and the paste was the source of the lilac smell. Someone had used some ingredients in a mortar and pestle to make it smell this way. Perfume or lilac oil, he guessed. He bet he knew where the mixing occurred and hobbled to the room that the doc kept as a pharmacy.

William walked into the makeshift pharmacy and started looking for anything out of place. He saw the mortar and pestle on the counter and two objects next to it. The first object was an amethyst-colored bottle labeled as "Cooley's Lilac Oil." The second object was a small bag filled with wet, clay-heavy soil. The person who had scrawled the message on the wall had used dirt and oil.

In that moment, William knew the killer was coming for him. There were too many coincidences. He sat down, dazed. Panic started rising in his chest, and he forced himself to breathe. Deep, slow in. Hold. Slow out. Hold.

"Solve the problem, William," he said to himself. "Focus on the clues."

The killer was telling William that they knew what he had lost and buried. The clay-heavy soil was the final straw. He would recognize that color of soil anywhere as it was the same color he spent hours in, face down, waiting for the attack to stop in the woods of Pennsylvania.

William kept looking around. There was something else. Something else didn't feel right. Up there on a high shelf. One of the jars had something in it. William resisted the urge to reach up and grab it, as he wanted to maintain the scene exactly as it was. William stepped closer and looked up. It looked like a finger in that jar. Amber glass with a small label on the backside would tell him what was in it. He had to see the contents. Was it another message to him? Was it a clue to the killer? Curiosity overcame his discipline, and William reached up to spin the jar until he could read the label.

'She's had enough' was written over the word 'laudanum' in bold pencil. Curious, William thought. Who was the 'she' this note was referring to? How much is 'enough?' What does this have to do with 'patience?'

William knew Doc Ferguson and Eunice both kept impeccable notes in the pharmacy logbook. William looked until he found the logbook. He grabbed it and laid it out on the counter and opened the pages until he found the most recent entries. The logbook was organized with columns for medicine type, the amount, the date it was used, the person who administered it, and to whom it was administered. William quickly thumbed through the book, looking for something. There were 2 recent entries that caught his eye in the same short, stunted script that was in Elizabeth's note and the writing on the wall.

- *Bromine, 1 bot – Oct. 22 (BS) – Luke*
- *Laudanum, 1 bot – Nov. 1 (BS) – Fergusons*

William was confused. He wasn't aware of any people with the initials BS that worked in this office. He couldn't even think of anyone in the town with those initials.

He thumbed through other pages. All the other entries had a graceful script that looked like JF. That was Doc Ferguson. The stunted script was the handwriting of the killer. William knew that if he found BS, he'd solve this case.

William mulled if this was likely a real name or an assumed one. He bet it was the real name. This killer had an ego. He had been daring William to find the messages in Luke's killing. He had been leaving notes. Creeping into Elizabeth's room meant a high probability of getting caught for a low payoff. Ego was the only explanation.

He left the small pharmacy and drifted around the rest of the main floor. Nothing else was out of place. He'd have to head upstairs. He started the climb slowly. Stairs were hard on him. He reached the top of the stairs and looked at the small kitchen, the living room and the dining room. Nothing was out of place, nothing was strange. William sighed. That left the bedrooms. He remembered this same feeling from when he had found Abigail, and a pit of dread formed in his stomach. Why did it have to be the bedroom?

Perhaps he should call for some help.

"No," William said out loud to the empty house. "This is my crime scene."

He could do this. He just needed to find the area of his mind that was welled off and saw everything as an object instead of a person. The spot of his mind that had seen his 11 squad mates laying in the mud in Gettysburg. The spot of his mind that had stepped over Abigail on the floor to find the note on the table. Lilac. That note.

I can't be here with you or without him.

That part always crushed him. Use that pain. Wall off your heart. He closed his eyes and slowed his breathing.

"Everyone in this world has left you, William. All you have left is you," he said aloud. He opened his eyes, ready for what was to come.

He pushed into the bedroom and was relieved to see that it wasn't another dismemberment. It wasn't pretty, but it wasn't as bad as Luke. Doc and Eunice Ferguson were in their bed. The sheets were stripped from the bed and piled in the corner, such that only the bottom sheet and the mattress were still on the bedframe. The two corpses lay there holding hands. Pennies were placed over their eye sockets. They were each dressed in their Sunday best, including shoes. It made it look like the two of them had gone to church, come home, laid in bed, and taken a journey to the afterlife together. William examined the bodies closer and saw that very little was out of place. Both of their hair was combed, and Eunice's makeup was done. Their fingertips and lips were blue, but otherwise they looked peaceful. There was no blood. No sign of a struggle.

Was this the same killer as Luke? This level of restraint didn't match. There was no rage here. There was no anger. There was only sadness and love. He frowned and stepped back into the hall. He went to the kitchen, where he looked around and finally saw what he was looking for. Doc Ferguson's house was lucky enough to have a telephone. William figured that the potential for emergencies put the good doctor higher on the list for telephone service. He walked to the telephone mounted on the wall, picked it up, and clicked the receiver twice. Soon he heard the familiar tone of an operator on the other end.

"How can I direct your call?"

"Connect with the police. Emergency line," William said.

"Right away," came the response from the operator.

After some time, a voice responded. "This is Deputy George Sullivan, what's the emergency?"

"George, this is Chief Smith. I need some help here at the Ferguson residence. Bring the undertaker and yourself. Don't let anyone know and lock the police station door behind you. Don't tell John he'll be alone."

William hung up the phone and headed back into the bedroom to look for more clues.

William hadn't noticed it the first time, but Doc Ferguson's index finger on his right hand had been severed at the middle knuckle, leaving a stump. The stump was fresh but there was very little blood pooled underneath the finger. William knew this meant the finger was removed after Doc Ferguson's heart had stopped beating. This made it almost compassionate as compared with Luke's severed genitals. William was betting the index finger in the laudanum jar downstairs would be an exact match.

William paced around the room until he came to the dresser. He noticed a piece of paper on top of the dresser, addressed to "Chief Smith." William's pulse skyrocketed. How did the killer know that he was going to be first on the scene? Or did he just want to be sure William got a message? William grabbed the paper and unfolded it with shaking hands.

They shouldn't have died but she didn't listen to me. This wasn't their fault. No more innocents will die if she just listens to me.

William left the bedroom and sat down in a chair in the living room and waited for George and the undertaker to arrive. The logbook connected the two crimes. The 'she' in the note as well as on the laudanum bottle seemed like it had to be Elizabeth Foster. She was the only other tie between the last scene and this one. He made a mental list of the other things in common between the two sets of murders. The notes, the clean crime scenes, and the skill with tools all hinted at an experienced killer who was toying with him. An experienced killer who was obsessed with Elizabeth Foster.

But what was it that she didn't listen to? What was it about 'enough' laudanum? He couldn't think of any connection between her and the laudanum. She seemed so well put together. Super smart, super driven, always composed.

She had to be hiding something, and it seemed that the killer knew her secret. Was there a chance she was the killer? It didn't make sense, but right now very little did about these cases.

William heard a knocking on the front door. He had forgotten to tell George that the front was still locked, so he yelled down for him to go around back. A short while later, William heard heavy footfalls coming up the stairs and saw George with the undertaker appear at the top of the landing.

William pointed towards the bedroom wordlessly. George and the undertaker went down the hall. George came back a little while later.

"Laudanum overdose, eh?" George asked William conversationally.

"How did you know that, George?" William asked.

"I spent some time walking the beat in Boston, Chief. I've seen the addicts take a little too much. The blue lips and fingers are a telltale sign. Still. Looks like the two of them went real peaceful. Laudanum deaths are supposed to be warm and gentle."

"I guess blessings come in all sizes," William responded, sardonically.

William stood up and took his leave of the crime scene. He walked down the stairs, unlocked the front door, and back into the street. The air was brisk outside, but William was looking forward to the long walk. William needed some time with his notebook to arrange his thoughts, but the walk would allow him to put the pieces together.

Besides, when he got back to the police station, he was going to grant John his freedom.

Chapter 35

November 1888 – Whitechapel, London

Ben returned home from the murder of Mary Kelly and fell asleep instantly, tired and satisfied. Besides, he had to work in the morning.

He was still conducting business for the Odessians street gang. As they had grown in power, he had moved up the ranks to help launder the money the gang received from protection charges. This involved working in a bank in the London financial district. The bank paid him well and the Odessians gave him a cut as well. He had adhered to Druitt's rule – take a job above reproach.

He stayed near the High Street to keep a watchful eye on Mistress Mary of the George's Street lodging house and sent her some money anonymously when he could. She had been kind to his mother in her last days and he wanted to return that favor. He would drop off an envelope filled with cash and watch from the street as she opened the letter, a look of elated shock spreading across her face. Strangely enough, the joy he felt from watching her face was the same joy he felt when he had cut Mary Kelly open. He didn't give it much thought but appreciated that he could have the depth of character that enabled helping as well as hurting. He was almost ready to leave for Medford to 'take what was his', but still had some loose ends to tie up.

The first of the loose ends was Druitt. While Ben appreciated the training Druitt had given him, he knew that having two of them could only lead to trouble. He knew Druitt was thinking the same thing each passing day that Ben stayed in

Whitechapel. One of them would have to go, and Ben quite enjoyed being alive. He had given great consideration how to eliminate his mentor during the moments after killing Mary Kelly, and if he did it right then the London police would have their scapegoat for Mary's murder.

Druitt had to go.

On the last night of November 1888, Ben left his flat at 10 pm to go find Druitt. Ben figured he'd be in his usual Whitechapel haunts and found the older man in a dark alley on Osborn Street.

"Ironic," Ben thought, "My story begins and ends on Osborn Street."

Ben sidled up to Druitt, interrupting his concentration.

"Bad night for it," Ben said. "Too clear and quiet."

Druitt jumped. "You're getting better, disciple."

"What can I say. I had a good teacher."

Druitt chuckled. "Do you want something? I need a whore tonight for slaughter, and if you scare them away I'll just use you."

Ben marveled at the man's lack of self-control. How was this man the scourge of London the papers kept painting as a criminal mastermind??

"Come have a drink with me in the Ten Bells. I have a present for you to say thank you. I'm leaving in the next week. Family matter."

Druitt nodded, and Ben couldn't help but think of the irony how not only was it on Osborn Street, but it was also the same pub he had followed Mary Kelly to that night.

"11:30 pm, whore," Druitt spat as Ben stalked away.

Ben arrived early. He found a table in the darkest corner in the back of the pub and situated himself so that the wall was at his back. He didn't trust Druitt at all. He ordered two drinks, paid for them, and waited for Druitt to show up. Druitt showed up at precisely 11:30 pm and sidled into the low booth that Ben had picked. Ben gestured to the ales, and they sat in silence for a while, nursing their cups and eyeing each other. It was Ben who spoke first.

"So. What makes me a whore?" Ben started, with a call back to the comment on Osborn Street.

"Boy, you must realize that you aren't a whore in my eyes because you're still alive. I could have gut you ten times over the last fortnight," Druitt responded.

Ben nodded and took another swig of ale. The man's ego was insufferable. It was time to start his plan. He waved to someone seated at the bar. Druitt turned to see who, which gave Ben the opening he needed. Druitt didn't see Ben's hand flash over his pint, nor see the drops of amber liquid swirl and mix within the pint. By now Ben was well connected in the Odessians. Obtaining liquid heroin was easy. Dispensing it was even easier when your quarry was distracted. Or trusted you. Ben wasn't sure which.

"Waving to your lookout, are you? Smart. Maybe you aren't as useless as I thought," Druitt said.

"I didn't think you'd agree to meet me, Druitt," Ben said.

Druitt hissed at him when Ben used his name and cuffed him across the face with the back of his hand.

"You don't deserve to use my name in a place like this. What if the whores figure out who I am!" he yelled quietly at Ben. The pub room was loud enough that no one seemed to notice.

The strike to the side of Bens' face caused him to start

bleeding. Druitt must have been wearing a ring, as the pain felt like a singular point high on his cheekbone. Ben reached into his cloak and withdrew a wrap of linen. He held it to his face to cover the bleeding and the slight smile on his lips. Druitt had fallen for the trick of vanity that Ben had planned. Yet again his mentor's ego was predictable.

"My apologies, sir," Ben replied. "Let us end this competition. I brought you a goodbye present."

Ben reached into his coat and pulled out something wrapped tightly in lamb's wool, stained red. He slid it across the table to the older man, who hesitated and then peeked beneath the wrappings. It was Mary Kelly's empty heart.

"These are good cuts, boy," Druitt said. "You mimicked my work very well."

Ben figured it was the closest thing to a complement that the man was capable of giving. Druitt rewrapped the heart and placed it in his coat.

"Step one done," thought Ben.

Ben raised his glass, inviting the older man to follow suit. Druitt obliged and gently clinked his glass to Ben's.

"To a world without sin," Ben said and drained his glass. Druitt smiled and did the same.

Ben stood up and made his way out the front door of the pub, tossing the serving maid a silver sixpence piece. Druitt rose and walked the other way, out the back door into the alley, retracing the same steps Mary Kelly had taken to service her John.

Ben counted in his head. The amount of heroin that he gave to Druitt would make him seem drunk in 3 minutes or less. Ben had carefully studied the doses listed in medical journals he had stolen. Maths had always been his strong suit. He waited another minute and then walked around the corner and onto the narrow Puma Street. He wound around to the back of the pub and saw the familiar outline of Druitt in the alley, leaning against the wall. It had worked.

Ben approached Druitt, who greeted him with an incoherent, "Whaddja doooota me?"

"I'm working on my scapegoat," Ben replied with a smile. The older man looked at him, confused.

"You took my mother away from me. She loved me with all her heart, and I loved her with all of mine. She wasn't perfect, but she was mine. How dare you do that to me. I am going to have to move to a new continent to try and find someone who was as wonderful as her. Someone who I can protect, and someone who will love me. Did you really think I'd let you get away with it? The heart from that whore is sending you a message, just like you taught me. Don't you ever think you can cut away my heart and live to tell about it."

A tear slid down Ben's face as he placed his arm under the shoulders of Druitt. They walked down Puma Street and then turned south on Commercial Street. He had a bit longer to go than he would have liked, but it was a nice night and the symbolism of starting at the Ten Bells was poetic. This is where Mary Kelly last had a drink, and rumors were that one of Druitt's earlier victims had drunk here as well. To the random passersby, it looked like a friend helping another friend home after too much time in the pub. They walked in silence for a while until the silhouette of the White Tower was clearly seen against a pale backdrop, the moon floating eerily over the city.

Yet again Ben felt too poetic. This tower that had held so

many criminals and thieves was going to be one of the last things that his mentor saw. He leaned over to Druitt and whispered in his ear.

"See that? That's where they take traitors and murderers. One of us will see it again after today, but it won't be you. You will lie beneath it, held in a dark suspension."

The looming towers of Tower Bridge were dark, metallic skeletons in the low light of the night. Tower Bridge would be a marvel when it was complete, with a draw bridge between two towers that could be raised to let larger ships through. Each side beyond the towers were accessed from the banks of the Thames by a smaller bridge that the locals called the approaches. The bridge approach on the northern end of the Thames was completed and spanned the distance to the skeleton of the northern bridge tower. Ben dragged Druitt over to the retaining wall by the approach. Ben reached down and picked up stones, sliding them into Druitt's pockets. Druitt still had a dumbfounded look on his face, but Ben didn't feel the need to explain.

He walked with Druitt further down the approach until they were over the water, a comfortable distance from shore.

"Thank you for the mentoring, but I've outgrown you," he said to the older man. He reached back in his coat and pulled out another vial of liquid heroin and poured more into Druitt's mouth. Druitt tried to resist, but eventually swallowed. Ben waited to see if the man had any stupid last words, but Druitt was already too far gone.

The two men stood there, arm in arm. Mentor and mimic. Ben felt Druitt go limp. The second batch of heroin must have taken over. Ben grabbed the man with both arms, thrust him against the weak guard railing, and pushed. Druitt fell for what seemed like an eternity, but eventually Ben heard a satisfying splash in the Thames below.

Ben had rid the world of Jack the Ripper. Now it was up to him to carry on his legacy.

Chapter 36

November 6, 1892 – Medford

Elizabeth was on edge.

Chief Smith had let John the butcher go free due to lack of evidence. The chief told the mayor that the two cases were connected by the same killer but wouldn't present his evidence to confirm that. John and Edna hastily packed their belongings, withdrew their savings from the bank, and moved to Ohio. Chief Smith had given them Luke's money, as they had the legal claim to it. It was found on their property. Elizabeth had thought this was a travesty, but her dad had assured her that Chief Smith was merely following the law. The town was glad to see them leave. Deep down, Elizabeth knew Chief Smith was right, as there was no way John would have written those notes.

The murders of the Fergusons set the town on edge. They were universally loved and cared for a large percentage of the downtown population. Their deaths increased pressure on William to find the killer. He was losing in the court of public opinion as well. The Mercury accused him of being soft on crime and demanded he resign. The paper stipulated he was too old for a modern police force, and it was time for someone new to take over. One opinion piece recommended that George take his place. William seemed to take it in stride but looked visibly tired with each passing day.

Chief Smith interviewed Elizabeth the day after the Fergusons were discovered, and she had confessed to taking laudanum. She also gave him the note that was left in her room the day before the Fergusons were murdered. Chief Smith didn't fault her for her actions but would have preferred she had shared the note with him sooner. They needed to trust each other.

He agreed – there was definitely someone stalking her and watching her every move. Every day thereafter he would check with her to see if she had received any more notes. That was 5 days ago. It wasn't fair. Someone had stolen her medication, and then they had killed her doctor. How could she deal with this stress without the help of that sweet amber liquid?

It wasn't fair. Nothing about 1892 had been fair.

She had lost a love, found a way to cope, and then lost her way to cope. It wasn't fair that she was in the middle of this. The killer was watching her, and she felt trapped. She felt like a hunted woman, and she didn't even know what the killer wanted with her.

"This will not define me," she repeated, over and over.

It was getting to be less effective at helping her focus. Instead, she tried to outsmart her stalker by keeping to herself, not wanting to endanger anyone else. Her life consisted of helping her family in the store, going to church, and meeting with Chief Smith. There was a silver lining, though, as the many hours in her room allowed her to study for college next year. She was anxious to be the recipient of one of the first women's diplomas from Tufts University. Her motivation to be bigger than these setbacks was still strong, it was just hard.

She was in her daily meeting with Chief Smith today, the 6th of November.

"Any notes last night, Elizabeth?" Chief Smith started. This was their routine, and a repeat of the same first question he had asked the last 5 days.

"Nope. No love letters. I did receive an annotated version of the history of the Spanish Inquisition, and 3 copies of Paradise Lost. Oh, and an illuminated Gutenberg bible. They were left in the privy," Elizabeth responded. She seemed bored with this exercise.

"Come on. Let's be serious," the chief responded. "We need to get through this so we can get on with our days."

Elizabeth slumped back in her chair and harrumphed. Chief Smith knew better to press the issue and decided to give her a few moments. It was remarkable how much this Elizabeth reminded him of his Lizzie. Poor Lizzie. Ripped apart when she was far away from home. A renewed wave of sadness crept over him. He had to protect this Elizabeth. He would make it up to his Lizzie and he had a bit of an idea where to start.

"Elizabeth."

She wouldn't look at him. She was sullen because she didn't want to be here. She didn't want to do this. She didn't want a life that was governed by police or questions or routine or murder. She wanted to make her own choices and be the guiding force in her own life.

"Elizabeth."

The Chief's pleading was more earnest. She could tell he wasn't going to just ask the next question on his list.

"Yes, Chief?" she finally responded, quietly.

"Look. We need to talk about something. If this thing ever gets to trial, I'm almost positive they're going to ask me to testify. I need to know what you want from me about these notes."

Elizabeth paused. She hadn't really thought that far ahead. Of course it was going to be public. Of course it could come out that she had started on laudanum. She would be painted as an addict. It made sense now why Dr. Ferguson hadn't recorded anything in the pharmacy book. There was so much possibility that the rest of her life in Medford would be stalked by accusations of addiction and weakness of character. It may impact her ability to get into Tufts. It may impact her ability to run a store or find a husband. As this crashed over her, she realized what she had to ask of the chief.

"I don't think I can handle the pressure from the town if the second note comes out."

She paused, and Chief Smith was gracious enough not to press the issue. He could tell that she wasn't done speaking.

"I think I'm ok with the first note. It doesn't say anything wrong."

William nodded and was about to open his mouth when Elizabeth continued.

"I know my father would do anything he could to ensure I was protected. It's hard to ask you this, Chief, but will you protect me like I was your daughter?" As she said this, she knew it was perhaps too far. But she had seen some parallels between her father and Chief Smith. He was a protector. He was just dealt an unfair life, filled with loss and regret.

"I'll consider it," was all that William could respond.

Now he was the one who needed a break. He stood up and hobbled over to the mailbox, where the overnight letters were stored. Near the bottom was a letter addressed to him. He grabbed it out of the box and headed back to his desk. He tore open the letter. His eyes dropped to the page and studied the words. The bottom of his stomach dropped out and his face must have reflected the news on the page.

"What's that?" Elizabeth asked. William barely heard her.

"Hey, Elizabeth?" he said, still staring at the letter.

"Yeah?" Elizabeth responded. She could tell something wasn't right, and that letter had delivered bad news.

"Don't go out tonight. Don't come here tomorrow. Stay in your room and lock your doors and windows."

"Chief, you're scaring me. Why? What's in that letter? What's happening? Who's the killer? Do you know?"

"I'm not telling you, but I need you to promise you'll do as I ask. Help me protect you. Tomorrow this could all be over, but I have to make a rather difficult arrest first."

William reread the letter and hoped this would mean it would all be over.

She left shortly after. Elizabeth did as he asked that night but spent all night trying to guess who was going to be arrested and what the letter said.

That night, William tilted into the whisky bottle, contemplating how far he'd go to protect Elizabeth. Would he commit perjury and lie under oath? Would he sacrifice his reputation for this girl?

"What do I do, Abi?" he asked to his empty bedroom. He didn't expect her to respond. She hadn't talked to him a very long time. He drifted off into the shallow sleep of an alcoholic. Right before he lost consciousness, the wind drifted through the trees, the sound cascading through the open window. He swore he heard Abi's voice cutting through the silence.

Protect her.

Chapter 37

November 7, 1892 – Medford

The next day, Deputy George Sullivan was arrested for the murder of Luke and the Fergusons. William had arrested him right as George was getting ready for closing time and placed him in the jail cell.

He was due to be arraigned today on November 7. Elizabeth was headed to the courthouse that morning with about half the town in tow. She was hoping for a gallery seat, and it appeared that the rest of the people parading down the street had the same idea.

She saw Jack walking about fifteen feet in front of her and called out to him. He turned and saw her approaching and waited for her to catch up.

"Nervous?" He asked her.

"No," she lied. She was terrified that her involvement in these cases was going to come up. She couldn't figure out the connection that George thought they had. She had always been nice to him, but never enough to genuinely believe that he was romantically interested in her. Jack saw right through her. She saw him staring at him out of the corner of her eye.

"Ok," she corrected herself, "I'm worried that things about the case will come up that will paint me in a very bad light. Things that will damage my reputation and make me a source of town gossip. I just want to get back to a quiet life led on my terms. This trial cannot define me."

"No matter what happens," Jack responded, "I know that you'll make it through. Minister DeLong and I are behind you for whatever you need."

"Is Henry coming today?" she asked, looking around.

"No, he's staying at the church, but has asked me to give him a fully detailed report." Jack looked at the size of the crowd as he finished saying this. "That is, if we can get in to see it."

Trials were held in the Medford city hall at the intersection of High Street and Forest Street. The road had been widened in both directions here, which meant that this intersection formed a natural square and had turned into an unofficial town center. This morning, the intersection was crowded as everyone converged through the same point. The city hall was a stout stone building that had been rebuilt in this spot after fires had claimed the old wooden building in 1839, 1850 and 1859. It had finally been rebuilt in stone and had stood for the last 32 years without suffering a similar fate. The front of the building was adorned by 4 columns of stone that provided an overhang for the main entrance.

Jack and Elizabeth pushed through to the front entrance under the overhang, where people were already being turned away. Chief Smith stood at the main door, supervising the officers that had been brought in from surrounding cities to help with crowd control. He caught the eye of Elizabeth and gestured for her to come forward. Jack followed her.

"This is absurd, Chief Smith," Elizabeth said. "Why are so many people here?"

"It's that madness in Fall River. The Borden Woman. People up here think this case is our version of that macabre killing and want a piece of the action. That was just 3 months ago when they found those bodies, and the papers have been having a field day with it. I'm honestly a little glad for it, as it's overshadowing our case. Feels like we have a friend in the press. Maybe it's just because the Borden Woman is rumored to have done the chopping. The papers always love an evil woman," William explained.

"Hopefully God's justice is served in both cases. How long do you think today will take, Chief," Jack asked.

"Not long. This is the arraignment, which means the judge will just read the charges and George will enter his plea. I wouldn't expect any fireworks," the chief replied.

He changed topics and pivoted towards Elizabeth. "I've made sure they saved a seat for you. I asked them to hold two, as I figured you'd be coming with your father or mother," his tone changed and was almost fatherly. "I don't know what's coming, but I'm glad you're here."

"They needed to mind the store. Can I bring Jack to sit with me?" She responded.

"Yeah, alright." He motioned to the officers at the door that the two of them were approved for entrance and they pushed forward into the town hall.

Offices lined each side, and Elizabeth saw entrances to the police station and the township board office. They wound to the back of the building, matching pace with the substantially smaller crowd. In the back of the building was a large antechamber that was used for dual purposes of town meetings and criminal trials. The room held about 50 people at maximum capacity, and from the crowd today Elizabeth was betting that every seat would be filled.

Elizabeth and Jack wound their way down the main aisle and found two seats about 4 rows back on the prosecution's side.

They figured that Chief Smith would have to sit much closer as the Chief of Police, so they didn't bother saving him a seat. They settled into their seats, too overwhelmed with the crowd to have much of a conversation.

Thirty minutes later, Chief Smith hobbled forward to the first row on the prosecution's side. He nodded to Elizabeth as he passed. The district attorney, Patrick Cooney, would be leading the case for the prosecution. Elizabeth knew Mr. Cooney by reputation only. He was a religious man but saw his duty as prosecutor to be a protector of corporations. She wasn't sure why he was involved in the criminal case instead of passing it off to one of his many assistants. Perhaps it was for the notoriety. He had run for congress about 10 years ago and lost in a very narrow election, and perhaps he saw this case as the launching platform to something bigger.

Conversely, the defense lawyer was a court appointed attorney, who looked too young and too inexperienced for such a high-profile case. The defense attorney looked nervously across the aisle at the DA.

The bailiff called for all to rise. This was to be a grand jury case, so it would be overseen by a three-judge panel. The chief justice sat in the middle chair while the other two associate judges took their seats shortly afterwards. The judge gaveled the court to order and asked for the defendant to be brought in. George came through the door and calmly sat on the defendant's side. He was shackled in handcuffs and leg irons. He looked cautiously around the courtroom and locked eyes with Elizabeth. He mouthed a "hey" in her direction, and Elizabeth quickly broke eye contact and looked at the floor.

The interaction rattled Elizabeth, and she could feel nervousness pulsating through her body. She wished she had some laudanum at that moment and grabbed Jack's hand looking for some sort of comfort. She gave it a squeeze and in his kindness he squeezed back.

Before she knew it, it was over, and everyone was rising to leave. George had entered a plea of "not guilty" to all of the charges and he was taken back to the jail house. A trial date was set for Tuesday, the 3rd of January. The judge had asked if the defense intended to post bail for the defendant, to which they had said no. George had nowhere to go and no family.

Elizabeth and Jack parted ways when they reached the General Store. She felt lighter for some reason, almost as if the mere act of charging someone with the crime in court was enough to alleviate her anxiety. Now George was behind bars. Tonight, she would sleep with the door unlocked.

Chapter 38

November – January, 1893 – Medford

The Fosters were greeted on Thanksgiving morning with 4 inches of fresh snow lining the streets of Medford. There was a jubilant feeling in the air as the town had the lucky convergence of a day off and fresh snow. Thomas, Clara, Elizabeth and James all bundled up against the snow and made their way to Medford Square to listen to music with the impromptu gathering of townsfolk. After the music, they walked down to the church, said a morning prayer, and donated their older clothes to the alms box. It had become their Thanksgiving tradition to fill the alms box with as many outgrown clothes as possible. The church was alight with other people doing the same, so the jovial atmosphere pervaded through the church. Medford felt alive, and Elizabeth felt as though the past two months had reached a conclusion, making her stronger and more capable than before. While she had told herself that she would be educated and move on to bigger things, she was finally able to consider this and feel like she had the strength of character to follow this dream. The trauma had not defined her.

After the merriment at the church, the family returned home to feast on roast turkey with cranberry sauce, accompanied by mashed yellow turnips, boiled onions, pickles, Indian bread, and pumpkin pie. It had been a good enough year at the store that Thomas even shared some coffee and chocolate with his family on the night of Thanksgiving. They stayed awake late into the night, reading books, playing games, and generally enjoying each other's company. Love filled the house, and Elizabeth went to bed under a mound of blankets, full and happy. She hadn't felt this happy in a long time.

One weekend in early December, Thomas convinced the family to walk into the woods, cut down, and haul back a Christmas Tree. Thomas loved the smell of pine and had thoroughly embraced the idea of a Victorian Christmas. Elizabeth thought of Luke during the trek, as Luke had also loved this new tradition from England to bring a fresh pine tree into their home. She felt pangs of loss and sadness, but they were not as deep or as intense as they had been. The oil lamps in her soul were not as brightly lit. Dr. Ferguson was right – time dims the lamps.

December of 1892 also saw Medford become an official city and elect their first mayor, Samuel Crocker Lawrence. Mayor Lawrence was a colonel in the Union Army and wounded at the first battle of Bull Run. His time in the army had inspired him to do better things for his community, and he ran on a platform of healthcare, infrastructure development, and education. He won by a landslide, and Elizabeth was looking forward to seeing how Mayor Lawrence brought Medford into the 20th century.

The Fosters woke early on Christmas morning and exchanged small presents with each other around the Christmas Tree. Elizabeth got a set of notebooks and pencils from her brother James, which was very thoughtful with her pending classes at Tufts. From her parents she received a fine lace shawl, which would be very helpful for summer nights. They made their way to the morning church service and sang carols with the rest of the congregation.

After the service, they planned to head back to the General Store for a merry afternoon and a delicious meal. As they were walking out of the church, Jack handed her a small parcel wrapped in brown paper and tied up with string. The line departing the church prevented anything more than a thank you. She tucked it in her coat and promised herself she'd open it when she got home.

They got home and Elizabeth made some excuse about needing to change her socks and retreated to her room. She had no idea what could be in the package, nor why Jack had decided to give her a present. She was unsure if he pitied her or fancied her. Regardless, she wouldn't know what it was until she opened it. She tore it open nervously and found within a small pocket bible.

"Well," she muttered to herself, "I don't think this is a gift you give a girl you fancy. Just a preacher giving a present to someone in his flock."

She opened the front cover and saw Jack's elaborate handwriting scrawl a dedication.

Elizabeth – it has been a trying year for you. Use this to find your faith. 1 John 4:1
-Jack

She thumbed to the page containing the referenced verse. This was even more confusing. Did he give these small bibles to all the people in the church? She read the verse.

Beloved, do not believe every spirit, but test the spirits to see whether they are from God. For many false prophets have gone out into the world.

"Clear as mud," she said to no one in particular. What did this mean? What was he trying to tell her? She broke it down, bit by bit.

Beloved – was that admiration? Lust?

Do not believe every spirit – did he think this was Luke? A spirit?

If they are from God and the bit about false prophets – that part was clear. It was to only believe in these 'spirits' if they are true. At least she understood that.

"He wants me to move on? Why doesn't he just say what he means!"

She threw the bible down on her bed and stood up. As she tromped out of her room, she realized the spark that had been her "love" for Luke had faded. She barely thought of him at all anymore. What did that say about her? Was she really that vapid where she could forget someone that easily? She knew she wasn't raised that way.

The rest of Christmas passed all too quickly, and Elizabeth had a hard time focusing for the rest of the day. Her mind started traveling faster than the trains from Medford to Boston, bouncing between Jack, Luke, Tufts, the future, her goals, and everything in between.

Soon it was New Years, and then it was January 3rd – the start of George's trial. Elizabeth hadn't had any additional notes in her room and Medford hadn't had any more murders. Either they had arrested the right man, or the killer was taking a break for the holidays.

"Maybe he decided to spend Christmas with his family of murderers in another town," she thought to herself sarcastically.

Elizabeth woke early, had a nice breakfast with her family, and trudged through more fresh snow to the courthouse. The courthouse was abuzz with the pending trial, and Chief Smith was out front yet again, helping direct the crowds. She was granted access again and went by herself into the courtroom. As Chief Smith walked in to take his spot near the prosecution, Jack once again slid into her row and sidled up next to her. It was a near perfect repeat of the arraignment day.

"Sorry I'm late," he said, his face red and flushed. "I fell behind on my chores and had to get them done before Minister DeLong would let me come."

She was glad to see him but couldn't tell him as such as the judges walked into the courtroom and gaveled the session into order.

Chapter 39

January 3, 1893 – Medford

Elizabeth knew that the first day of the trial would likely only be jury selection and opening arguments. District Attorney Patrick Cooney traded questions all morning with the young lawyer defending George, Leander Brown. They dismissed jurors during voir dire, and everything seemed to be progressing politely and appropriately. Elizabeth was bored with most of the process, as there didn't seem to be any scandals in the selection of the jury. She spent time looking around the courtroom at those in attendance. She saw Mayor Lawrence among the crowd, sitting rigid and nearly at attention. She avoided looking in the direction of George again, not ready for a repeat of what had happened on his arraignment day.

People had known both Luke and Doc Ferguson but didn't seem to know the details of what happened. Chief Smith had done a good job of keeping the details quiet. As a result, finding a fair and partial jury wasn't difficult. The 12 white men selected by the end of the process were seated, and opening arguments could begin. Patrick Cooney turned to address the jury.

"Gentlemen of the jury, I come to you today to talk about the guilt of George Sullivan in the gruesome murders of three people."

He pointed at George, who was sitting at the defense table. It was clear to Elizabeth that Patrick Cooney knew how to control a room.

"I will outline for you the way that he mercilessly stalked

and killed his victims, and the horrible things he did with their corpses. He is a depraved lunatic, and I believe that by the time I present my evidence to you, you will all agree that he deserves to hang for what he did."

As Patrick spat out the word 'hang', Elizabeth saw Chief Smith wince. There was something about that word that set off Chief Smith. Maybe he had an oil lamp of his own. She had heard from her dad that his family had died, but she never knew the details. He didn't talk at all about his family. She thought she also heard of a living son in Boston named Charlie, but Elizabeth didn't know if Charlie spoke with his dad anymore.

Elizabeth mostly tuned out Patrick after that, thinking about other things. She mentally drifted in and out of his lengthy opening statements but didn't really care. Soon it was over, which meant it was Leander's turn. Leander stood up and nervously looked at the jury while he smoothed the front of his suit and buttoned his top button. His voice was quiet and shaky. Elizabeth wasn't sure he had ever done this before.

"Gentlemen. Today I stand before you and urge you to consider your job. You are to weigh the merits of this case with the term 'reasonable doubt.' That means that if you have any doubt at all, you will be sure to find my client not guilty." Leander seemed to warm up and started to find his voice.

"You will hear stories about my client, a good man named George Sullivan, who only wants to help people. He has served this community faithfully since he moved here from Boston. He isn't capable of the things that the prosecution will tell you about. He is a gentle soul."

Just like during Patrick's opening statements, Elizabeth quickly lost interest. She started looking around the courtroom again at the others. It seemed there were people from all walks of life. She saw wealthy town magnates next to common workers. The timing of this trial enabled a lot of people to attend who may not be able to in the summer, but early January was still before school was back in session. She also spun around to see several reporters frantically making notes and trying to keep up. Finally, her eyes rested on Jack, who was rapt with attention at every word that Leander said.

As Leander finished, the judges dismissed the court until the next day, when the prosecution would call its first witness. A murmur arose from the court as everyone gathered their things and made for the door. As Elizabeth stood up, she asked Jack his thoughts.

"It was very interesting," he started. "I think that Mr. Cooney won this round. He tried to paint George as a villain, and all Mr. Brown could do in return was to paint George as a saint. I think that is short sighted by Mr. Brown," Jack paused. "No one is a saint."

"I guess you will need to fill me in each day this case proceeds," she said in response. "I didn't get that at all."

"What is in that head of yours, Miss Foster, if not that?"

"Ribbons and pretty things," Elizabeth responded playfully.

Jack flashed her a sly smile and made his way towards the exit. Elizabeth was looking forward to seeing him tomorrow.

Chapter 40

January 4, 1893 – Medford

The next morning, the prosecution called their first witness. Her name was Mrs. Cooper, and she was the owner and landlady of the triple decker house in which George lived. There were no tenement houses in Medford like there were in Boston, but there were triple deckers. The landlady or owner of the house would live on the ground floor, and there was a staircase that connected the two upper floors. Each floor was split into a common living space and 2 – 3 rented rooms. This meant that each floor became a community unto itself. It also meant that the landlady knew the ins and outs of her tenants.

After Mrs. Cooper was sworn in, Patrick Cooney started questioning her. Elizabeth could tell he was proceeding gently. She wasn't sure why but figured there were going to be some things in her testimony that would paint George in a bad light. There had to be a reason she went first.

"For the sake of the jury, please describe your relationship with George Sullivan," he asked.

"George is one of the tenants in the house I run," she replied.

"Thank you, Mrs. Cooper. How long has he lived there?"

"Oh, since he moved to Medford. About a year."

"Do you know if he's ever lived anywhere else in Medford?"

Leander interjected with an "objection, irrelevant" at this point, which the judges sustained. If Patrick was flapped at all by this, he didn't show it.

"Let me try a different question, then," Patrick said, glancing at Leander. "George makes a decent wage as a police deputy. Did he ever discuss moving into place of his own?"

This objection for relevance from Leander was overruled. Elizabeth realized that although Leander may not be great at speaking or opening arguments, he was very sharp when it came to court proceedings. Maybe he wasn't going to be such a pushover after all.

Mrs. Cooper answered carefully. "George didn't always have a lot of spare money. I don't think he would have been able to afford a place of his own."

Patrick looked shocked. Elizabeth was pretty sure it was for the benefit of the jury. "Do you know where he spent his money?" Another objection was raised by Leander as conjecture and speculation, and Patrick addressed the judges directly. "This is relevant, your honors."

After a nod from the judge to Patrick and then a similar nod from Patrick to Mrs. Cooper, she continued. "George had an opium habit. I found him passed out a couple of times per week and always found empty bottles of laudanum in the trash cans for his floor."

"And how did you know it was laudanum?" Patrick prodded.

"It was written on the side. It looked like it came from a doctor, but I could never figure out which one would give him so much."

This objection from Leander to the judge on speculation was overruled, and so Patrick abandoned this line of questions.

"How long did you know about his habit?"

"I knew about his habit since he moved in. I don't judge, see, as long as he pays on time. George always paid on time," Mrs. Cooper continued. "He was quiet, and he was gone most nights. That's the life of a policeman, you know. I liked having him in the building because people wouldn't try weird things with a copper around."

The questions and the cross-examination proceeded until the lawyers had decided they were done with Mrs. Cooper. She was dismissed and the judges called for a 10-minute recess before the next witness. Elizabeth honestly wasn't sure why Mrs. Cooper was put on the stand, but she was very curious to see who was next.

Chapter 41

January 4, 1893 – Medford

The trial was called back into session and Patrick was allowed to call his second witness. Elizabeth hadn't left her seat or stood up. She had spent the time considering what was said by Mrs. Cooper. George was addicted to laudanum. She thought back to her conversation with Chief William and hoped he'd protect her secret. She didn't want anyone in this courtroom to think the same things about her that she was currently thinking about George. She was shaken from her thoughts by Patrick Cooney's announcement of the second witness.

"The prosecution calls Sergeant Samuel McCarthy to the stand."

A hushed whisper went through the crowd. No one knew this name, and they were all trying to figure out the connection between this person and George Sullivan. The court swore in the sergeant and let the DA Proceed.

"Sergeant McCarthy," Patrick began, "Can you please tell the court what you do and how you know the defendant."

"Sure thing. My name is Sergeant Samuel McCarthy, and I'm a police sergeant with the Boston police force. George Sullivan was formerly under my command." The sergeant's voice had a slight Irish lilt, but it was barely noticeable.

"Did George Sullivan have a nickname on the force?"

"Aye, we called him Big Sully," the sergeant responded.

"And why did Mr. Sullivan leave your command?"

"George Sullivan was fired in 1891 from the Boston Police

force. He left my command at that time." The sergeant was clearly well versed in courtroom proceedings, as the outline of facts didn't draw any objections from Leander.

"Can you explain the details behind Mr. Sullivan's termination?"

"Aye. He was fired for use of excessive force during a labor strike in South Boston. He was found to have beaten a protestor to death."

A gasp went through the courtroom. This was not what they had expected. Elizabeth looked over at George and saw his shoulders slump. The big man had clearly tried to run from his past, but the presence of Sergeant McCarthy was the past bringing judgement to bear.

"Can you provide any more details about the case that led to his termination?" Patrick continued.

"Sure. There was a gang of protestors in the rail yard outside of Boston. We was sent in to quell the strike and get the people home. We moved in, but the workers didn't want to leave. I told them they could start roughing up a few of them to send a message." The sergeant paused and turned his head to the jury before continuing. "This was based on orders from our captain then. He told us that the railway was more important than the workers and if we didn't break them up, the National Guard was to be sent in."

He turned back to the DA. "George was a little more excited about this than some of the others. He moved in fast and started roughing up some of the strikers. I watched him thump three or four of them with his club. This caused the workers to start moving away from their picket lines, but they soon stopped.

George had knocked one of them to the ground, see, and he stood over the man and just kept thumping him. Musta hit him 12 or 15 times before some of the boys pulled him off."

"What happened then?" Patrick asked. Patrick was good at acting as if this was the first time he had heard this story, and the jury followed suit. Elizabeth watched them lean forward in their chairs, clearly rapt with attention.

"Well, I came up to the man on the ground, but there wasn't much left of him. George had smashed his skull open, and the man's blood and brains were just sitting there, oozing into the rail yard. I looked at George just then, and the man looked wild. I backed away slowly with my hands up so George wouldn't come after me. I've never seen someone look so much like an animal. Then he..." The sergeant stopped talking.

"What did he do then, Sergeant? Please remember that you are under oath." Patrick was guiding the man's conversation, but the whole of the courtroom held its breath in anticipation, waiting to hear what was coming next.

The words that came out of the sergeant's mouth had lost their bravado, and the man's Irish accent came out.

"He bent down an sure as rain picked up tha man's eyeball. It ha fell out the man's skull, from the beatins, see. He sure stared at it for a long time, now. All the tother workers an tha coppers were watchin him so. They conna look away. Tha man had been beaten ta death and tha body was bleedin into the dirt, an there be George wit tha man's eyeball in his hand. George looked at the protesters an started yelling at them."

The sergeant shook his head, reliving that day. The murmur through the courtroom was eventually quieted by the insistent banging of the gavel from the panel of judges. When the sergeant resumed speaking, the Irish accent was gone.

"What did he say, Sergeant?"

"He said something like 'I'll be keeping my eye on you if you don't break this strike right now.' Only when he said the word 'eye,' he threw the man's eye at the crowd. I've never seen a crowd run so fast. They were terrified of him."

At this point, Patrick Cooney gave a knowing nod in the direction of the jury and informed the judge he had no further questions. The defense elected not to cross-examine. The damage had been done and the defense knew better than question this official record.

The next witness to take the stand was William, and the prosecution spent their time asking William to fill in the details of the crime scenes. Elizabeth was impressed with William's recollection of the facts and described all the details of the crime scenes vividly. William never mentioned the notes left in Elizabeth's room.

During the cross-examination, the defense spent time checking small facts within William's story but was unable to score any points. All in all, the testimony of William served as a setting for the facts and little else. Just the way it should have been.

Elizabeth breathed a heavy sigh of relief. Her laudanum usage and the notes left in her room had never come up. Chief Smith had protected her secret.

After William testified, the prosecution called one more witness – Jack.

Chapter 42

January 4, 1893 – Medford

Jack calmly strode from Elizabeth's side and took the stand. Elizabeth was confused – what could an assistant Minister do to help this case, one way or the other? She found herself holding her breath, curious to see how this would play out. She knew this was silly – Jack wasn't on trial. Still, this made her stomach flutter, and she found herself surprised that she was nervous.

Every day that went on, she remembered Luke less and less. It seemed that the feelings she had developed for Luke just weren't there anymore. Instead, she found herself thinking of Jack at strange times, wondering what he was doing and if he was thinking of her. She brushed this off, knowing it was little more than a passing infatuation. Besides, as an assistant minister, he wouldn't have time for a relationship. She wasn't even sure that she had time for a relationship. She was going to be a college girl.

Elizabeth's attention refocused as Jack was sworn in, and Patrick started his questioning. "Good afternoon. Please state for the court your full name and occupation."

"Jack Taylor, assistant minister at the Universalist church of Medford."

This was the first time Elizabeth had heard his last name. How did she not even know his last name? She barely heard Patrick's next question.

"Can you describe your role in this town and how long you have been here?"

"Sure thing. I joined as an assistant minister about 9

months ago. Before that I had been in the seminary in Fort Plain, New York at the famous Clinton Liberal Institute. I moved to Medford to try and gain acceptance to the Crane School at Tufts University. So far my application has been denied, but I have been working at the Universalist Church under the tutelage of Minister Henry DeLong ever since."

"And what has your role been since you came here?"

"I mostly assist Minister DeLong – Henry – with services and help with chores he needs done around the church. This includes things like replacing candles, cleaning the nave, laundering the robes and taking care of the building. Henry is getting old, and he can only do certain things now," Jack continued. "Our church doesn't make enough in the offering plate to contract out these jobs, so it's left to me to be the Jack of all trades."

The jury and the courtroom laughed at this obvious pun.

"Thank you, Jack," Patrick said, through a smile. "Will you please tell us where you were on the night of October 22, 1892?"

"Yes. I was at the church. Henry had asked me to replace all the candles and check the hymn books for missing pages."

"And did Luke or George visit you at church that night?" Patrick continued.

"Yes, both of them."

Elizabeth saw Chief Smith perk up at this comment. She wondered why this statement garnered a reaction.

"What was the nature of their visit?"

"Luke came to light a candle. He did that about once a week. He told me it was for his mother, as she had died about 10 years before. He wanted to honor her memory. Each week he would come to the church and spend about 30 minutes in prayer. That night was no different."

Elizabeth paused here. She thought she had remembered Chief Smith telling her that Jack had no memory of Luke visiting the church that night. Perhaps that is why Chief Smith looked surprised.

"And George?"

"George came in shortly after Luke and sat in the back of the pews. He left right after Luke left."

"Did anything seem different about George that night?" Patrick asked.

Elizabeth was surprised the Leander didn't object to that question, but perhaps it caught him off guard.

"Yes, he didn't seem himself. I waved hello to him and said hi. He responded, but he seemed like he was suffering from soldier's disease," Jack responded.

"Can you explain this?" Patrick said.

"Yes. In my time in Fort Plains, we spent time caring for some old war vets," Jack started. "Some of them were known to be opium eaters, and we always referred to what afflicted them as soldier's disease. They're detached and just stare into the distance. They will respond to you, but it's always a little slow and a little removed from reality. They seem like half of themselves."

"Objection – speculation," Leander cried. "Overruled" came the response from the judges. It appears that Jack's background had made him enough of an expert to judge when someone was suffering from opium addiction. It made more sense to Elizabeth why Patrick had wanted him on the stand.

"Do you think that George was following Luke?"

"Objection," Leander said, frustrated. "Leading the witness."

This objection was sustained very quickly by the judges. Patrick was non-plussed.

"Did you see where George went after he left?"

"No, sir. I went back to my chores since the nave was empty. Replacing the candles can sometimes be loud, so Henry doesn't like it when I do it if there are people praying."

"Thank you, Jack," Patrick said, walking towards the jury box. "To recap, on the night of Luke's murder, you saw Luke come in, light a candle for his dear deceased mother, say a prayer, and then leave. You saw George Sullivan leave shortly after that. What happened then?"

"I fell asleep in the pews but woke up a little later and resumed my chores. Nothing else happened until 3:32 in the morning," Jack replied.

"How do you know it was 3:32? That's oddly specific," Patrick asked.

"Yes, sir. Well, I have this pocket watch my dad gave me on his deathbed. It's all I have from him, you see, and it keeps really good time. After I woke up, I opened all the doors to the nave. I like the rain and the chill in the air is a good way to stay awake. I was doing my chores, I heard this scream, and the first thing I did was look at the time. I didn't know what time it was until I did, but I remember seeing it as 3:32," Jack explained.

"Go on."

"About 5 minutes later, Edna from the butcher's shop comes storming into the church, white as a sheet. She told me something awful had happened and I needed to go get Chief

Smith. I ran to his door, woke him up, and then walked with him back to the butcher shop. Then I stayed outside, leading the crowd in prayer."

"And did you see George at all outside of the butcher shop?"

"Yes, I did. He was standing in the crowd when the prayers started. I didn't see him walk up or anything, though. He went into the butcher shop to help Chief Smith shortly after."

Jack concluded his summary of that night, and Patrick signaled that he had no additional questions. Leander Brown stood up in the courtroom and approached Jack.

"Mr. Taylor," he started.

"Please, call me Jack," Jack smiled at the jury. "I'd have to stop being a Jack of all trades if you didn't." The jury smiled back.

Elizabeth saw what natural charisma Jack had with a crowd. He seemed to be able to bend the wills of the people to what he wanted. He adapted to what was needed. She was impressed and thought of how good of a minister he would be if Harry died or retired.

"Fine," Leander responded, "Jack. Some of your story doesn't really add up, and I'd like to see if we can fill in the blanks."

"Sure, go ahead."

"First, you said that you saw Luke and George in the church that evening. Is that correct?"

"Yes, that is correct." Elizabeth noted how Jack struck a balance of calm and cocky. He was indestructible up there. The jury and the crowd were playing directly into his hand. He exuded ease and confidence.

"What time was it when Luke was in the church," Leander asked.

"He arrived at 9 pm. Before you ask, I know this because 9 pm is the last bell we ring at the church. I had just hung up the sally and was heading back to the nave. When I walked in, there was Luke."

"And how much later did George arrive?"

"It must have been no more than 10 minutes later," Jack explained.

"Didn't you check with your fancy pocket watch?" Leander asked snidely.

It was Patrick's turn to object. "Objection – speculation, conjecture, argumentative, and relevance."

The head judge sustained the objections on speculation and argumentative. Leander withdrew his question.

"How do you know that it was 10 minutes later?" Leander asked.

"That was an estimate, sir. I didn't look at my watch because I had my hands full of candlesticks. To replace the candles, you must first gather all of the sticks." Jack looked triumphant in this response. Elizabeth saw the jury nodding. The jury had not taken a similar shine to Mr. Brown that they had to Jack nor to Mr. Cooney.

"That's the part that doesn't make sense to me," Leander continued. "That night George Sullivan was on duty at the police station for the night shift. That is from 6 pm to 6 am. If he was on duty, then how do you explain his appearance at the church?"

"Objection – speculation," Patrick interjected. The cry of "sustained" was repeated from the bench.

"All right, I'll ask a different question," Leander continued. "You mentioned that George seemed different that night. I believe you used the phrase 'detached and staring into the distance.'"

"Yes, that's correct," Jack responded.

"Did you spend much time with George to know he was acting differently?" Leander asked.

"Yes sir. Henry insists we tend our entire flock, and that meant we would do outreach to the triple decker where George lived. There are 9 people who live there, including George and Mrs. Cooper. He would come to our services and usually sang as part of the hymns. I'd also seen him on Sundays when his schedule allowed for it, and he always sat in the back and sang loudly with that nice, booming voice of his. Sometimes we would talk after the service, as I always wanted to make sure I told him thank you for keeping the town safe," Jack said.

Elizabeth noticed a change in Mr. Brown's body language. While Jack had remained calm and collected, Mr. Brown seemed flustered. He was looking for an opening in the testimony but could not find any cracks.

Mr. Brown seemed to realize this as well, as he abandoned his course of action and merely said "No further questions."

Jack was dismissed from the witness stand, and Patrick calmly stated that with just three witnesses, the prosecution rested. The judge dismissed the trial for the day, with the defense set to go the next morning.

Jack walked back to his seat near Elizabeth.

"You did well, Jack Taylor," she teased. "Next time tell me you're going to testify before you do, though."

"You act like we're best friends, Ms. Foster. And besides,

you think there will be a next time?" he replied. "I'm hoping I never have to testify in a court, ever again. I didn't like seeing George look at me like that. I felt like I was breaking a confessional seal, giving away secrets of what he did in the church."

"Psalms 34:16, Jack," Elizabeth said, a glint in her eye.

The face of the Lord is against them that do evil,
to cut off the remembrance of them from the earth.

He clearly recognized the passage, for he returned the sly smile. Elizabeth continued, "Would you like to come to my house for dinner, Jack? I figure it's the least this town can do for the testimony you just gave."

"I wouldn't miss it for the world," Jack replied.

Chapter 43

January 4, 1893 – Medford

Jack and Elizabeth walked the short distance to the General Store, making small talk. The store was still open, so Thomas and Clara were both milling about, tending to customers. They looked up as Elizabeth and Jack walked in, and then looked at each other quizzically. Elizabeth went to her mother first.

"Can Jack join us for dinner tonight? He testified against George today, and it feels like it's the least we can do to say thank you."

Clara glanced at Thomas, who gave a small nod. "That works. With the store closing, we plan to sup around 7." She turned her attention to Jack, "Can you come back around 6:45?"

"No problem, Mrs. Foster," Jack replied politely.

Jack turned on his heel and exited the store. Elizabeth was struck again with how well Jack could read a situation, always able to apply the right amount of grace and politeness, knowing when his stay wasn't welcome.

She spent the rest of the afternoon helping her mom and dad around the shop. Around 6 pm, she went upstairs to start some of the basics of dinner. She enjoyed cooking, but she realized this was only because it was a novelty. She couldn't imagine living on her own and cooking for herself every night. She seemed she would run out of food ideas and revert to the same 3 basic meals. Nightly dinner was just so boring.

While most Medford families made lunch their most extravagant, the Fosters would have the previous night's leftovers for lunch and then made a larger dinner. They just couldn't afford to close the store for lunch, which tended to be some of the busiest hours of business. Tonight, the Fosters had planned a nice, rich pork stew with fresh farm potatoes, carrots, and turnips. That sat on the stove, simmering away nicely. Elizabeth had decided to make some bread to go with the stew, and spent the afternoon mixing, kneading, proofing, and baking in their small, wood-fired cookstove. By the time Thomas and Clara came upstairs, the second floor smelled of stew, freshly baked bread, and the warmth from the oven gave the Foster's home a cozy feeling against the chill of the January night.

Elizabeth went to her room and changed into one of her nicer cotton dresses and reset her hair. She glanced in the mirror and noticed she had flour on her nose from the baking. With a smile she wiped it off. She didn't want to go all out for Jack, but at least wanted to look presentable. Her eyes drifted down to the nightstand where she had found the note about the laudanum. Chief Smith hadn't mentioned any of the notes today in the testimony, and she was grateful. She still felt guilty asking for protection from the old policeman, and she wasn't sure why. Regardless, it had saved her the embarrassment of connection to this trial. She couldn't imagine herself up there on the witness stand, having to think about how to respond to any questions the lawyers could come up with. She had to figure out a way to thank Chief Smith.

With one last glance in the mirror, she headed downstairs to wait for Jack in the now-closed store. She glanced up at the clock in the store and heard his rap on the front door at exactly 6:45. As she let him in, she said "quite punctual, Jack."

He smiled and pulled out a silver pocket watch on a chain.

"Yeah, remember that thing about my father's watch from the trial?"

She led him upstairs, where they joined Thomas, Clara, and Elizabeth's younger brother James. Thomas sat at the head, with Clara and James to his right. This left Elizabeth and Jack next to each other on his left. James had been working in the brick factory in the afternoons after school and had arrived home but had not yet had time to change. He looked tired, but since he had started working at the factory, he had always seemed a little tired. He was starting to bulk up from the manual labor, and the extra mass suited him. Elizabeth was sure that soon he would be very popular with the young ladies of the town. James didn't seem to want to take over the store but would likely live a comfortable and quiet life of his own after he graduated from High School in May of this year.

Jack led them in a prayer, and then they all tucked into their food. They ate quietly and politely for a short time before a conversation inevitably turned to the trial. Elizabeth was pretty sure a similar conversation was probably happening across many of the dinner tables in town.

It was Thomas who started. "So, Jack, we heard earlier that you testified in the trial today. How was that?"

"That's true," Jack responded. "It was quite the experience. One I don't think I want to repeat again, honestly."

"He's being too modest," Elizabeth interjected. "He was a natural. He was calm on the stand and had the jury eating out of his hand."

"Where do you think the case will go from here? The prosecution rested, correct?" Clara asked.

"That's correct," Jack began. "I think the defense has a long and uphill battle. If I look at the basics of the murders as Chief Smith described, there are several things the defense will have to disprove."

"Like what?" Thomas asked. Everyone had stopped eating at this point, waiting to hear what Jack had to say.

"First, in the case of Luke, there was the matter of location and timing." Jack reached over and squeezed Elizabeth's hand quickly under the table. Elizabeth appreciated this but didn't really feel any apprehension about the conversation. She felt like she couldn't find the sadness within her anymore. "Luke was unaccounted for between 9 pm and 3:30 am. That means that the person that killed him had to know where he was coming from and going. By placing George at the church with Luke at 9:30, it narrows the suspect list considerably."

"And that was Jack's contribution to the case," Elizabeth added. She felt proud of that. Why did she feel proud? She was still a stranger to Jack.

"Just a small detail I was able to provide," Jack replied modestly. He continued with his analysis. "The second element is the access and knowledge of laudanum. Who else would know the dosage appropriate for murder than someone who was addicted to it? I think the only other person qualified to make that sort of decision would be someone with medical training like Dr. Ferguson."

"The final major consideration that the prosecution had to establish was if George had a streak of violence capable of murder." Jack proceeded gently with this portion. "The small detail that was important about the Boston incident was the eyeball." Thomas, Clara, and James looked confused, so Jack paused to explain.

"Sorry for this at the dinner table, please forgive me. There was a police sergeant from Boston who testified about how George was a strike buster. He beat a worker to death and threw their dislodged eyeball at the other workers to bully them into compliance. Sounds like it worked, too." Thomas and Clara looked shocked at this macabre detail. Clara put down her spoon, apparently losing what appetite she had left.

"Details also came out from Chief Smith about similar things that happened to Luke. It forms a pattern of violence that each member of the jury is probably thinking about right now."

James looked up from his plate and spoke for the first time since sitting down for dinner.

"The prosecution established opportunity and means, but not motive. Why would George target these people?"

Jack thought about this for a long time. "I don't know, James. But I'm not sure it matters to the jury. It definitely won't matter in the court of public opinion. Regardless of the outcome of the trial, George won't be welcome in Medford ever again."

The rest of the dinner they talked about other small topics and happenings around Medford. At the conclusion of dinner, Elizabeth walked him back downstairs to the front door of the store. She bid him a good night after he thanked her for the kind invite and the delicious meal.

As he turned to walk back to the church, Elizabeth went onto her toes and gave him a brief kiss on his cheek. They both flushed and as Jack left, Elizabeth locked the door and went back upstairs.

Chapter 44

January 5, 1893 – Medford

It was 4:15 in the morning when the knocks roused William out of his whisky-induced sleep. It had been a hard day, and by the bottom of the first bottle he believed that he had told Abigail everything she needed to know. He had drifted off to a half sleep, half dream state and had the dream where he was chasing his Elizabeth through the snow again. He had been having this dream more and more lately, and he was wondering if Abigail was trying to tell him something. He just couldn't figure out what it was.

He got up, luckily still dressed from the day. He brushed himself off, grabbed his cane, and hobbled to the front door of his apartment. It was the bailiff from the court, a no-nonsense man who was also named Smith. William could never remember his first name, though.

"What can I help you with, Marshal Smith."

"Sorry to wake you. It's about Sullivan. He broke out." The Marshal handed Chief Smith a Colt revolver, butt first. "We think he may be trying to find you. Keep this close."

The usage of revolvers was not common in Medford, and William hesitated before taking it. William was obviously no stranger to firearms, but he had hoped he had put that phase behind him. It appeared not. William checked the barrel and noticed it was loaded with 6 rounds. Marshal Smith handed him another box of the .45 caliber rounds.

"We have authorization from the judge to shoot on sight," Marshal Smith concluded. "We'll fill you in if we find anything else."

    The Marshal turned around and left Chief Smith standing in the doorway, trying to figure out what just happened.

Chapter 45

January 5, 1893 – Medford

The unknown man crept back into Elizabeth's room, watching her sleep quietly. She breathed gently, in and out. He noticed the delicate way that the blankets outlined her body, his eyes tracing the curves from her shoulders to her waist to her hips and then tapering off to her feet. She was sleeping on her side, legs together in the fetal position.

He could smell her, and it made him flush. She smelled of summer strawberries and the earth after a rain. She smelled of the cold silence at night during a snowstorm when the earth is asleep. It was a smell of heaven, hearth, and home, He wanted to bask in that smell more than anything in this world.

He quietly paced around the room, being careful not to set off the boards that he knew creaked. He had been in this room so many times, and yet one day he hoped to be in this room with her permission. She stirred, and he froze. He slinked back against the wall and pulled himself into his trusty overcoat and turned up the hood. He was near the corner of her room that was the darkest and knew that she wouldn't be able to register his presence if he was still. It didn't matter, though. She turned onto her back and drifted back to sleep. Soon her chest was rising and falling rhythmically again. He stood, staring at her chest, wondering about what lay beneath the blanket and further beneath her clothes. He wanted to lay his hands and his head on that chest. He wanted to place his skin on her skin and meld together, down to the marrows of their bones. He wanted to be with her completely: mind, body, and soul. He wanted to hear her heartbeat and hear her heart quicken when he was near. He watched her breathing and was mesmerized by the regularity – sucked into the pattern of her breathing that captivated him like a cheap carnival hypnotist.

The last time he was here, she had smelled of that awful laudanum. It had tainted her pores and overwhelmed his nose. The smell turned his stomach such that he couldn't get within 5 feet of her. He was so glad he got her off that stuff, even if he had to kill two innocent people. They were the most regrettable and he hoped they met a peaceful end.

Luke wasn't innocent. It was the worst after Luke's dates with Elizabeth, where Luke would go home and pleasure himself over and over. It was impure, and he had known Luke's obsession with Elizabeth was purely physical. Luke didn't value Elizabeth as a person, only as an object. Luke never asked Elizabeth about what she wanted in life. Luke didn't know that she wanted to be a student or that she wanted to take over the store. Luke just wanted an attractive wife to follow him wherever he went. Luke's obsession over Elizabeth was nothing compared to his, and for that reason alone he had to murder Luke. He wanted to be sure he sent a message with Luke's mutilated body. Anyone with such a purely physical attachment to Elizabeth would meet a similar end. He had taken off Luke's favorite plaything while Luke was still alive and oh, how Luke had screamed. He had used his dullest knife. He had almost gotten caught with how much Luke screamed, but he knew what he was doing. He had been taught by the best. Besides, the hard rain and thunder covered the worst of it.

His mind snapped back to the present as he finally stopped watching Elizabeth breathe. He reached out a hand in the night, wanting more than anything to touch her. He wanted to hold her, kiss her, love her. He knew that if he did that he would have to kill her. His obsession with Elizabeth Foster was so much more than physical. It consumed his entire soul. They needed to be together, but she couldn't know about him. Not yet. She had to be preserved in her innocence. He felt so protective of her, but it had to be her that came to him. He knew that.

Once she came to him, he would treat her like an equal. He would ensure she had everything she wanted in life and ensure that they did everything together. They would never be apart, and they could rule this town together. They could build a family, and if anyone got in their way, he could always kill them. He was good at removing loose ends.

The plans were falling into place. The trial had been a setback, but he was done with that now.

He had watched her at dinner that night, smiling at that fool named Jack. Jack was half the man he was, but he seemed to have fooled the entire town today. There was no way that he would let Jack win, especially since Jack had skated into town and found himself next to the wonderful Elizabeth Foster at a family dinner.

He left her room as silently as he had come. As he got back outside, he removed the cloth from his shoes and walked towards the church. It was time to get rid of Jack. Only then could he be with Elizabeth.

Time to get to work.

Chapter 46

January 5, 1893 – Medford

William had managed to get a few more hours of sleep after Marshal Smith had woken him. He knew that today was going to be a long day with an uncertain end. George was out there, and he needed to be found. His mind went through the checklist of possible places George could be. The triple decker where he lived was unlikely as most of the residents knew the big man was on trial. The train station was unlikely as well. George would be recognized and would realize that was one of the first places that Marshal Smith would look for him. There were a number of places to hide in the woods, though, and William figured that was as likely as any other place. That meant that if George came back into town, he'd be looking for those that caused his pain. That would be Mrs. Cooper, Sergeant McCarthy, Jack, and him.

William removed Sergeant McCarthy from his mind, as the Boston man had caught the evening train back to Boston and William didn't have the capacity to worry about another city. He wasn't worried for himself, either, so that left Jack and Mrs. Cooper. William would start with Mrs. Cooper.

He got to the police station, knowing it may be difficult to find enough people to cover all the places he needed to cover. However, he was pleasantly surprised to find it already packed with about 25 people, made up of veterans, police from the surrounding towns, and a couple of army men. Marshal Smith was there, coordinating the manhunt for George. The younger Smith had plenty of energy and was clearly in charge of this hunt. William knew that whenever he decided to retire, Marshal Smith would make a good replacement.

"They wouldn't even have to replace the name badge on the door," William thought to himself. He chuckled quietly but was brought out of his trance by someone calling his name.

"Chief Smith," the newly elected Mayor, Samuel Crocker Lawrence, called to him. "Care to see our plans?"

"Sure thing, Mayor."

"Come on over here and let's talk about it," the mayor said, waving him over with a hand.

William walked over to the group of men around the table. As he got closer, he saw it was an annotated map of Medford, with several squares drawn in dark ink. Each of the squares had a number in the middle of it, numbered from 1 to 10. William recognized this as a map of the many neighborhoods of Medford. Marshal Smith was talking.

"We need two people per neighborhood, at least. That's 20. We want you knocking on doors and looking around in alleys and other obvious hiding places. We're going to pair civilians up with someone who has the authority to carry a firearm."

Marshal Smith paired off people and directed them to West Medford, Hillside, Wellington, South Medford, North Medford and Glenwood. He paused as he reached Chief Smith.

"What about you Chief, think you can search?" Marshal Smith gestured at William's cane.

"No. I can't tolerate that much activity. I'd like to request one to two people, and we want to check out some of the most probable locations first – the triple decker and the church. I think that if George was really escaping, he'd be targeting the witnesses from the stand."

"That puts you on that list, too, Chief," Marshal Smith said.

"Don't worry about me. I've seen a fair share of scrapes in my days," William responded with more confidence than he felt at that moment. Truth be told, he had been shaky lately, probably a result of his increasing whisky habit.

"Right. Take Thomas and James Foster. You know them and are comfortable with them," the younger Smith directed. All three of them nodded at each other.

Marshal Smith continued around the circle, assigning people to Fulton Heights, Lawrence Estates, and Brooks Estates. He took Medford Square himself and paired himself with the mayor. He handed the mayor another Colt. The mayor was a colonel in the war, but in a different regiment than Chief Smith. Now that people had received their assignments, they started filing out of the police station to go start the hunt. There was an air of excitement surrounding them, and William really hoped they wouldn't abuse their power. He stepped towards Marshal Smith and the mayor, gestured he had something to say, but waited for everyone else to leave.

"First, thanks for arranging all of this. I was trying to figure out how to coordinate a manhunt on the way over here without any idea of resources."

"They were here when I showed up this morning, Chief," Marshal Smith said. "I think people are scared, and some people rise to action in the face of fear. I hope I didn't overstep your authority."

"No, I'm not worried about my ego. I clearly cannot spend too many hours searching." William tapped his leg with his cane for the effect. "That's one reason I came over here. After this hunt is done, I'm done too. I'm handing in my resignation to you, Mayor Lawrence, and I'd like you to consider this man as my replacement. I can't keep up anymore."

The mayor and Marshal Smith both nodded. It was the mayor who spoke first. "You know that we don't blame you for this, Chief Smith. You've made this town safe over the last 17 years. We won't forget that."

"Thank you, Mayor. Now let's go catch this bastard."

William turned and hobbled to meet Thomas and James in the hall. They had a bit of a walk to get to the triple decker. William reached down and checked that the Colt was easily accessible, ready for whatever this day would throw at him.

The walk to the triple decker was subdued. James carried an axe handle, and he would periodically thwap the handle into his other hand as a nervous tic. William could tell that Thomas and James were itching to get there faster, but they respected the rule of law enough to stay with William. William was walking as fast as he could, but it was clearly only about ¾ of the pace the other two men wanted.

They arrived at the triple decker where George lived and paused at the front door. William knew from conversations with George that Mrs. Cooper lived on the ground floor. William was glad he wouldn't have to worry about stairs at this first stop. He broke the silence with the other two men.

"Listen. I'm going in first. That isn't negotiable. I want one of you to stay out here in the street, ready to run back to the station or find another person if things go wrong in there. Thomas, will that be you?"

The older Foster nodded his head, and William continued.

"I've been given authority to shoot, but I want to hear what the man has to say. He was my friend. James, I want you to stay behind me. Make sure you're always in a place where you can swing that," William gestured at the axe handle, "and don't get trapped in any hallways. The most important thing you can do is stay behind me. Don't confuse bravery and stupidity. Got it?"

James nodded, and William drew the Colt. He opened the front door and walked in, not knowing what he would find.

Chapter 47

January 5, 1893 – Medford

What hit William first was the absence of the sounds of life. It was way too quiet for a triple decker. It wasn't as packed as the tenement houses of New York and Boston, but it shouldn't have been this quiet. The uneasy calm put William on high alert, scanning with all of his senses, searching for signs of life.

As William walked in the front door, there was a closed and locked door to his left and the stairs directly in front of him. The door to the left led to where he expected to find Mrs. Cooper. Up the stairs on floors 2 and 3, he would find two to three bedrooms per floor with a shared kitchen and living space. There was also a shared bathroom, but sometimes the rooms would have a private bath, which demanded double the rent. Each of the bedrooms had their own locking door to maximize privacy. William remembered that George lived on the second floor with two other people. Three total rooms. William had a choice to make; Investigate Mrs. Cooper first or look for some clues about George first. He chose to protect the potential victim, so he smashed the window of the door that led to Mrs. Cooper's apartment, unlocked it, and swung the door open. He raised his Colt to be ready to fire if needed and left his cane at the entryway. He'd have to make do without.

He stepped into the apartment, which was dark except for the light filtering through the curtains. He heard a faint, slow dripping noise, but it didn't sound like it was coming from the sink. It sounded like water was striking something wooden. Something hard. William put the noise out of his mind and went back to an orderly visual search of the scene, looking for anything out of place. He moved carefully through the living room and the kitchen one belabored step at a time – both were clean and tidy. He hobbled through the living space and towards the back of the house where the bedrooms should be. He paused and leaned on the wall, trying to will feeling back into his leg while he considered the next steps. The darkness was oppressive, and every small movement of the curtains put him on edge as the light danced on the floor. The hallway presented a door to the right. He nudged the door open and swung his body around the corner, letting the colt lead the way. It was a small half bath, completely empty. William retreated to the wall and leaned on it for support, out of breath.

He was feeling old. The rest of the hall revealed three remaining doors, all closed. There were two doors on the left and one straight ahead.

William guessed that one led to a bathroom, and two led to two different bedrooms. He opened the first one and his suspicion was correct. It was an empty bathroom.

"Two doors left," he said to himself.

He chose to open one of the bedroom doors and saw Mrs. Cooper used this room for storage. Boxes were piled from floor to ceiling, but the room was otherwise empty. William closed the door behind him, reasoning that if he missed someone in there, he wanted some warning.

He pushed open the door to the master bedroom. It was a medium-sized room with a window along the back of the house next to the bed. There were clothes strewn on the floor, and there was someone in the bed. The dripping noise was louder in here. William watched the form in the bed for signs of life but saw nothing. He shuffled forward and pushed against the shape in the bed with the barrel of his gun, finger on the trigger. The shape didn't move. William knew he would need to figure out who or what was in that bed, but he had to finish his sweep of the room first.

William backed up and crouched down to peer under the bed. This proved to be too much for his tired muscles, and his leg gave out. William fell on his backside awkwardly and sat there, mad at himself. He was glad no one else was around to see that. William started to get up off the floor but glanced under the bed again. He had finally discovered the source of the dripping. The bottom of the mattress was blood-soaked and had pooled into a single point. Droplets of blood were falling from the mattress and hitting the floor periodically. A sizeable pool of blood was on the wood floor, but William could tell that most of the blood had run through the floorboard cracks to an unknown destination. It was clear that the person in the bed wasn't going to be rising again.

William rose to his feet and holstered his gun. He grabbed the sheet and blanket that covered the mass and threw it back. Mrs. Cooper lay there in the bed, face up, a look of terror and pain plastered on her dead face. Her eyes were open, and her mouth was in the shape of a scream. Her arms and legs were bound to the bedframe with thick leather belts, making her completely immobile and helpless against what someone had done to her. She was split from groin to ribcage with a deep, clean, efficient cut. Whoever had made that cut had the same precision that had cut up Luke. Her intestines and other organs spilled out onto the bed, with blood draining from her chest cavity down to the mattress. She had suffered. William had read about this type of killing before. The victim was bound and then cut open, and gravity would keep most of the organs and blood in the body. However, the pain from the cut would cause the victim to thrash around, which would eventually spill the blood out of the body and result in a faster death. If the victim overcame the pain, the death would be just as painful but slower. It was a cruel way to die, and the killer had wanted Mrs. Cooper to suffer for what she had done.

Something was left on Mrs. Cooper's chest, right between her breasts. William poked it with the tip of his revolver. It was a tongue. The killer wanted Mrs. Cooper to stop talking. This painted George in a very guilty light.

William didn't have time to look for more clues. He left the bedroom and went back to the entryway, where James waited patiently with his axe handle. William picked up his cane and spoke to the young man.

"Mrs. Cooper is dead. Don't go back there. It isn't pretty. I didn't see anyone in that apartment, but I need to check the other two floors."

James nodded silently as William grabbed his cane from the wall and started his way up the stairs.

Chapter 48

January 5, 1893 – Medford

The second-floor layout was like the first, but there was no entryway door. The staircase emptied into the common living space and kitchen area, and a quick scan revealed there was no one visible. On this floor, though, one of the private rooms was near the front of the house and two were near the back. William had yet another choice to make and chose to go for the room at the front of the house first. As he pushed open the door, it was clear that he had found George's room.

The room was small – almost too small for anything more than a bed, but George had managed to fit an end table in the room and a chair in the opposite corner. William saw George's police badge on the small table on top of a letter. The letter was addressed to him. William pocketed it, not ready to read it. He still had two more rooms to sweep on this floor. As he turned to exit the room, a board on the ground on the opposite side of George's bed caught William's eye. The board stood next to an open area in the floor. It was a false floorboard storage spot, just like he had found in John's room. No wonder George had been able to find that false floorboard so easily – he had one of his own.

William reached into the hold and pulled out two things. A bottle of laudanum and a newspaper clipping. William turned the clipping over and saw it was a picture of Elizabeth Foster, torn from a copy of the newspaper on the day she graduated high school at the top of her class.

'Local girl bests boys to be top of class.'

Things were looking even worse for George's innocence.

William pocketed the two things and went back to sweeping the rest of the second floor. He opened the smaller of the bedrooms, which was equipped with thicker curtains than the others. As a result, only the faintest of light shone through. As William's eyes adjusted to the darkness, he saw another shape on the floor. He poked it with the tip of his cane and the shape didn't move. William walked over and drew back the curtain to illuminate an unknown man lying face up, a blunt knife sticking from his neck. The man lay in a pool of his own blood and looked like he had fallen out of bed in the struggle to make sense of the pain while his life force was pumped from his body. These were clues. William's mind raced.

The blackout curtains.

The man in bed.

A second shift laborer probably lived here, which would explain the blackout curtains. Someone murdered them while they slept by stabbing them in the neck with a blunt knife. The one who killed them ran out of the room, but the location of the stab meant the victim wouldn't be able to cry out for help.

"Efficient. Stealthy. Quick," William thought.

William moved to the larger bedroom which had a dedicated bathroom. The room itself was empty, and William turned to enter the bathroom. He swung the door open and saw a young woman, naked in a filled bathtub. The water had turned red, and the woman was dead. One arm draped out of the bathtub and William saw that her wrist was slit from the joint halfway up towards the elbow, following the line of the arm. William bet that if he examined her other arm, he'd find the same. This woman didn't stand a chance. It clicked into place why the house was so quiet. Everyone was dead.

William couldn't handle a third floor of gruesome scenes. He started back down the stairway and met up with James, who hadn't moved from his spot in the hallway.

"Do me a favor, James. Go upstairs and call out to see if anyone answers. Everyone is dead on the second floor and George's room is empty. I need a rest."

James dutifully ascended the stairs two at a time, and William heard him crashing around on the third floor for a few minutes before he came scampering back down the stairs.

"Ahhh, the resilience of youth," William thought.

"Find anything?" He asked James.

James looked at him, all color drained from his face. "All dead. Murdered. 5 more bodies up there. Blood everywhere. So much blood."

William hung his head and shook it slowly. This was a spree. 8 bodies in this one house. 8 lives cut and ended. There was no need for this much loss of life. It wasn't worth a silly infatuation with a local girl. He gestured to James to head back outside and meet up with Thomas. As they stepped outside, James paused to retch into the bushes to the left of the front porch. William was betting this was the first time James had seen death. He remembered his first, way back in Manassas at the Bull Run river, 30 years ago. He was getting really tired of death.

While James finished emptying his stomach in the bushes, Thomas ran to make sure James was ok. Thomas stood behind his son, patting him on the back and comforting him. William took that moment to open the letter that was addressed to him. He looked down and saw the same short, stunted writing he had seen in the notes about Luke and the Fergusons that had been left in Elizabeth's room.

Chief Smith—

I did it. I did it all. It was all to get closer to Elizabeth. I would leave love notes on the headstones of a thousand people if it would get me closer to her. I wasn't ready to hang. Take this badge and find a better person to hold it. I'm sorry.

George

Chapter 49

January 5, 1893 – Medford

It was a solemn walk back to the police station. Once there, William turned to the two men.

"Wait here."

He turned and went inside to discuss what he had found with Marshal Smith and the mayor, who were taking a break from the manhunt to eat some food. William stepped into the police office and the two men looked up from the desks at which they were sitting.

"Any luck?" the mayor asked. His face fell as he saw the somber look on Chief Smith's face.

"Not unless you consider bad luck. You'll need to call the undertaker."

"Mrs. Cooper is dead, then?" Marshal Smith asked.

"Aye, and 7 others in that household," Chief Smith replied bluntly. He no longer had the energy for pleasantries.

"Eight more bodies? Jesus Christ," the mayor said, a look of shock on his face.

"I don't think that our Lord had anything to do with what we saw in there. It was a massacre and there is no other word to describe it. I haven't seen anything that bad since the war," William said.

"Did you find any hard evidence, Chief?" The Marshal asked.

"Yes. I found a bottle of laudanum and a picture of

Elizabeth Foster from the paper." He handed both of those to the Marshal. He turned and handed the note over to the mayor. "There was also this."

The mayor read the note a few times and passed it silently to the other man in the room. Marshal Smith read it a few times as well and then placed it down on his desk.

"Seems we need to guard our dear Miss Foster," the Marshal finally said. "Someone is hunting her."

"I still have to check the church to see if Jack is ok, but I can send Thomas and James to go watch her. If they know someone may be coming, they can lock that house up pretty tight."

"Understood, but I'll join them. It'll be nice for them to have a gun in the house," Marshal Smith said.

The three men nodded in agreement and William turned to head back out.

"Chief, wait," the mayor said. "Stay a bit and talk with me. You can have some of my food as well."

"Yes, sir," William replied. Marshal Smith took the opportunity to head back outside and presumably tell Thomas and James to go locate their sister. William figured that Elizabeth would not be too happy with this arrangement. She was a strong-willed girl – it was one of the things he admired about her – but sometimes a strong will gets in the way of common sense.

The older man sat down at his desk and rubbed some feeling back into his leg. Jack would have to wait at the church. William hoped he could fend for himself or buy some time if George was chasing him. The mayor handed half of a pork sandwich over to William, who accepted it gratefully and took a bite. The meat was tender, and the bread was light and airy. It was accompanied by fresh lettuce and had a mustard spread with a hint of wild horseradish within. William took several more bites, hungrier than he realized. The mayor watched with amusement at the ravenous nature of the older man.

"I've been reading about you, Chief Smith. You've seen quite a lot of death in your life," the mayor started. It wasn't a question. William continued to eat, the energy from the sandwich giving him new drive and motivation for the hunt that was to come. The mayor continued. "Part of Lincoln's army, served at the second Bull Run, Antietam, Fredericksburg, Chancellorsville and Gettysburg. You lost a son and a wife. Your daughter moved across the sea and your other son moved to Boston to make his fortune. Do you still keep in touch with them?"

"No, sir. My daughter is dead, sir. Murdered in the streets of London 4 years ago, we think by Jack the Ripper. My son refuses to talk to me. Says I'm nothing but a sad, old man whose only love is the bottle and the police work." William was surprised with his honesty at this moment. He didn't know this man. All he knew was that he was a colonel in the Army, and apparently that was enough for him.

"Why do you ask about how much death I've seen, Mayor Lawrence?"

"Please, call me Sam. I do have one question though," the mayor responded, his tone suddenly turning serious. "In the last few months, someone you trusted to watch your back turned into a violent and depraved murderer, right under your nose. He has now taken 11 souls from this town. On your watch. How did you miss it?"

William thought for a long time about how to respond, taking a few more bites of sandwich. Mayor Lawrence was watching him closely. He took a swig from the glass of water that was on his desk, swallowed his food, and said "I've seen horrors in my life that will make most men turn and vomit. I've seen young kids laying in the mud, bleeding out of several holes from enemy fire. I've seen legs blown apart, stomachs ripped open, and heads severed from necks by cannon fire. One time I watched a young man lying on the ground, trying to scoop his intestines back into his body. He packed so much mud within him by the time he bled out that I'm sure he weighed at least 10 pounds more on the corpse cart. I've walked into my bedroom where I conceived three children to see my wife's lifeless body swinging from a rope with no explanation except a note blaming me for my son's death. I've managed to see the worst that this life has to offer, and it has broken me. I drink so much whisky to numb the pain and help me sleep without dreaming that I don't even know what would happen if I stopped. In the mornings my hands shake and in the evenings my leg burns with a fire that cannot be quenched. My life is hell."

He took another drink of water and continued.

"The only thing that kept me going was the kindness of the people in this town. And that included George Sullivan. George would always help around the office with little things, so I didn't have to walk as much. He'd bring me food and carry the heavy loads. He'd ask me intelligent questions and always seemed like he wanted to learn more about the craft of police work. He was kind to the people in this town, but it is clear to me that he led a double life. There was a darkness within him that no one registered. At most his landlady thought he was a laudanum addict. That isn't directly illegal if the medicine is obtained legally. And for that I'll always question if I did the right thing in hiring him. I don't know how much more violence I can take, but I know that there just isn't much left that I could see that would damage me further."

William put down his glass and looked at the mayor directly in the eyes.

"I will welcome Death when she comes for me, for every day I am already in hell. That's how I missed the devil."

Chapter 50

January 5, 1893 – Medford

William left the police station and headed toward the church, somewhat refreshed. The sandwich that the mayor had given him had hit the spot. The conversation had not. William knew he wasn't blameless in all this. That was a common theme in all the major events in his life – he was to blame. What the mayor couldn't figure out, though, was that William was a survivor and William was working as hard as he could to improve this town for the next generation. That was his penance for a life lived of violence and disappointment. He just had to figure out how to get George to stop. No matter what.

William vowed he'd go home after he warned Jack and made sure he was safe. William wasn't ready to tell Jack about what he saw in the triple-decker house, but he could dance around it. William walked to the Universalist church slowly, despite his rush of energy from the lunch break. By the time he arrived, he had the outline of a plan.

He walked through the main door of the church into the nave. He heard a wail. He also detected a faint smell of smoke. Something was wrong again. There were two shapes near the altar, but William couldn't make out who or what they were doing. His plan went out the window. Was he too late?

He dropped his cane and the clang of the wood on the floor rang out in the open space. One of the figures looked up just as William drew his gun. It was Jack, tears running down his face. Jack wasn't wearing a shirt, and William couldn't figure out why.

William approached slowly, keeping his gun fixed on Jack while also scanning the rest of the room for something out of place. He scanned the open pews as he moved, and sometimes would pause to shift his weight and try to get his leg to wake up. He'd be sore for a week after today.

As he got closer, the scene pulled into focus. The other figure was Minister DeLong. Someone had bashed him in the back of his head with something heavy, and it appeared that Jack had wrapped Henry's head with his shirt to try and stem the bleeding. From the tears and the amount of blood that had soaked through Jack's shirt, William could tell that it hadn't worked. William kept the gun trained on Jack while he tried to make sense of it.

"Tell me what happened. Now." William said at Jack. William sat down in the first row, needing the rest. William's colt never wavered from Jack.

"I came in here. As part of my chores," Jack started. He was speaking in short, choppy sentences, with a rasping inhalation of breath between each one. "I saw someone big. Run at Henry. They had the cross from the altar. They hit him. He went down. The big figure saw me. He yelled. 'That was supposed. To be you.' I chased after the figure. They got away. I ran back to Henry. He was bleeding so much. It was just pouring out of him. I saw his brain. I had to stop the bleeding. I couldn't keep the blood in his head. There was so much blood. I just had to put the blood back in."

William looked around, as if to check some of the details of Jack's story. Sure enough, the heavy brass cross that sat in the middle of the altar table was on the floor, a gleam of red on one of the three arms of the cross. Some of the pews were knocked over between the altar and the door, looking like someone had run out of here in a hurry and run into a couple of the pews on the way.

"Why does it smell like burning?" William asked.

Jack looked up, puzzled. He hadn't smelled that yet. His eyes darted around the congregation, settling on the narthex near the back of the church. An area where people lit candles for lost ones, the same place where Luke had lit a candle, those short months ago. William turned to look where Jack was looking and saw the source of the smell. Someone had knocked over the candles, and they had caught fire on the banner proclaiming the joy of Jesus. Flames were already licking the ceiling and building quickly. William hadn't even seen them when he came in.

"Right," William said. "We're getting you out of here. Grab the important relics and follow me."

Jack reached down and grabbed the heavy cross with Henry's blood still on it, hesitated, and then wiped off the blood on Henry's clothing. He grabbed the cross and nodded to William that it was all he was going to take. It was too cold outside for Jack to go out without any covering. William looked around for something for Jack to wear and saw a heavy coat lying in the pew near the altar, probably left by someone. He grabbed it and picked it up. It was heavy. And lumpy. Whatever.

William threw it to Jack, who quickly put it on, understanding exactly what was needed. They made it outside just as the flames broke through the room. They stood in the street in a state of shock as the fire brigade started to arrive. William could already tell the church would have to be rebuilt, brick by brick.

The two men stood there, speechless, watching the orange dance against the fading light of the January evening. It was as destructive as it was enticing. Finally, Jack turned to William and said, "Were you looking for me, Chief?"

"Yes, I was," William responded, almost dreamily. He hadn't looked away from the flames yet. "I was coming to warn you that you were in danger. I was at George's triple-decker earlier and I have reason to believe he's hunting you."

"Seems that you're right and I am in danger," Jack said, calmly. "What did you find at George's?"

"That doesn't matter anymore. We got you out and you're safe now. We have people guarding Elizabeth and I'll stay with you. Did this big man who killed Henry say anything else?"

"Yes. He said, 'tell the Chief to find me where his joy began.'" Jack snapped out of his trance. "Wait, what about Elizabeth?"

"No worries, Jack."

"I have to go, Chief Smith. I have to make sure she's ok. I won't let that freak spill her guts."

Jack ran off towards the Foster's store. William watched him go and thought it was an odd turn of phrase given what had happened to Mrs. Cooper.

Chapter 51

January 5, 1893 – Medford

William had to find George before someone else was killed. William searched his brain for any thoughts of where he could find his former deputy. Jack had said something, and it had to be a clue.

Tell the Chief to find me where his joy began.

Another clue from the killer spoken in riddles.

"One of these days I'll get a criminal who's too dumb to speak in riddles and just tell me what I want to know," William exclaimed, frustrated.

Where had he felt joy?

He briefly retraced his life. It started in Medford in the General Store to parents who were kind but not joyful. Their love drifted away and left the house cold. Then he got married.

Abi.

Abi was his joy. Where did his life start with Abi? It was the church – stolen kisses in the afternoons after church service. But he was just in the church, and now it was on fire.

"Think, William, think."

Joy came with the birth of Ben, which lifted life's anxiety from William's chest. The birth of Ben told him and Abi that his parent's curse wouldn't befall them. That means...

The cottage. He had to get to the cottage.

They had sold the cottage when his parents died, and they moved back to the General Store to run it. It was amazing how life started to fall apart as soon as they started living in that damned General Store. He had sold the cottage to Charles Tufts, and as far as William knew, Charles Tufts had let it rot. Tufts was looking for the land, not the house.

William grabbed his cane and hobbled as quickly as he could in the direction of the old cottage. It was a 10-minute walk on a good day and with two functioning legs. It was just past 6 pm and darkness was setting in. It would probably take 30 minutes tonight, longer if he didn't have light. He stopped by city hall on the way out and grabbed a lantern. No one else was there but William knew this part of the hunt was set up for him and him alone. The personal touches left at each killing had enabled a final climax between him and George. He'd have to ask the big man how George had known such small, intimate details about William. Bromine. Lilac. These were things he didn't speak aloud. After Abi died, he had only ever put them in his letters pleading to Lizzie to come home.

As he walked the rough roads and trails that would lead him to his old cottage, William tried to think about what he would say to George when he found him.

"Hey, buddy. I know you killed everyone, but let's talk about this so I don't have to shoot you."

No, that probably wouldn't work.

Before he knew it, William was rounding the bend and saw the dim outline of the cottage on the edge of the woods. There was a light inside. William knew it wasn't wired with electricity, so there had to be someone in there with a fire or an oil-lamp. As he got closer, the telltale flicker of an open flame made William believe it was a fire. Good. He was cold right now from a long day spent outside. The cold made his leg muscles ache, too. There was so much pain. William was ready for this day to be over.

William hadn't been to this cottage since they sold the land. He had almost immediately gone off to war and when he got back, he found he couldn't come out here. The painful memories of Abi were just too much. Tufts had done absolutely nothing with the place, and the years hadn't been kind to the cottage. All of the windows had been broken and dead vines and creepers had started to pull apart the walls from the foundation. The roof had holes in it, which allowed the fire within to illuminate the lower canopy of trees that had grown over the top of the cottage. Nature had started to reclaim the land.

The dilapidated cottage and the light bouncing off of the trees gave off shadows that belied an eerie feeling upon the entire surroundings. William shivered, not sure if it was from the cold or the creepiness. William knocked on the door loudly. There was no answer.

He drew his Colt and opened the door. It protested its hinges and creaked as it opened.

"So much for the element of surprise," William said out loud, not caring if he was ambushed or not.

The floor was rotted out and the ground was visible beneath. A fire burned in the middle of the floor, stoked with pieces of floorboard. There was no furniture in the small house, and the walls were cracked. The small pieces of wallpaper that him and Abi had been able to afford had long peeled away.

The room was empty.

Or was it? The firelight cast shadows on the wall, including a large shape that swung slowly back and forth. William looked up.

For the second time in his life, William had found a dead body, hung from the rafters of his home. Deputy George Sullivan hung from one of the roof rafters that was still intact, a toppled chair beneath him. He was dead.

William sighed. It was over. He reached up and grabbed George's leg.

"Goodbye, old friend. May you find peace in the next life from the pain that clearly tormented you in this one."

William turned and started the long walk back to the town. He let the fire burn. He didn't care anymore.

Chapter 52

January 5, 1893 – Medford

Elizabeth sat at the kitchen table in her home, bored. They wouldn't let her leave the house and wouldn't tell her why. Thomas and James had come home about an hour ago, and James looked sickly and ill. He hadn't left her side since then and was gripping an axe handle tightly.

"Why are you carrying that, James?" she'd asked him.

"Oh this?" James responded, "this was downstairs during inventory, and I brought it upstairs by mistake. I'll take it back down soon. I'm just holding onto it so I don't forget about it."

When her dad had come home, he told her mom that they should expect Marshal Smith for dinner. She didn't ask why, but a look was exchanged between them, and they vanished to their room a short while later. Elizabeth walked past the closed door and heard urgent, hushed voices. Clearly something was going on. She plopped back into her seat at the table and let out an exasperated sigh.

"Hey, Elizabeth, want to play some cards?" James asked.

"Sure," she replied, and he went off in search of the cards they kept in the living room. He returned a short time later with a deck of cards and a cribbage board. They dove into the game and soon Elizabeth's boredom vanished. She barely noticed Marshal Smith come into the kitchen and sit down at the table. He studied their game but didn't say anything. She won the first game by a small margin and skunked him the second. She picked up most of her points in pegging, which meant James was distracted and not thinking clearly. Pegging is all about thinking ahead.

The second game ended, and Elizabeth heard an urgent rap on the front door. James and Marshal Smith both bolted upright and nearly in unison told her to stay put. Clara came out of their room dabbing tears from her face and ran to Elizabeth's side. Thomas stood in between and waited at the top of the stairs while the other two men descended into the store. James still had his axe handle, and she was pretty sure she saw Marshal Smith draw a revolver from his belt. Out of the corner of her eye, she saw her dad slink into the kitchen and pull a knife out of the drawer.

"Ok, WHAT is going on?" Elizabeth asked.

She was shushed immediately by everyone in the room. Fear started to creep into her mind. She heard the front door open, then closed again, followed by the unmistakable latch of the lock. She hadn't heard anyone come in the door, though. That was odd. Usually, she could hear someone walking across the floor from upstairs. The downstairs floor was old enough that it creaked on nearly every board. James reappeared up the stairs, followed by Marshal Smith and then another figure in a coat. He was disheveled and not wearing a shirt, but she instantly recognized his face. Jack.

She ran to him and hugged him, happy for another familiar person in this uncertain time. He barely hugged her back, though.

"Ok, what is going on. You owe me an explanation," she finally said, darting a glance between her dad, James, Marshal Smith, and Jack. Her mom came over and stood next to her, squeezing her hand in a protective manner.

"You may want to sit down for this, Elizabeth," her dad said.

"No. I'm not sitting down. I'm not going to play more cribbage. I'm not going to eat food. I'm not going to be quiet until someone tells me what in the HELL is going on."

Thomas Foster let out a large sigh. He glanced at Clara, who gave him a brief nod, clearly authorizing the truth. "You're being hunted." Her father paused, letting that sink in. "We are pretty sure it's George Sullivan who is hunting you, and he's doing whatever it takes to get to you. He's in love with you and says he won't stop until he has you."

The air went out of Elizabeth's lungs, and she sat down in the nearest chair. She stared into the distance, trying to make it all make sense. She had talked to the big deputy maybe 5 times in her life. She had no connection with him at all. Why was he coming for her? It didn't make sense. Something wasn't adding up.

"I thought he was in jail," Elizabeth said, flatly, "How did he get out and what has he done so far?"

Marshal Smith picked up the conversation at this point. "Yesterday during dinner time, the guard opened the cell door to get the previous meal's dishes. George overpowered the guard and knocked him unconscious. He ran from the cell and vanished. No one has seen him since."

Elizabeth noted that the man had declined to answer the second part of that question. She turned to James. "That's why you're carrying the axe handle. You're trying to protect me." He nodded and she stood up, ran over to him, and gave him a hug. She continued to put pieces together.

"That's also why you're here, Marshal Smith. To try and apprehend him. But why not Chief Smith? He's been with me since the start of this and we know him."

"That's where I come in, I'm afraid," Jack interjected. "Chief Smith was sure that George was targeting each of the witnesses who testified against him. That includes me. He came to find me in the church, but George had already gotten there. George used the big altar cross to hit Minister DeLong in the back of the head and kill him." Jack paused here, trying to recover against unseen tears and unspoken grief. "Me and the Chief are pretty sure he thought Minister DeLong was actually me. He mentioned you were in danger, and I ran over here. The more hands, the better."

Elizabeth walked over and embraced Jack, holding him tightly. He nuzzled into the crook of her neck and stayed there, squeezing back. The world vanished and for a little bit it was just the two of them. Thomas cleared his throat, perhaps louder than necessary. As she pulled away, Jack blushed and drew his coat tighter against himself.

"Sorry, I realize I am not wearing a shirt," he said. "That wasn't very proper of me."

James silently left the room and gestured for Jack to follow him. They returned about two minutes later, with Jack wearing one of James shirts. He had ditched the overcoat in James' room. Clara went to the stove, checking on the dinner. In all the madness, Elizabeth looked up to see the clock on the mantle nearly at 8.

"Dinner's ready," she said. "Everyone needs to eat."

Clara's tone made it clear there was not any room for debate.

They sat down at the table and Thomas said a quick prayer. Clara served them stew made with beef and potatoes. It smelled marvelous, and soon the motley crew of protectors tucked into their bowls. They were tired enough that they didn't speak. For a while the only noises were the clinking of spoons on bowls and a dog barking in the distance.

Despite the situation, the meal ended up being rather relaxing. Elizabeth was seated between Jack and James, and soon they sank into comfortable familiarity. Marshal Smith ended up talking with Thomas and Clara, which left the three youngsters to their own devices. Jack spent most of the time talking to James, trying to get to know him better.

"You're working at the brick factory now, but what's your longer-term goal?" Jack asked.

"My passion is actually architecture," James responded. "I figured spending some time with bricks would help inform my future. I'm hoping that when I'm done with high school, I can get an apprenticeship in Boston with a firm."

"Well," Jack interjected, "there's a possibility it'll be a little sooner than that. I'm pretty sure the church will be a near total loss, which means it'll be time to rebuild. We'll need to employ an architect. If I'm still around, I can put in a good word for you."

"Wait, what do you mean if you're still around?" Elizabeth asked. She had heard what he said but couldn't believe there was a chance he would be leaving Medford. She felt herself getting closer and closer to him. Living without him didn't really seem like a good possibility at the moment.

"Well, with Henry gone, the congregation has to choose a new minister. There's no guarantee that they'll want me, and I'm not sure if I want it. Medford has a darkness within it right now. Especially for me."

Elizabeth looked at him with an exasperated expression. She couldn't believe he was making this about him, when they were putting her under house arrest because a psycho was trying to murder her to fulfill an infatuation. She let him know of her frustration, losing what little patience she had left.

"YOU think Medford has a dark tone? What do you think I feel right now? The man that I thought I loved was butchered in his place of work. My doctor was forced to overdose on opium. My brother is so worried that he is carrying around an axe handle and I have a Marshal eating dinner in my house, wearing a GUN." Everyone else had turned to watch her meltdown. "I've been shushed, lied to, coddled, and patronized. I don't want to hear you say anything about Medford right now, Jack Taylor."

Her voice had steadily risen until she was yelling, and the urgent hushes from all the others in the room was an indication this may have been a mistake. There was a knock on the front door again. Spoons clanked to plates as they were dropped. Marshal Smith drew the revolver, and James went to the other room for his axe handle. Thomas went back to the kitchen for a knife, and Jack joined him. Thomas handed Jack another knife. They stepped between Elizabeth and the stairway and Clara stood next to Elizabeth again. It was clear – they would have to go through all four men before getting to her. Elizabeth was immediately sorry for her outburst, realizing how much she really was protected.

Marshal Smith and James crept downstairs, trying to see who was at the door. They vanished downstairs and the four remaining people held their breath. They heard the door open and close again. This time Elizabeth heard the telltale creaks across the floorboards as someone entered. She also heard the unmistakable thud of a cane. Chief Smith had arrived in the general store.

Chapter 53

January 5, 1893 – Medford

Chief Smith slowly climbed the stairs and appeared in front of Marshal Smith and James. The latter two men looked a lot more relaxed than they had when they went downstairs. Elizabeth wondered if the presence of the older law man had the same calming effect on them that he had on her. She would have to ask them sometime. Thomas offered Chief Smith a chair, which he gladly took. He set his cane against the table and rubbed feeling back into his bad leg. Elizabeth noticed that the chief refused to look down the hallway towards the bedrooms. He seemed very uncomfortable in the home above the store. Marshal Smith was the first to speak.

"Tell them what you told me, Chief."

"George is dead," Chief Smith said. "He was found hanging out in an old cottage in the woods. The manhunt is over. Jack, Marshal Smith, you're free to return to your normal lives."

Elizabeth couldn't help but notice there was a wavering in the chief's voice when he said this part about the cottage. She couldn't figure out why, though. The chief continued.

"Elizabeth, I'm very sorry for how this all turned out. I want to figure out George's connection to you, but not tonight. Tonight, I am going to head to my apartment and sleep. This day has taken a lot out of me."

Elizabeth felt a mix of joy and exhaustion and let out a breath she didn't know she was holding. The ordeal was over.

The chief stood up, grabbed his cane, and started back

down the stairs. "I wanted to let you all know that today is also my last day as a chief."

He left them in stunned silence, and they heard the front door open and close again.

The rest of them stood in the kitchen for a long time, processing what just happened. Eventually Marshal Smith thanked Clara for the food and took his leave. James went to his room, grabbed Jack's coat, and gave it to the young assistant minister. Jack started to follow Marshal Smith downstairs and out.

"I'll walk you out," Elizabeth insisted.

They walked down to the main floor and approached the door. Marshal Smith had come and gone, and they were the only ones on the shop floor. It was fully dark outside now, but the High Street was gently lit by the dim glow of electric lights. Jack reached for the doorknob, but Elizabeth grabbed his arm. He turned to face her. She was acutely aware of how close they were together. She could feel his warm breath. She could smell him, and she was aware that her heartbeat had quickened. He reached out and brushed some hair from her face and swept it behind her ear. Electricity sparked through her body, focused on the spot where his fingertip had touched her. She needed to think of anything other than him.

"Where will you stay?" Elizabeth asked, her voice raspy.

Jack thought about this for a bit and then responded. "I'll stay at the parsonage tonight. Henry didn't have a lot of stuff, but it would be better for the house to be occupied. I'll figure out what to do in the morning."

Elizabeth didn't let go of his arm. "Promise me something."

"Anything," he said, in a forced whisper that had an air of

urgency.

"Promise me you won't leave Medford without us talking about our future."

His eyes sparkled. "Oh, so you're saying we have a future?"

She tilted her head up and drew his head to her. Her lips found his. Her lips parted slightly, and the tip of her tongue lightly licked his lips, searching for the tongue she knew was there. She found it with hers and felt his body rise against it. They pulled away from the kiss and he wrapped his arms around her, holding her tightly. Safely. For a long moment she stood there in the embrace, just letting herself be held. Finally, Elizabeth wrapped her arms around him and squeezed back. She felt the telltale poke of excitement between his legs, at which time she broke the embrace.

She didn't need to say any more and turned on her heel to head back upstairs. She heard him walk out of the store and into the street. As she mounted the first stair, though, she went back to the front door and locked it. She couldn't be too careful.

Chapter 54

December 1888 – Finsbury Park, London

Ben knew it was time to go to Medford. It was what his mother wanted. He already knew he'd need a new identity and likely take two or three stops on the way. He would need to start going by something generic like Paul or John or maybe George. Something overtly biblical made everything easier with strangers. He planned to change his last name as well, as even though Smith was a common enough name he wanted to avoid any connection at all to his extended family.

Even after he rid the world of Druitt, there was still one loose end that nagged on him. Over the course of two months, Ben started to stockpile his savings and withdraw money from the various banks in London.

He had amassed almost 2000 pounds in his time working for the Odessians. He was able to withdraw 1200 pounds without arousing suspicion, and he split them into three piles of 400 pounds each. He realized there was something he needed to do to separate himself from the inhumanity and evil of Montague Druitt. He had to use his alter ego for some good in this world, trying to rid the world of sin in the light as well as the darkness.

The first stack he delivered to Mistress Mary one night, thanking her for the kindness she had shown his mother. The old woman sat in shock as Ben placed stack after stack of bills in front of her and said nothing. Ben gave her a hug and vanished into the night. He never heard what she did with the newfound money, but he hoped she used it to make her life better.

The second stack he sewed into one soft-sided travel bag where he stored his worldly possessions. He kept the lye tin from his time in the lodging house, a kerchief from his mother, and two changes of clothes. He would need to travel across the Atlantic in a third-class berth to avoid suspicion, and as a result he didn't want to flash any of his money at risk of being robbed or killed.

The third stack was destined for his sister, Sarah. She would need the money after he tied up the loose end that was his father. He wanted to do for her what no one else had ever done for him: change her trajectory. Ben took the train out of Whitechapel to Finsbury Park and spent the next two days planning. He watched his father's habits and realized this was going to be the easiest murder yet.

He saw Sarah, now 10, forced to work behind the bar cleaning glasses. She looked miserable. Ben always remembered Sarah as a warm and kind girl who was quick with a smile. She was a far cry from that girl, and as Ben stalked his prey, he saw the way that Tom leered at his own daughter. It was obvious that Tom liked his quarries on the younger side, and the thought of what was to come as Sarah got older turned Ben's stomach. Incest was never excusable, but a father taking advantage of his daughter is the worst kind of sin. The world would be better without him in it.

On the final day of Ben's father's life, Ben spent the morning at the prestigious North London Collegiate School and arranged for a place for Sarah using the stack of money he had set aside. By the time he left the campus, her tuition was pre-paid for the next 8 years, and a trust was set up in Sarah's name for the remainder with a local bank that had ties to the school. She would leave an educated, grown woman with a sizeable fortune to start a new life. He would try and reach out to her someday after he had settled in his new life in Medford. Maybe she'd come live with him, and they could be the happy family neither had ever had.

That evening, Ben donned his pocketed cloak and prepared his instruments. He packed his favorite knife, but all he wanted to use tonight was the pull handle from a beer engine that was used to draw ale from casks. Tom Smith still had his habit of drinking with his patrons, and there was no way anyone could remain sober with as many rounds as he shared. Ben's plan was solid. While there was always space to improvise, Ben wasn't thinking he'd need to.

Ben found a single table near the back of the pub and started ordering ales from the serving girl. The serving girl looked young – likely around 15 or 16. Ben shuddered to think what Tom had already done to her. His sister wasn't at the bar tonight, and Ben was glad. She shouldn't have to see this.

Each time Ben ordered a pint, the serving girl would deliver it, and Ben would take a drink. Then he would get up and start a rousing song with the rest of the bar and pour bits of his beer into other patron's cups. If they ever noticed, he would give them a hearty cheer and order another round on him. As a result, by closing time he had drank very little and spent enough money that Tom took notice. Ben sidled up to the bar at the end of the night to close his tab.

"What's the damage, barkeep?" Ben asked. He intentionally slurred some of his syllables together.

"50 pence," replied Tom.

Ben knew this was a lie. He had ordered maybe 5 pints, and each pint ran around 3 pence. Tom was trying to shake down an out of towner. It wouldn't matter much longer.

Ben opened his pocketbook, allowing Tom to see the stack of 10-pound notes within. 10 pounds would have paid for 800 pints at 3 pence apiece, and Ben was counting on his father's greed. Ben mumbled to himself while he closed the pocketbook and started slapping his pockets, looking for something else. He pulled out two crowns and laid them on the bar.

"Keep the change," Ben said. Two crowns were worth 120 pence. Ben had just given Tom a rather large tip. Any ordinary barkeep would feel lucky to get such a tip on top of overpriced ale, but Ben knew his father wasn't an ordinary barkeep. Tom nodded his head at this young man, and Ben left through the front door, knowing he'd be followed. Nothing attracts thievery quite like an outward display of being loose with your coin.

He walked slowly down the street and heard footsteps approaching. He pivoted to see Tom, club in hand.

"I think you better be leaving that pocketbook behind, sir," Tom threatened, slapping the club against his open hand.

"I'd rather not. My sister could use the money. You know. Sarah," Ben replied. "Hi, da."

Before Tom could register what happened, Ben charged his father and knocked him down. Ben ran past the man and ducked back into Tom's bar. He hid and waited. A few minutes later, Tom came into the bar, flushed from the chase.

"So you've come back to take a swing at me, eh boy? Come out where I can see you and I'll beat you like I did that whore of a mother you had. Yeah, I saw the papers. Ripped apart, dead in the street after one too many cocks. Serves her right. She never could keep her legs or her mouth shut."

"YOU were the problem, you fat ignorant piece of trash,"

Ben screamed back at him. "YOU were the reason she left, and YOU were the reason she had to sell herself for a chance at life. I've watched you. You are a sick pervert who wants to screw his own daughter," Ben yelled, tears welling up and streaming down his face. Ben hadn't realized how much of his life he'd spent in the shadow of this man's oppressive thumb. So much of his life was spent in fear of a man he didn't know.

"Now I'm going to have to beat you harder. Yer not very smart, thinking you can hide in me own pub," Tom said, all the while slapping his club against his open hand.

It had felt good to scream at him, but Ben knew he was in danger of turning into Druitt. There was too much emotion. He had to calm down. He had to keep his wits about him. He had to execute his plan and then get to Medford. None of that would be possible if he was dead. Ben knew he needed to make the larger man a little madder. Weakness comes through emotion.

"So, tell me, fat man, why do you think you'll be able to catch me?"

Tom didn't take the bait. Ben stood up out of his hiding place and placed a table between him and Tom.

"You probably haven't had to work this hard since you raped your last serving girl and promised her a better life. Was it that 15-year-old girl that served me drinks tonight? She looked like she had been abused by you. Tell me, can a fat lard like you even still find his tiny member?" Ben realized the emotion was gone. He was having fun now and let out a peel of laughter.

Where the taunting had calmed Ben, it had equally enraged Tom. In his anger, Tom put the club down on the bar, grabbed the table between them with both hands, and threw it out of the way.

Ben quickly went the other way and vaulted the bar so that the bar was between him and Tom. The bar was about 10 feet long and in the shape of an L, with one end that opened into the room and one end that was closed off to the room. Ben removed a can of oil from his jacket and emptied its contents on the floor, about 2 feet from the open end. He hoped this would work. If it didn't, Ben had his favorite knife still tucked away in his coat, and he wagered that he was faster with his knife than Tom was with his hands.

Tom chased Ben around the open end of the bar as Ben was putting the oil can back in his coat and laughed.

"I have you trapped now, you bastard," Tom said. "I'm going to show you what a real man does with a petulant child."

Tom advanced towards Ben slowly, arms outstretched. Ben vaulted over the bar and back into the room. The speed with which Ben did this confused Tom, who started running and took two quick steps towards Ben. The second step Tom took was right in the slippery spot where Ben had put the oil on the floor and Tom fell forward at great speed, right onto his face. As the large man fell, Ben jumped back over the bar and approached the large man, withdrawing the pull handle from his coat.

"Time to die. But before you do, I want you to know the only thing you ever gave me was a last name. But names can be changed."

Ben started beating his father in the head with the pull handle, over and over. He lashed out with all the rage he had stored up over the last 15 years. All the rage from being born into the wrong family. All the times he had to stand by while his mother had been beaten. All the times where she would tell him of a better life in Medford. All those times she read to him letters from her father, William, talking about the family she had left behind. All the times she would leave at night to service unknown numbers of anonymous men and come back smelling of semen and alcohol. All those times she got a black eye from a rough John and he had to help her heal so she could make them money. All those holidays he missed, and all the moments since his mother had died where he just wanted to talk to her again. Each of these things and more earned his father a blow to the skull. Whack after whack Ben brought the pull handle onto his father's skull until he had no more rage. He yelled at the prone shape of his father, a yell that came from Ben's soul. A yell that changed him. A yell that killed the Ben that had been in London for 15 years and gave birth to a new person, ready to sail across the Atlantic and take what was his.

Ben looked down. The body was still twitching, but Ben kicked the man to ensure he was dead. The lifeless corpse rolled over on the floor and Tom lay on his back, blank eyes to the ceiling. The pull handle was bloody but still intact. As a final blow, Ben took the handle and jammed it into Tom's open mouth, through the soft pallet, and out the back of his head. Blood began to pool at the bottom of the bar.

Ben saw a glint of silver in Tom's waistcoat, reached down, and extracted a silver pocket watch.

"To remind myself to be better than you, all the time," Ben said to the corpse on the floor.

Ben took out the can of oil again and spread it over the rest of the bar. He took out a box of matches from another pocket, lit one, and dropped it into the oil. Flames danced over the dead body of his father and licked at the bottom of the liquor bottles. This place would be an inferno in under 3 minutes taking with it the last memory of Tom Smith.

Ben left the bar and walked to what was now Sarah's house.

Sarah was likely asleep at this time, so Ben removed a note from his coat and left it in their mailbox.

> *Sarah-*
>
> *I have watched the way your "father" treats you and decided that you deserve better. You must leave before his desires become physical. I know that your mother is dead, and I cannot find your brother Ben. He was involved with the Odessians, and they likely eliminated him. That doesn't mean you need to be an orphan.*
>
> *You will find 8 years of tuition paid for with a small trust in your name at the North London Collegiate School. Do better than your father. Make a better future.*

He hoped the note found Sarah before Sarah found Tom. He walked into the darkness and saw the flames of the Tailor's Tape illuminating the London sky. Ben had eliminated all traces of him in London. He remembered the last words his mother had said to him.

"Go to Medford. Take what is yours."

He intended to do exactly that.

Chapter 55

January 5, 1893 – Medford

William walked slowly from the Foster's to his apartment. It wasn't very far, but each step felt like a journey. His body was tired. He was glad that he was going to retire tomorrow and turn in his badge. Maybe he'd move down to Boston and see Charlie a little more. Maybe he'd ride the train out west to see the other ocean. He had heard wonderful things of San Francisco. Maybe he'd take a steamer to London and go find this Miss Mary who had written to him about his Lizzie all those years ago. His brain was full of maybes by the time he walked in his front door.

He put his keys on the entryway table and unbuckled his gun belt. He hung the belt on a coat hook behind the door and unholstered the colt and set it on his end table next to his bed. He would return it in the morning to Marshal Smith. William sat down and ate some of the day-old bread to fill his stomach, but his main course tonight would be the new bottle of whisky that sat on his kitchen table. He washed down the bread with a glass of water, drained the glass and opened the whisky bottle. He poured a healthy measure and went over to his armchair to make some more notes in his book. He slipped off his shoes and grabbed a lap blanket that Abigail had made when they had first moved into the general store. It felt later than it was, and he was physically and emotionally exhausted.

He started making notes in his notebook but set the book down soon after. Something was sticking in the back of his mind – something he couldn't get over. The same thought tumbled over and over in his mind, so he wrote it down in his notebook. William used visualization sometimes as a key to solving a puzzle.

*George Sullivan couldn't have had enough of a
motive to involve Elizabeth.*

William looked at the murders in a new light. He had been focused on the common threads that connected the victims, but from the perspective of the killer. He shifted tactics and made notes weighing the involvement of Elizabeth against all the murders. He started making frantic notes in his notebook, chronologically numbered by victim.

1. *Luke – nearly engaged to Elizabeth, likely killed for his romantic involvement with her. Attempted to frame John. Killer passed up almost $1000. Killer does not need money.*
2. *Doc Ferguson – prescribed laudanum to Elizabeth to help her sleep and get over Luke's death. Killed with laudanum. Killer robbed nothing and killed Edna in the same manner. Sent a message to Elizabeth to stop using laudanum and made it clear that the killing was a result of her disobedience.*
3. *Mrs. Cooper – no connection to Elizabeth. No note left. Connection to George.*
4. *7 other residents of the triple-decker – no connection to Elizabeth. No note left.*
5. *Henry – clubbed to death with large cross. Sloppy compared to the other killings. Rushed.*

William hesitated before writing down a final name.

6. *George Sullivan – hanged. Made to look like suicide? <u>Connection to Elizabeth?</u>*

He underlined this last question twice in his notebook, as

this was what was sticking in his brain. George didn't have a connection to Elizabeth, despite the hard evidence in his room.

The picture.

The laudanum.

George's room.

What if George wasn't the killer? William took another drink of his whisky, the familiar burn of a kind friend in a dark night. He took another. It was already helping alleviate his stress. William's mind went back to the notebook.

What if the things left in George's room were actually clues left by the real killer? Chief Smith owed it to his former deputy to ask this question and examine the case from all angles.

William's mind went back to George's room – there was a note left and a picture found of Elizabeth. What if the killer had left the note, finalizing the frame job?

William took another sip of whisky. The glass was empty, and he rolled this question around in his mind while he went back to the kitchen table and refilled the glass. What if George's "hanging" was actually his execution?

Ok, William thought. Let's assume for a second George is innocent, deftly framed by someone else. Who could it be that has a connection to Elizabeth? Luke? No, he's dead and the killings continued.

William took another drink.

Someone in her family? No, they seemed very loving, very tight knit.

Jack?

William mulled this name around. What if Jack had killed

Henry and set the fire in the church? William had never pressed for more details about the 'large man' that Jack claimed he saw. Jack stood to gain the most from all these killings if Elizabeth was his true quarry. They had been a lot closer in the past few weeks. She sat next to him at the trial, and he was pretty sure he caught them holding hands at least once. He saw the way she looked at him. Jack made infinitely more sense than George.

William drained the glass. Tomorrow he would delay his retirement and arrest Jack Taylor. He would describe all of this to Marshal Smith and the mayor. He would end his career catching a serial killer who just had a hard time talking to a girl. William thought of the stupidity of it all – Jack would rot in prison or get the hangman's noose because he was too chickenshit to talk to a girl he liked.

The rush of solving a case wore off quickly. William was tired, probably from his day of close calls and the half bottle of whisky. The arrest could wait until tomorrow.

William yawned.

Most days he could tolerate more whisky, but tonight it was almost as if his arms and legs didn't want to move of their own accord. He was so far beyond tired.

William changed quickly into his night clothes and climbed into bed. He laid the lap blanket from Abigail across the top of his body and basked in the comforting warmth. The joy from figuring out this case had acted as an analgesic. He couldn't feel his leg throbbing. There was no pain anymore.

He heard a soft noise in the distance, and figured it was Abigail coming to listen to his day. The dream about chasing Lizzie through the snow had to be Abigail telling him to join them in the heaven that the memory represented. It was Abi telling him she wanted him to come find them. Abi wasn't mad anymore.

"Not quite yet, Abi," he thought. "Soon."

He smiled as sleep took him. Jack had been a worthy adversary, but William had won.

Chapter 56

January 6, 1893 – Medford, MA

In the end it had been so easy to get away with. George played into his hands perfectly and served as the perfect patsy. Jack was so lucky that his patsy had a backstory that included drug addiction *and* a history of violence. Jack Taylor smiled, thinking back to what his mentor had said.

"Murders only need two things: a victim and a scapegoat. Once you've found the person to blame, the rest is easy."

He had adopted the name Jack Taylor when he moved to the United States. Jack was an homage to his mentor and Taylor was a bastardization of his father's pub. He had found a forger in South Boston who did quick work and provided Jack with cheap papers of immigration and birth. He stored those documents in an old lye tin under his bed, along with the remainder of the money from his old life. It turned out that blending into Medford was a lot easier and cheaper with two names that didn't mean anything to its citizens.

Jack Taylor, who was also Ben Smith, walked out of the General Store on top of the world. He was pretty sure Elizabeth would be his now, of her own choice. He would be able to have her and start a new life with her, and would never be alone, ever again. He was going to ask her to marry him tomorrow and confess that he was born Ben Smith, grandson of Chief William Smith, her guardian angel for these last two months. He would get rid of Jack and become Ben again.

Much like he had thought after he killed his mentor 5 years ago, just one more loose end. He had hated his grandfather from the moment he arrived in Medford. This was the man he truly blamed for his mother's death. If William Smith hadn't driven Elizabeth Smith away, she never would have stumbled into the hands of Jack the Ripper. Ben still had those sob story letters William had sent his mother, also in the lye tin beneath his bed. They reeked of a weak, pathetic man who refused to take accountability for the death of his daughter.

There was another universe out there where he and Sarah had a better family, right here in Medford. This was the family he would make with Elizabeth Foster. This was what was owed to him, and so it was what he would take. His mother would be proud.

He pulled out his silver pocket watch and smiled to himself. If his math was right, and it always was, Chief Smith was already half-way done with the spiked whisky bottle, which means he was very sleepy right now. Time to go bury the hammer. Jack crept in through the front door of William Smith's apartment.

It had finally come to the confrontation that Ben had wanted from the start. He was about to murder the man who had left for a stupid war of his own accord. The same man whose morals caused his wife to kill herself. The man who had alienated his other son and drove his daughter to London for a lifetime of abuse and an unjustified murder.

It was the man who didn't catch Ben and believed his trusted deputy was capable of the genius that Ben had just acted out. The deaths of Henry and the Fergusons were regrettable, yes, but they had helped to cement the manhunt for George. They were necessary. It wasn't for sport.

Henry's murder was the hardest. Ben had looked up to the man and Henry had taught him a lot about how to work a crowd. Ben thought about how he had grabbed the heavy cross from the altar under the pretense of cleaning it, but Henry had seen right through it. He did nothing to stop it.

William Smith would be found in the morning with a bullet through his brain. There would be a short investigation that would conclude suicide was the logical explanation. Ben was good at his craft. He could mimic so many crimes, and he would prove it again. Everything was falling into place like the second hand on his pocket watch that a boy named Benjamin Smith had taken from his father's lifeless corpse so many years ago. That boy who took a steamer and crafted a new life, using a new name to cement his future and take what was owed to him.

Ben looked at his pocket watch again and checked the time. The appointment with his grandfather was right on time.

Acknowledgements

Every summer since my kids were very little, my wife, Rayna, puts together a summer reading challenge. It's loosely based on library and bookstore summer reading challenges but provides prizes for tasks related to reading. In the summer of 2024, Rayna had an element on our yearly challenge titled "Create an outline for your own novel." It was worth 20 points, so of course I did it!

I was also desperately trying to get back into shape at the time, attempting to chase away the pains of the middle-aged man. Thanks to long runs and an easily distracted mind, I started turning the outline into a story, thinking of all the things I wanted to say and all the ways I wanted to put it in writing. I wanted a book that was historically adjacent and something that could fill in the mysteries of history as I saw them. Those chapters that I composed while running eventually became the portion of the story where Elizabeth Smith was murdered by Jack the Ripper. From there, I realized there was so much potential in the US, as the 1860s through 1890s represented such a change. The story just kind of poured out of me after that. It has been a labor of love and has awakened a passion I honestly didn't know I had.

To say thank you, it must start with Rayna for the inspiration and for valuing reading for us and our kids, J and Rosie. Rayna is to whom this book is dedicated, and her support in this writing process has been instrumental. Whether it's taking care of the "clunky" bits or challenging me on early anachronistic mistakes, she has been there for me as my biggest critic and my biggest cheerleader. It has brought me joy to write this story for her and brought me joy to realize that I was also writing it for me.

I'd also like to thank Sahaja Patel, for providing feedback and discussion points that proved vital to polishing the story. The cover was created by Evgeniia Gurcheva, who was easy to work with on my first cover.

Finally, although they can't respond (we hope), I did want to thank Microsoft Copilot. Copilot helped me distill the historical facts around the 1890s, Medford, and London down into easy to read, easy to summarize, salient points. It makes an author's job so much easier when they can simply ask "who was the district attorney of Medford, MA in 1892" and instantly get a response of "Patrick Cooney" instead of spending hours trawling through the corners of the internet to find a reference. I admit that this doesn't mean my references are vetted, and I won't claim historical accuracy, as the premise of the book is based in speculation. As a result, I'd like to say that the history in this book is correct adjacent or historically inspired. Let's be clear, though. I didn't use AI to <u>write</u> a single word in this book. That's not what AI is for. Art and literature (and whatever this book is) should be left to humans, but the research and the summaries can receive help from the machine.

I hope you've enjoyed this little piece of fiction I created, and it made you say "oooh" at least once. The hardest part of all of this was using Oxford Commas. I think Vampire Weekend summarized my feelings about those pretty accurately. Thanks for reading and may all your oil lamps dim over time.

Scott Ehlert is a husband, father, quality geek, and engineer. He has enjoyed writing this book and hopes people will buy it. In his other life, he has worked in several industries and has a Master's Degree in Mechanical Engineering. He lives in Cincinnati with his wife, two children, and husky.

He can be found online at @EhlertWrites.